ONE FOR HELL

When Willa Ree emerges from the boxcar, he is broke and ready for a fresh start. And Breton looks to be a town full of fresh suckers. Ben Halliday is not one of those suckers, or so he thinks. One of the town leaders, he needs a new cop with adjustable morals. Ree is the perfect fit. Unfortunately, Ree is even less subtle than Halliday had hoped. Because Ree has plans of his own. Now that he's a cop, he intends to steal every dollar he can lay his hands on, and seduce any woman he wants. This Texas oil town is ripe for the picking on all accounts. It's Willa Ree's town now, and nothing that Halliday—or anyone—can do will stop him.

JADA M. DAVIS BIBLIOGRAPHY

One for Hell (Gold Medal, 1952)
The Outraged Sect (Avon, 1956)
So Curse the Day (unpublished, 1981)
Midnight Road (unpublished, 1987)

"Stark House is the best thing to happen to hard-boiled noir since the first California housewife got the idea to team up with a door-to-door salesman to off her husband and collect the insurance money. Each new volume is cause for celebration among mystery geeks everywhere — including this one."

Duane Swierczynski, author of *Severance Package*

One for Hell

JADA M. DAVIS

STARK
HOUSE

Stark House Press • Eureka California

ONE FOR HELL

Published by Stark House Press
2200 O Street
Eureka, CA 95501, USA
griffinskye3@sbcglobal.net
www.starkhousepress.com

ONE FOR HELL
Originally published by Gold Medal Books as a Red Seal Book
and copyright © 1952 by Fawcett Publications, Inc.
Copyright © renewed 1980 by Jada M. Davis
Reprinted by permission of the Jada M. Davis Estate

Introduction copyright © 2010 by Mark Davis

ISBN: 1-933586-30-3
ISBN-13: 978-1-933586-30-4

Text set in Figural and Dogma. Heads set in Egiziano Black.
Cover design and layout by Mark Shepard, SHEPGRAPHICS.COM
Proofreading by Rick Ollerman

First Stark House Press Edition: October 2010

Reprint Edition

Jada M. Davis

BY MARK DAVIS

There are parts of West Texas where the land is so flat you can sometimes be stricken with the dizzying sense that you are about to fall upwards into the blue, featureless sky. Against such a horizon, individual human beings seem larger than life. Like actors projected against an enormous drive-in movie screen, ordinary people take on the dimensions of giants.

A bullying police chief who liked to frame others for his crimes. A couple of dime-store plutocrats who were in on the next sweet deal brewing at city hall. The cynic who imagined he was clever enough to get his part of the action and yet stay above them all.

This was the landscape that my father, Jada Davis, knew as the editor of several daily newspapers in the 1950s. A journalist's immediacy and unrefined raw observation characterizes this novel of the outlandish oil boom days of West Texas.

As a journalist and as a novelist, Jada was an instinctive muckraker. His wife, Mary Alice, wrote the society columns and helped out with the grueling work of running hot-lead presses. It was around this time that Jada turned out *One for Hell*.

He had no lack of raw material for his writing. As a journalist, Jada had exposed corrupt land deals, as well as the local police practice of blaming unsolved crimes on any convenient black youth. More than once my mother, Mary Alice, came running from the courthouse to say one young man or another had appeared in court beaten half to death. More than once, my father had been taken for a ride—literally—by a local police official in menacing silence for daring to complain about such violations of constitutional niceties.

It was dangerous, hard work—and it was great while it lasted.

Jada Davis was born in 1919 on a West Texas farm to a sharecropping family, one of eleven children. After running through the gauntlet of the usual boy names—Jack, Tom, Bob—my grandparents named their tenth child after a popular ragtime song, the one with the refrain, "*Ja-Da, Ja-Da/Ja-Da, Ja-Da, jing, jing, jing.*"

The family of Jada Davis had deep roots in the American past. Jada's grandfather, who had served in Hood's Brigade as a teen-ager, often sat his grandson on his knees to recount horrifying stories from the Civil War. Jada's father, Elijah, by then well into his forties, was old enough to remember his pioneer parents grabbing him by the suspenders and throwing him under the bed while they fought off a Comanche raid. Jada's mother Sally was a dark, beautiful woman whose Cherokee ancestors had avoided persecution by marrying whites.

While Jada's father Elijah made a little money trading knives, horses and mules, Jada himself was hired out with the other Davis children to pick cotton. At age ten, Jada labored in the fields under the blistering Texas sun, his hands raw and bleeding. While suffering in the heat, Jada Davis fantasized that someday he would awe and humble his neighbors by driving around his little West Texas town in a big, expensive car.

The Davis family had at one point become so hungry that out of desperation, Elijah shot a possum. Sally dutifully cooked it up with sweet potatoes. The pot of possum meat sat stewing the middle of the table, the hungry family glumly staring at the bowl. No one could bear to eat it, so they all went to bed hungry that night. Jada later observed that he was so poor that the Great Depression brought no observable differences in his family circumstances.

When he could escape farm chores, Davis was a voracious reader of novels, histories and poetry. He found that he could make extra money by writing short pieces for magazines and newspapers. He briefly attended a small college before signing up for the U.S. Army in the 1930s. In the ill-equipped Army of that time, Davis trained in a cavalry unit in horseback deployments across the deserts of the Southwest. Later, when my brother and I were growing up, my father enchanted us with his stories of the horse cavalry. He would tell us how his sergeant would station all the men with their horses before troughs and cry out, "Don't feed till I say feed... FEEEEED!" (In my childhood, this became our family dinner cry.) My father also told us how an old cavalry horse, Mayberry, once saved his life by bracing herself in front of him to protect him in the middle of a 500-horse stampede.

At the beginning of World War Two, Jada was stricken with tuberculosis. So while his comrades went on to fight in steaming jungles (with typical Army logic, men trained on horseback for desert warfare were sent to the Philippines), Jada spent the duration of the war in a sanitarium reading classics. When he recovered at war's end, he felt a need to perform a heroic service for his country. Jada volunteered for medical experiments being performed on servicemen at that time. He allowed his chest to be bombarded with atomic radiation.

After marrying a long-legged gal named Mary Alice, Jada went on to earn a degree from the University of Texas at Austin. It was in Odessa and other West Texas towns, however, that he had the adventure of his life as a newspaper editor and paperback novelist.

After some success with *One for Hell*, Jada's agent and editors urged him to move to New York, where his raw, self-taught writing-style would be sharpened in the company of the best. Television was already thinning out the ranks of dime-store novelists. To make it as a writer, Jada Davis would have to undergo the painful process of constant criticism, revision and learning. This would be a whole new start for him, with study at the City College or Columbia, and then a job in publishing, television or a magazine.

Jada Davis turned down the offer. Partly, he turned them down out of sheer stage fright. Like many charming and charismatic people, his easygoing exterior hid a raging inferiority complex—Jada Davis feared being ridiculed before such sophisticated company as a hick, a half-Indian kid from the fields with no real middle name (the "M" in Jada M. Davis was his creation). I believe another concern was also at work. New York would not just be an adventure. It would be a whole new life for his wife and sons. He saw disruption for his family. I believe he saw more financial struggle ahead, perhaps divorce. A new life that would come with costs.

With a family and a mortgage, Jada opted instead to accept an offer to join the telephone company, where he worked as a PR executive until his retirement. He had taken the easy path, opting to keep the life and family that he had.

In time, Jada's work for Southwestern Bell/AT&T made him a virtual creature of New York. He had the best of both worlds, his home and family back in Texas, and his separate life in Manhattan, with his executive circle, his steakhouse and martini haunts. He had a big job with a big expense account. He became a legendary and much loved figure in AT&T. He outfoxed some of the nation's most rapacious trial lawyers on the witness stand, and befriended powerful politicians. But like so many of us, he never lived up to the high standards of his youth.

He never fulfilled the promise of *One for Hell* to become the writer he had always wanted to be.

In time, Jada Davis would live out one ambition. After his retirement, Jada and Mac moved back to their small, West Texas town. He drove around that town in a big, silver Cadillac that far exceeded his youthful cotton field dreams.

He would drive around town, shake his head and laugh. It was nothing like he imagined it would be.

Jada Davis died in 1996, a victim of the radiation experiments compounded by his addiction to smoking. As his life wound down, Jada puttered around his little town in his Cadillac, mostly content. But his happiness was always edged with a slight trace of disappointment. He had not gotten everything that he had wanted. But he had got everything that he had chosen.

We can now be grateful that one of his choices was to write *One for Hell*, a tale that is both a period piece of a Texas long vanished, and an indelible portrait of human cupidity.

McLean, VA
September 2009

One for Hell

BY JADA M. DAVIS

To my Mac—
And to Jeffry Brett,
Now three years old,
Whose determined aid
Made it possible
To complete this story
In only twice the time.

Chapter One

Ree heard the whistle and cursed the engineer.

The far away whoo-ooo-ooo, whoo-ooo-ooo, whoo-ooooooing was a going-away echo, faraway faint and going away fast.

Half asleep, he sat up and groped for the bundle he'd been using for a pillow, found it and curled up on the hard boxcar floor. His back ached, head ached, throat scratched, and his stomach was emptier than empty, sick empty and heavy. Soon he'd have to find food, but sooner he'd have to find water. Food he needed. Water he had to have.

Again the whistle skimmed the night, and he wondered why the hell the engineer would hoot his whistle out in the middle of nowhere leading to nothing.

Maybe at cows.

Or maybe at some bypassed whistle stop of a town sitting like an ugly boil on the bare face of the desert.

The train had stopped not long ago and someone had boarded the car. He had heard the door slide open and had heard the pantings and gruntings of a man climbing aboard. Then he hadn't wondered why the train had stopped, but now he remembered that the road maps had not shown a town on the tracks.

A water stop, maybe.

"Shut the door," he'd growled. And the newcomer had obeyed.

The man had made no noise, and Ree guessed he had dropped to the floor to sleep. Anyway, there was plenty of room.

It was stuffy in the car, and he couldn't sleep. The clickity-clicking of the wheels, before unnoticed, now drummed in his ears. The car swayed, gently rocking his body, and no position was comfortable.

A slithering sound.

The man?

It had to be the man. The sap had waited a long time to make up his mind. Too long. And, suddenly, Ree remembered the dime in his pocket and shook with silent laughter.

He separated the clickity-clicking of the wheels and the tortured rumblings of the car from the slithering, until the slithering was a loud thing to hear. He tensed, not laughing now, and waited while the man slid his body across the car floor, nearer and nearer....

A hand touched his hip lightly, so lightly, and was withdrawn.

Ree didn't move.

He could hear the man breathing and marveled that the breathing was so loud. Before he had heard only the slithering of the man's body across the floor, but now the breathing sounded like the rasping of a file on soft wood.

Inside himself somewhere, deep inside, he talked to himself and cursed the darkness of the car. He strained his eyes, willing himself to see, but only flashes of light danced before his eyes and he knew the light was in his head, behind his eyes.

The hand touched his leg, again so lightly, and crept toward his hips.

Ree caught the hand in his left hand, grasped hard with fingernails biting deeply, twisted back hard and harder still, and reached out with his right hand to grasp the wrist.

The man groaned.

Ree twisted the hand back, pulling at the wrist, and the man screamed.

And then the man wrenched away, his feet flailing the darkness and grazing Ree's chest.

Ree dived forward, exulting and his widespread arms caught the man's legs.

They fought silently, gouging and butting and biting, unseeing and uncaring.

And then the man was gone. Ree could hear his breathing across the car, in the darkness, but when he advanced the breathing circled away.

"Come on and fight," Ree said.

"Why?"

"Well, why not?"

"Don't see no point to it. I ain't got nothing against you."

"You wanted my money."

"Well, that's cause enough for you to be mad but it ain't no reason for me to be mad."

Ree laughed.

"Maybe you've got a point there," he said. "Open the door and let's get a little light on the subject."

"You won't try to throw me out?"

"Not if you don't start anything. Anyway, you might be twice as big as I am."

"I doubt it. I felt you."

The door slid open, and the lighter dark of the outside made the car only half dark on the inside. The man was big. He stood in the doorway, silhouetted, his arms long and dangling and his shoulders broad and hunched. Ree couldn't see his face, but his head seemed too big for his body.

"You wouldn't have made much of a haul off me, mister," Ree said. "I've got one thin dime between me and starvation."

The man laughed. "I've got a quarter."

Ree stepped to the doorway, leaning against the edge. Cool air rushed at him, plucked at him, and moved around and away in front of some evil-smelling something. He sniffed.

Gas.

Moments later he saw the flares, hundreds of them, like the lights of a far-off city, and knew this flatland was oil country.

Where there's oil, there's money. And people to spend it. So this was it. Red light. Bottom of page. End of journey. No need to make decisions or weigh pros or cons or consider this and that. There was a dime in his pocket and a rumbling emptiness in his belly. Here he'd make money. And this time it would be different from last time and the time before and the time before that and the time beyond that time.

No more slipups, no more mistakes, he promised himself.

He looked at the far-off flares and marveled at the flatness of the shadowed landscape. It had taken a long time to get this far, but there must be a town somewhere lying ahead. Where there's oil there are towns, near railroads, for oil wells need pipe and bits for drilling and machinery and men and towns.

It will be different this time, he thought.

After all, he was no stranger to oil or oil country or oil towns. Especially oil towns.

He'd been orphaned in an oil town.

There'd been an oil town once, long ago, and a home in a tar-paper shack. He remembered the mud, seas of mud, and the hogs that wallowed in the mud of the streets. There'd been huge wagons loaded with pipe, lumbering and monstrous things. The drivers were fearsome men, bearded and dirty and huge. They'd used long whips which popped and crackled and their oaths had been their chief weapons against mud and hogs and rock-throwing boys.

He'd been alone in that town, later. At first there had been a man and a woman, but his memory of them was more a feeling than a memory. They'd been there and then they hadn't been there, and he'd been alone in the town of mud and hogs and wagons and men and women who had no time for boys alone in their town.

Memories were sharp after that, for they were memories of cold and hunger, loneliness and emptiness and fear. He'd been ill once, broken-out and red-spotted ill, and that memory was a dim memory of fever and thirst in an abandoned shack.

There'd been big cities then. Cold cities and hot cities, dirty cities and clean. Papers to be sold, groceries to be sacked, things to filch and things to steal and things to beg for and whine for.

And then it had been easier. Still empty and still lonely, but easier. Plenty to eat and warm places to sleep and good clothes to wear, because there'd been more things to steal and fewer things to whine for or beg for or ask for.

"My name's Murdock," the big man said.

"What?" Ree had forgotten the man.

"My name," the man said. "It's Murdock."

"Oh."

"What's your name?" The man's voice was sharp.

"Ree. Willa Ree."

"Glad to know you, Willie."

"Not Willie. Willa. W-i-l-l-a."

The man laughed.

Ree hit him, hard, and the big man sprawled on the floor, slid on his back, and rolled to his knees, cursing feebly.

"Don't ever laugh," Ree said. "They laughed when I was a kid, but they don't laugh now. My old woman couldn't spell, they told me, and wrote it like she said it. And that's all right. It's all right, so don't laugh. Don't ever laugh."

"I'll never laugh again, bub. My jaw's broke."

"O.K. Forget it."

The man snorted.

"You've served time," the man said finally.

"How did you know? Does it show?"

"No. Besides, I can't see you good. It's a feeling, I guess."

Ree stepped to the doorway again. The man moved up beside him.

"Have a cigarette, Willa."

"Thanks."

The man flipped a match with his thumbnail and gave Ree a light. He cupped the match in his hands and held it to his own cigarette. He was a Negro.

"I'm sorry I hit you," Ree said.

"Aw, 's all right."

"Where you headed?"

"Who knows?" the big man asked. "Or cares?"

"I'm getting off at the next town."

"It's a free country."

Ree turned back into the car and found the bundle that held his spare slacks and tie. The slacks were wrinkled and dirty. They'd have to be cleaned.

It had taken a long time, but this was what he wanted, where he wanted to be.

He'd followed the spidery red lines on road maps, and the red lines had been deceptive. He'd followed the lines by slow freight and the distances had been amazing. He'd been in the boxcar a day and most of this night. During the day it was hot, burning hot, and the wind had whipped stinging sand before it, until his face was burned and his eyes red raw. The night had been cool at first, almost cold, but turned warm, and the car had retained the heat soaked up during the day.

There were town lights ahead.

Ree crouched to jump, but changed his mind. He straightened and relaxed and again leaned against the car door. When the train neared the station lights and slowed, he stepped back into the car, out of sight. Not until the train was at a dead stop did he jump to the ground, parcel of clothes under his arm.

"Take it easy, Buster," he called.

"So long, Willie," the Negro said and laughed softly.

The first gray light of day flicked darkness aside and outlined the station, train, empties, and dingy buildings that are part and parcel of any town's railroad area. The sign on the station said "BRETON."

Chapter Two

Ben Halliday couldn't sleep.

He cursed himself for a fool.

The bed floated in circles each time he closed his eyes, dipped and swayed and spin span spun, sickeningly. A hollow place formed at the pit of his stomach, heavy and dead.

How many beers had he had?

Not many.

Twelve, maybe.

There was a time, a time, a time when a dozen beers wouldn't have made his head spin. No matter what medical science had to say about it, there was a time when he could drink more than he could now.

What was it he'd read in the paper?

There is no such thing as building up a tolerance for alcoholic beverages by regular drinking, the paper said. A man's capacity is based on the bulk of his body, and not on his drinking habits. Age has nothing to do with....

Nuts!

There'd been a time, once upon a time, when he could drink all night and every night and sometimes during the day, and it never made him sick. And he never, never, never, ever had hang-overs.

Except now and then.

And what about the bulk of the body?

Wasn't he heavier at forty than he'd been at thirty? Not fat. Not paunchy. Just a little heavier, all over heavier.

The clock in the hall ticked away, and his mind ticked with it. Back and forth, back and forth, to and fro.

If he could only take his brain out and rub it.

Martha stirred, moved on her bed, in the darkness there, somewhere in the darkness, over there or over there, somewhere to hell across the room.

He didn't know where, because his head was spinning.

A groan welled up from that heavy place in his stomach and climbed up through his chest and throat and out between dry lips.

Nora would tell Martha in the morning. Not that she'd want to, but no doubt she'd feel duty bound to tell. After all, her conscience would say, you're Martha Halliday's best friend.

Ah, Nora Byrd would tell her. She'd approved at the time, even asked him over to their house for dinner and drinks.

Poor Nora.

But in the shape Sam Byrd was in, stayed in, he couldn't satisfy himself, much less a woman like Nora. Drunk or sober.

And Nora needed a man.

Sam was too drunk, slobbery fall-down drunk, to do anything but fall asleep. Why Nora'd ever married that slob, with her looks, and her figure, was more than.... Well, Sam was a friend, fellow businessman, member of the town council and all that, but too weak to hold a woman like Nora.

Someday, wait and see, Sam'll pass out and Martha'll be out of town. Like last night. Only last night Sam hadn't passed out.

Someday, wait and see.

No, it wasn't Nora last night. It would have been, could have been, except for Sam.

Why did Nora plan last night?

Because, don't be a fool, because Martha was out of town and she knows Martha's colder than an ice-box and because she wanted to see just how far things could go if the opportunity presented itself.

She almost found out, too.

Martha stirred again, somewhere in the darkness, and Halliday lifted his head from the pillow to listen.

Even the darkness began to spin, and he let his head fall back.

It might be better to get up and go on to the bathroom and be sick and get it over with.

The spinning slowed. He felt better, except that his throat burned and his lips felt thick and parched and cracked and the inside of his mouth felt lined and slick.

There had been Martha, hours away, sky high, on a plane, dozing in her seat, flying home.

Martha had wired that she'd be in on the one A.M. plane, and he knew that it was too late to find a woman. Unless he went to a hotel, and he didn't want to do that. Bought woman was the same as no woman, almost, yet not altogether. But bought woman wasn't the same, somehow, and anyway besides, bought woman left a bad taste in the conscience.

Every night he'd thought of going out, meeting some lovely girl at a night club or in a café and making a conquest. Hell, she wouldn't even have to be lovely, just young, good figure and young.

But, as the nights passed and the date for Martha's return neared, he realized that he'd have to buy a woman.

Or forget it.

But he couldn't forget it.

His body, his mind, cried aloud, or almost aloud, the need for woman.

He'd tried, even tried, picking up girls on the street. And that had failed. Because, when he tried, he could see himself as the girls must have seen him. And that made him feel like the fool he felt the girls felt he was.

Too old and too awkward and too tongue-tied.

Finally, sick with desire for someone young and pretty, but old, not loving, (not Martha, old with young body, but old, just suffer in silence like a good wife) he'd tried a night club.... No luck.

Too old.

Too old.

Well, might as well wait and love Martha, though the love in return would be nil, no more and no less than he could get at a hotel for ten or twenty bucks. At least, a tramp pretends enjoyment. Martha wouldn't even do that.

Here he'd worked and slaved and made money, lots of money, a hell of a lot of money, and she gave nothing in return. Here he was, respected and wealthy, a member of the city council, a director of the chamber of commerce.

All for Martha.

Hell.

His head was spinning. If it didn't stop spinning, he was going to be sick.

Maybe he'd feel better if he smoked a cigarette. Groaning, gagging, he sat on the edge of the bed and found cigarettes and lighter on the table.

He inhaled—it tasted good, for a moment.

Sweat on his face—sick.

He must have made a noise for Martha stirred again. If Martha knew...!

He laughed inside, hating her, hating her for withholding what she had and he wanted, and for having what he wanted and couldn't have and was wasting.

His conscience didn't bother him, not a bit, and had never bothered him. He'd always said, if you can't get it at home, get it where you can.

Not that he didn't love Martha.

But if she knew, oh, if she knew!

Tonight, last night now, hadn't been the first time and wouldn't be the last.

Dinner at the Byrds' had been mostly beer, and he and Nora had watched each other, and he knew that she wanted him too.

Sam got drunker and drunker but he didn't fall asleep, so at ten o'clock he left the Byrds' and went to a hotel. He wondered what time it was.

Martha stirred again, moaned softly.

The thing is, he thought, that Martha has the body and all a woman needs to make a man happy, but she either didn't know how or wouldn't even try to please him, and a man with guts would leave Martha.

At twelve he went to the airport.

The plane had been on time, and Martha stepped off looking fresh and young and beautiful.

He hugged her and tried to kiss her but she turned her head.

He noticed what's-his-name, the manager of Johnson's Tool Company, get off the plane. What's-his-name nodded and he nodded back.

Martha needed one look, just one look, and knew he'd been drinking. He could feel her scorn, but she didn't nag, but even though she didn't nag he knew she was scorning him.

They'd gone home and straight to bed, in separate beds, like always.

And he thought, If I hadn't had what I had, I wouldn't have had a damned thing.

At first, for an hour or so, he had slept. But then he came wide awake, half sick and more than sick without being sick at his stomach, really. When he closed his eyes, though, the bed began to spin, making his stomach more queasy, and all he could do was make himself think about other things.

He finished the cigarette, scraped the floor with his feet until he found his slippers, and stood up. He tried to orient himself in the darkness. It was hard to think, and finally he began to walk with short sliding steps until his knee hit an end table. He knew where he was, then, and his hand found the wall.

It was easy going down the hall, easy knowing how many steps to take before reaching with the left hand and touching, surely and accurately, the handle on the bathroom door. And then he closed the door quietly before switching on the light, lest the light and noise disturb Martha.

Must not disturb Martha, he thought.

The light hurt his eyes and he felt a headache coming on. Not a hangover, but a headache. Migraine, maybe.

Four o'clock by his watch. He'd slept longer than he'd thought.

He doused his face with cold water, sloshing it on the back of his neck, wanting to drink it from cupped hands, but knowing better, and only wetting his mouth and swallowing a little.

After he'd dried his face, burying it in the towel and blotting gently (deep dark warm darkness with nowhere light), he looked in the mirror.

Not bad at all for forty, he decided, and sick as hell, at that, and after a hard day's work before a hard night that was, in a lot of ways, harder work than the day's work had been.

And then, suddenly, he bent over the basin and vomited again and again until the sick feeling was gone from his stomach and the dizziness from his head.

His throat and mouth burned, but the weight was gone from his stomach and the swaying dizziness from his head.

It was wonderful to drink cold water, wash his mouth out and gargle and drink. He felt weak, but not sick any more, and except for that and rawness of throat and mouth, he felt fine.

Coffee, now, he decided, and scrambled eggs and toast and jelly.

On impulse, he almost called Martha to ask her to have coffee with him. He checked himself—foolish.

Martha wouldn't do it, he knew. She'd be mad as hell at being disturbed, and she'd refuse.

He wondered if only the bitches of the world understood men and enjoyed life and love as do men, lived under the same code as do men, and had the ability to make men happy.

If only Martha would get drunk one time, and lose her inhibitions.

He snorted at the thought of Martha drunk. He sighed.

Trying to be quiet, he was clumsy. In the kitchen he was unknowing and unfamiliar, and he banged and clattered pots and pans.

Maybe, he thought, something in my subconscious is causing this noise-making, trying to make Martha hear.

The eggs were good, moist and soft as he liked them, and never had food tasted better. Drinking his coffee and smoking, he was conscious of the deep stillness of the night.

How long had it been since he'd had time and inclination for a thing like this? Or just for thinking?

A long time.

Money he had, and prestige. City councilman, solidly entrenched, and fingers in several pies. In fact, the man to see if things needed doing.

But I'm not honest....

Well, who is? Who can be, and make money? What is honesty, anyway? A code.

Maybe I'm not honest, but I'm ethical....

He left the dishes on the table and went to the bathroom. There was a chance that a shower would disturb Martha, but he needed a bath.

Not a bad physique for a man of forty.

His mind went back a step, and he wondered why had thought of himself as being dishonest. Not dishonest, just not honest. Unethical might be a bad word, at that. It's possible to be honest and not be ethical. Or is it? Anyway, it's good business, and if it's good business, it's not dishonest. Or if it is dishonest, there'll be a lot of company in hell.

"Oh, a hell of a hell of a hell of a lot of company in hell," he sang, almost gaily.

Thirty minutes later, clad in khaki shirt and slacks, he left the house and walked.

Flares in the fields twinkled like city lights, friendly and beckoning in the distance. The sky was not so dark now, though there was no moon, and he realized it must be almost five. Nearly dawn.

Maybe he should go back to the house and dress for the office.

Did the council meet today, or next Wednesday?

He couldn't remember. They were supposed to get some street paving started. Some wise guys were beginning to yelp about paving money disappearing faster than paved streets appeared, and it was time to pave a few blocks to lull the suspicious to sleep. Well, no matter. Sam Byrd would call about the paving today. Poor old Sam, old worried Sam, scared-as-hell Sam. Not too scared to take a slice of the graft, but scared.

Sam would bear watching. Scared men make mistakes.

Well, maybe Sam was right to be scared. Something would have to break some day. Someone would slip, or some wise guy would run into something.

A few more months and he'd slide off the council and take Sam with him.

Everything had gone smooth as silk for three years now, with no slips. And it had been so easy, so damned easy.

Except for Chief Bronson, it had been easy. But the Chief wouldn't play ball. And he was getting wise.

It hadn't been easy to fool Bronson, and it had been damned hard to organize a town behind the police chief's back.

He needed someone—someone hard.

Not that things, on the whole, hadn't run smoothly. There'd been rumors, ugly rumors, of course. Rumors of kickbacks, pay-offs, fund splitting.

But nothing ever happened. People don't get excited until they suffer a personal loss.

Still, it might be better to get out while the getting's good. Sam Byrd's scared, and Sam's no fool.

Oh, nuts! Get someone tough on the police force and organize things big.

The damn fools in this town don't care. They wouldn't care if somebody walked off with the city hall. They're too busy making money, fighting for money, spending money.

Typical oil town.

The air was fresh and clean, almost cold. He shivered and wished he'd worn a jacket.

A milk truck passed.

Two paper boys, on bicycles, called a greeting.

Far off, faint but clear, a train whistle mourned the passing of the night. Whoo-ooo-ooo, whoo-ooo-ooo, whooooo....

Main Street was just ahead, dark and silent. His shoes clop-clopped on the pavement, gray with the drifted sand gutter and in the recessed doorways of the stores.

It was darker here, amid the buildings, and the dawn seemed far away. Ahead of him, down the street, a café's neoned front flickered bluely.

He decided to have some coffee, and then take a cab home to change.

He went into the café.

Chapter Three

Willa Ree stood beside the boxcar for several minutes. He wasn't big, wasn't tall, but his shoulders were broad and he looked strong, as some men look strong because of an inner something that makes itself felt. It may be that he was more compactly formed than others, or it may have been the way he stood or moved or held his head. It could have been the look on his face, or the expression in his eyes. It could have been all these things or none of them, or some of them, or it could have been the very presence of him that tickled or irritated the unused and forgotten danger senses of other men.

Willa Ree.

He was, perhaps, five feet and ten inches tall, and weighed, perhaps, one hundred and seventy pounds. His hair straight and black. He smiled, as he almost always did, and his lips were thin and his mouth wide. His teeth were white and strong. His skin was tanned, and he was hard and brown. His nose was straight, a bit too thin and a bit too long, but his eyes were widely spaced. They were brown, and the brows above them were bushy black, curving and ending outward and upward in sharp points, giving him a somewhat rakish appearance. He wore a white shirt, once clean white but now dirty white, and a pair of khaki trousers. Both shirt and trousers were wrinkled, but his shoes were shiny brown and good.

Willa Ree.

He walked up the street, passed dingy-fronted cafés and beer joints, dark and closed, and hock shops and liquor stores.

A dog, dirty and thin, ribs showing and hipbones stretching its skin, sniffed at his heels before trotting out into the street.

A car came around a corner, going fast, and the driver made no attempt to miss the dog.

"The son-of-a-bitch," Willa Ree said curiously.

Blood oozed from the dog's mouth and nostrils. Willa Ree picked it up in his arms, heedless of the blood, and carried it to the curb. He put it down, going on hands and knees to pat its head. And then he walked away.

The dog whined.

Willa Ree stopped, looked back, and returned to the dog. He picked it up, muttered soft curses, and bashed it against the curb. He threw the body into the gutter and walked away.

Two blocks, and the buildings were larger and in better repair. A café was open, filled with work-clothed roughnecks and drillers, but he did not stop.

Two more blocks, and he was in the main business center of the town. He passed by two banks, several jewelry stores, and glanced at signs fronting clothing stores, hardware stores, theatres. He passed a four-story hotel.

The streets were deserted.

At a corner, he stopped and looked back down the street, as if wondering whether or not to return to the railroad. With a shrug, he turned down a side street and walked slowly for half a block. There were no cars at the curb, no other person on the street. Wind played idly with a loose newspaper, turning it over and over and sliding it along the gutter.

Ree walked on, his footsteps clicking on the pavement, slowly clickity-clicking on the pavement. He slapped at a parking meter idly, paused and looked up and down the street. No one insight. He went over to a store window and looked at a display of wrist watches and rings.

Almost casually, almost slowly, he lifted his right foot and kicked the window. Glass shattered and fell tinkling, loud in the empty stillness of the street. With his left hand, he snatched three wrist watches and two rings.

And then he was running down an alley and across the street at the next block. Walking now, not hurriedly, and whistling a little.

He reached the neoned café, opened the door, and entered. He sat down at a booth near the front, ignoring the man seated across from him.

A waitress came. He ordered coffee, looked around the room, felt for a cigarette with a hand that knew there was none.

"Have one of mine," the man across the table said.

Ree took the cigarette and leaned across the table and accepted the man's proffered light. He sucked in smoke, held it, and exhaled. He drank his coffee and smoked.

"New in town?" the man asked.

"Fairly new."

"Looking for a job?"

"Depends on the job."

"Well," the man said, "there's lots of work in the fields."

"Not for me." Ree laughed and shook his head. "None of that for me. I'm no oil man. I'm a policeman."

"A policeman, huh?"

"That's right."

"An, ah, unattached policeman, eh?"

"For the moment."

"More coffee?"

"Yeah," Ree said, grinning. "Thanks."

"You had breakfast?"

"My belly's growling, mister. From hunger."

"How about ham and eggs?"

"Sounds good."

The man called a waitress and ordered. Turning to Ree, he held out his hand. "My name's Halliday."

"Glad to know you. My name's Ree. Willa Ree."

"I believe I might be able to help you, Mr. Ree. In fact, you may help me, too."

Willa Ree ate. The man smoked in silence.

When he finished his breakfast, Ree accepted another cigarette and light. He barely glanced at the policeman coming through the door.

The policeman was short, fat, graying. His red face was covered with perspiration. He grunted his way across the room, scanning the faces of the diners, and waddled out again.

Willa Ree snuffed out his cigarette. "You need a new watch, Mr. Halliday?"

"You sell watches?" Halliday's eyes were amused.

"Yeah." He slid his hand into his pocket and pulled out a wrist watch. He slid it across the table.

"Ten dollars."

"Just for you, fifteen. And breakfast," Ree said.

"Fifteen and breakfast," Halliday said. He drew bills from his pocket, peeled off a ten and a five, and gave them to Ree.

"Think you could use a ring? Another watch?"

"I guess that'll be enough bargains for today, Mr. Ree. Now I'll offer you a bargain. You go to city hall and ask to see Chief Bronson. Tell him I sent you. I have a hunch he can use you on the force."

"I'll do that."

Ree turned to leave, but Halliday called, grinning, "You stole the watches, didn't you?"

"I don't know what you're talking about."

"Don't kid me, son."

Ree shrugged. "Then I might as well blow."

"You see Bronson in the morning," Halliday said. "I think I need a man like you around."

Chapter Four

The mayor heard the whistle, the whoo-ooo-oooing, shrilly whoo-ooo-oooing whistle, and sat up in bed.

"I told you not to eat so much supper," his wife said.

The mayor grunted. If he could just get that weight off his stomach, that leady dead weight, he'd be all right, he thought, and burped.

The trouble was that his apparatus was worn out, he thought glumly. And yet, other people still had regular elimination, people no younger than he—maybe not so young. Maybe he wasn't getting enough of the natural juices, maybe that was it, and maybe some doctor could tell him something to take that would allow him normal elimination.

It was getting to the point where he sized people up by their regularity. Healthy-looking people, those people with a lot of energy and get up and go, he figured, were as regular as clockwork. The mayor resented people like that.

When a man had his natural juices and normal elimination, what else did he need? It would be easy for a healthy man to get to the top, but hard as hell for a man who hadn't had normal elimination for twenty years.

Take a man like Halliday, for instance. There was a man who... Well, there was a man who—that's all there was to it—a driver, a pusher, full of vinegar, a getter of things done, a man who wanted something and didn't know what he wanted, but who settled for money.

Give him a good case of indigestion and he wouldn't be so damned pushy. Make him so constipated he'd go around feeling as if his mother's milk was still in his stomach, packed down by all the steaks and beans and potatoes he'd eaten in all the years since he was a baby, and he wouldn't be so eager to tie the town in a neat package.

Take Messner, the sheriff. There was a normal man. Hell, he probably had rocks in his stomach, like chickens, to grind the food to paste, and gravity did the rest.

The mayor groaned out of bed and padded to the bathroom, his potty little stomach jiggling gently, side to side with a slightly up-and-down motion so that it was more circular than side to side or up and down.

He sat for thirty minutes, hearing the whoo-ooo-oooing of the train fade away.

Finally the mayor padded back to bed.

"I told you not to eat *so* much," his wife said.

□   □   □

Arthur Fry didn't hear the whistle, but his wife did. And that was just as bad as being awake and hearing the whistle, because his wife heard it every morning and every morning she couldn't go back to sleep. And so she lay there thinking.

When she thought, which was often, her thoughts invariably turned to the sex-filled magazines she read constantly. And, invariably, she shook her husband awake.

"Let's have a party," she said, as always.

"Leemy alone," Fry grunted.

"Let's have a party," his wife said.

"Oh, hell!"

"Well, if you feel that way about it!"

"That's the way I feel, damnit!"

She turned over and pouted, and now there was no use trying to placate her or love her up because she'd pout until the damned train came through whistling its brains out the next morning.

Arthur Fry couldn't sleep.

He'd worried before going to sleep, and now his mind took up where it left off, rethinking thoughts he'd thought before he went to sleep, churning the same thoughts, chewing the same thoughts, and he couldn't go to sleep.

That damned Messner! And that damned Halliday!

They'd come to his office and asked him to pick a man for chief of police.

"What's the matter with Bronson?" he'd asked.

"Too old, for one thing," Halliday said. "Won't cooperate with Sheriff Messner for another. Just won't play ball."

"Well, you need one honest man in a front job like that," Fry had told them. "Let Messner do the work and let poor old Bronson browse along."

"He's getting in the way," Sheriff Messner said.

"Well, why come to me?" Fry asked. "After all, I'm the county attorney, not the police commissioner. It's your job to pick a man, Halliday."

"I've racked my brain," Halliday confessed, "and I can't think of a man."

"In other words," Fry said, "you want a man with a good name and a good following, but who's got sense enough to take orders and play ball."

Both men nodded.

"Well," Fry continued, "what about one of the sheriff's deputies?"

"Punks," Halliday said.

"I'll think about it," Fry promised. "I'll come up with somebody."

Halliday patted him on the shoulder in that patronizing way of his. "I knew we could count on you," he said.

But now, in bed, with his wife pouting because he couldn't get romantic before breakfast, Arthur Fry couldn't think of a man. There were lots of men, but none with a following, no vote getters.

Well, hell, he thought, let Halliday and Messner lose sleep over it.

He shifted his thoughts to his island, dream island, far out in the South Seas somewhere. It was an old day-night dream, one he'd never been able to complete, but though he dreamed the same parts over and over and always swore to finish the thing, he never did. He always went to sleep.

It started on a yacht, with a beautiful girl cutting him, scorning him, giving him the cold shoulder. It ended with a storm, with him being knocked unconscious, and while he was unconscious all the other members of the yachting party put off in boats, all but one girl, the girl, the beautiful girl. The yacht was blown into a quiet harbor, floating in deep water to the very shore of a beautiful island. And he was hard to get and the girl used scant clothes and practically no clothes to capture him, but he was hard to get and gave her the cold shoulder. She was lovely....

Arthur Fry nudged his wife gently and said, "Honey."

She didn't move.

"Honey?" he called again.

She was still pouting.

"You still want to have a party?" he asked.

She flounced, shaking the bed, and Arthur Fry returned to his dream.

Chapter Five

Chief Bronson heard the whoo-ooo-ooo, whoo-ooo-ooo, whoo-ooo-ooo-ing of the train and was glad that morning was on its way.

How many mornings, sleepless mornings, twisty-turny-tossy sleepless mornings had he heard it? Too many.

He reached for the blanket at the foot of the bed, pulled it up to his chin, and snuggled into warm drowsiness, thinking, this damned country, this funny so damned hot in the day and cool at night almost cold in the morning country.

Thinking, I'll quit and get out of this damned place and raise chickens, maybe.

Thinking, should have quit long ago before they tried to rope me in on their lousy thieving.

"I'll quit," he mumbled. "I'll resign before that damned Halliday fires me. Or frames me."

Catherine reached over and patted his chest. "Go to sleep," she said. "Stop worrying."

"It's that they want me to steal for them and I won't do it," he said. "It's that I won't clip the tramps and the pimps and the bookies and smalltime chiselers. Halliday and Byrd and the rest, the whole damned rest, want me to do their dirty work now."

"Don't worry about it," Catherine said. "We'll buy a farm and forget this town."

"I've seen it coming a long time," he said. "And now they've made it pretty plain."

"I thought the sheriff did their dirty work."

"Some of it. I don't know. Maybe he keeps the graft, or most of it, and they want to muscle in. Or maybe he's getting scared. Or maybe they want to use me and make me the goat in case they get caught."

"We'll buy a farm."

"Chickens," he said. "That's what I want. Buy a little place and stock it with a couple thousand chickens, maybe more. Grind my own feed and raise fryers and sell eggs. Have a few cows, too. Sell butter and milk and chickens and eggs."

She patted his shoulder. "That's what we'll do, then. Just make up your mind and stop worrying about this job. Chuck it! Throw it in their faces!"

"An honest cop hasn't got a chance here," he said. "They're not used to honest cops! Don't expect to have honest cops! Don't believe in honest cops!"

"Stop worrying and get some sleep."

He threw the blanket back and sat up. "I'll make some java."

Catherine thought his voice was tired, resigned. "No," she said. "Not now. You need your rest. Lie down and try to go back to sleep."

"What I don't understand," he said, "is why they want more money! Halliday and Byrd, those two, why they're rich. Old Halliday owns half this town, I guess, and Byrd's got nearly as much. Messner has bought himself a ranch, a big one, and on a sheriff's salary. In a pig's eye! And Arthur Fry, with his houses and apartment buildings— Think he bought them with the three hundred a month he gets as county attorney?"

"Go back to sleep."

"They've got plenty," he said. "Why do they want more? And if they want more, why do they have to rope me in?"

"They'll not rope you in. Go back to sleep. Stop thinking about it."

He stretched out, pulled the blanket up, and went to sleep....

The sun was streaming through the window, and Catherine was standing by the bed with a cup of coffee in her hand.

"Sit up and drink this," she ordered.

She lit a cigarette and gave it to him. He sat on the edge of the bed and sipped the steaming coffee.

The phone rang.

Catherine answered it.

"Bronson residence," she said.

He blew on the coffee, sipped it, and dragged at the cigarette.

"Yes," Catherine said into the phone. "He's awake. Just a moment."

He put the cup on the night stand and stood up.

"Halliday," Catherine said.

He took the receiver. "Hello."

"Bronson?"

"Yes."

"Halliday. Sorry to disturb you, but there'll be a man in to see you today about a job. Name's Ree. Willa Ree."

"Don't need a man."

"Yeah, I know. This is different. Listen, he's the man we've been looking for. To, uh, do the job we want done. You understand?"

"What job?"

"The one you don't want to do! This Ree can handle it, and you can forget the whole thing. Put him on the force and he'll take care of the whole deal. You can go right on like you've been doing, see, and he'll do the, ah, the work we've been talking about."

"You want him in uniform?"

"Put him in plain clothes. We've been needing a detective squad or whatever you call it. Give him two or three men."

"Well, you're the boss, Halliday. I don't like it, but you're the boss. Way I look at it, you can do it with or without me. It might as well be with me. For a while, anyway."

"Glad to hear it, Bronson."

"I'd like this understood though, Halliday. Whatever's done is done without my knowledge. I don't want any part of it and I don't want to hear about any of it."

"That's fair enough. You put this Ree on and then forget the whole thing."

"O.K."

He finished his coffee and cigarette standing up, without enjoyment.

After he'd shaved and bathed and dressed, he went to the kitchen. Catherine was frying eggs and bacon. The clock above the icebox said nine o'clock.

Catherine smiled. "Sit down. Breakfast'll be ready in a minute."

"That was Halliday."

"I know."

"He told me to hire a guy named Ree. Wants him put in plain clothes."

Catherine transferred the eggs from pan to platter. "I thought Wesley had been promised that job. He'll scream to high heaven. This Ree must be—very competent."

Bronson snorted. "He's going to handle the graft! I'm to hire him and forget it."

"Well, that's a worry off your mind."

"It'll give us time to sell our house and find the place we want," he said. "I can't keep that job when I know there's dirty work going on."

She poured coffee and passed toast to him.

"No, Catherine," he said, "this is the beginning of the end. I'm going to see a real-estate man today and put this house on the market. Halliday's crowd will use me for a front for a while, and then when they get things going like they want—pfft—out I'll go. This new man, Ree, will step up into my place."

"Why don't you quit now?"

"Maybe I should. But I might just as well draw a salary until we get the house sold. Another month's pay, or two, will buy a lot of baby chicks."

"Eat some more."

"Had plenty. Think I'll go on down to the office and see what kind of character Halliday's found."

The sun was high in a cloudless sky, but the wind came from nowhere to whip and circle in gusty breaths. The smell of gas was strong. He stood on the front porch, hat in hand, and watched the heat waves lancing over the top of his car. The lawn needed watering, but he knew it would be a waste of time to water it now. The sun would soak up the moisture before it had a chance to soak through the hard crust of the soil.

A stray dog scratched a hole under the chinaberry tree.

A gang of kids, barefoot, came down the street, sticking big toes into the heat bubbles of the asphalt.

He could, from his front porch, see the courthouse and the hotel, over the tops of houses, clear and plain and neat looking. And beyond, as far as the eye could see, oil derricks sprouted in disordered profusion.

A hell of a town, he thought. Shacks and tents and trailer houses, flanking expensive homes. Shacks and tents and trailer houses, with new cars parked in front and good furniture inside.

A hell of a town.

Maybe Catherine had been right. Maybe, taken it all in all, it would be better to resign now. It would be nice to leave this town, this county, this flat forsaken country. Go away. A long way away, where it rained, snowed.

He sighed, put hat on head, and went to the car.

Chapter Six

The train whistle sounded fuzzy and dreamy to Laura Green, the whoo-ooo-ooo, whoo-ooo-ooo, whooooo-oooing lonesomely lonely and by itself.

Like Laura Green.

Something soft rubbed her cheek, and she realized that she was hugging the pillow tight in her arms.

Need a man, a man, a man, she thought. Never had a man, but need one.

She was on her side, her left side, legs doubled up, body in a curve, pillow held tight.

The whoo-ooo-ooo of the train faded away, but later she felt the vibration of the train as it roared into town. The windows rattled.

She pushed the pillow away and rolled over on her back, knees up. Her hands cupped her breasts.

I wonder, she wondered, I wonder what's wrong with me. Inhibited, probably.

A girl with a body, like this body, and a face, like this face, and legs, like these legs, should have plenty of men.

All that's necessary, all, is give a look or say a word or wiggle in the right way in the right places at the right time.

But the trouble is that it's not just a date that's wanted, or needed. But a man, all of a man, here with me. And unknowing how to go about it and afraid to date because it won't be just a date.

Is it un-normal to be like this? Are all girls like this? Or do other girls go all the way? Over-sexed? Heard that somewhere or read somewhere.

And how could one know what one wants if one never had it? Maybe, if a man took the place of this pillow, it would be revolting and nasty. But how could one find out?

Try it and see.

What was it Rita had said—"there is no such thing as a nice girl. Any girl can be had by the right man at the right time in the right place..."

Rita should know.

Laura Green reached out for the pillow, her face hot.

The men called her Legs, sometimes, when they talked to other men, never to her face. But she wouldn't have cared.

"Hey, Laura," Rita had said one day. "You'd never guess what the guys call you. Legs. Last night my boy friend—you know him—Jerry Maddox. A dream. He's a driller and, boy, has he got a good-looking boat! Spends money—throws it around like water! Well, we went to the Haven last night and he said, 'Say, how is Legs these days?' And I said, 'Who do you mean?' And he said, 'You know, Legs. The gal with the legs.' And I said, 'You must mean Laura Green. She's got the loveliest legs I've ever seen.' And he said, 'Sure, that's the one. The tall girl with the brown hair and the body beautiful. She walked down the street the other day,' he said, 'and I was standing at the curb. She was between me and the sun and she might just as well have left her dress off, because I could see right through it and the slip, too, if she wore a slip.' 'Well,' I said, 'that's Laura Green, all right....'"

"I had on a slip," Laura had protested. "It was sheer, I'll admit, but I thought the dress was thick enough."

But after that, always after that, she knew her figure was all right, and she walked with a conscious grace.

Still, no men. Somehow, when they talked to her they got scared. Something about her voice froze them.

Well, after all, when your father's a preacher and most of your life, your young life, was spent in church or going to church or coming from church, what can you expect?

Her hands, cupping her breasts, knees bent, thighs pressed close together, in the darkness in the bed with pillow against cheek and the lonely lonesome whoo-oooooo of a train fading.

Get ready for prayer meeting, Papa said on Wednesdays. Get ready for Sunday School, he said on Sunday mornings. Get ready for church, he said on Sunday nights....

Papa didn't believe in dates, except with nice young sons of church members. And only then when the date was a "to church and home early date."

In high school, even then, boys liked her legs and figure. She knew it. She didn't know how she knew it, but she knew it. And, knowing it, swung her hips when she walked and held her shoulders back to make her breasts push against the full-necked dresses Mama cut down for her.

For some reason, boys thought preachers' daughters were bad girls. And, in her thoughts, she was bad.

But, one night, a rare night, she walked home with a boy, or the boy walked home with her. From a party. And the boy kissed her, caressed her body with hot hands, until she cried and ran away.

Later, in bed, safe in bed, she was sorry she had run away.

Boys tried dating her, a few found the nerve to call at the house. Papa saw to it that they never came back.

Whose boy are you? Papa always asked.

I'm Lute Bingham's son, the boy would reply. Or Jesse Smith's boy, or Flirt Craddock's son.

Oh, Papa would say. Yes. Mighty fine man, your father, I've heard. Tell me, son, are you saved?

Then would follow a dissertation on smoking, drinking, dancing, thinking about girls. Once, and only once, because Mama dared stand up to Papa and order him to stop it, he lectured on the evils of masturbation.

(Laura and the boy looked the word up in the dictionary and never spoke one to the other again.)

Usually, by the time Papa had finished his lecture, it was too late to go anywhere. Or the boy would be too scared to do anything except go home. Laura would cry and stamp her feet, or shut herself in her room and sulk.

Papa sent her to business school after she graduated from high school. There was a depression and she got a job in a café to help pay her way. Papa lost his church and had to take a smaller one in Rockford. And he never got over losing his church, and he became old. Older and kinder and more tolerant.

Laura saved three hundred dollars.

She heard there were plenty of jobs in Breton, and quit school to become a file clerk in an auto-parts store. For thirty dollars a month she rented a garage apartment. The furniture was shabby, but she hung curtains and pictures, and it didn't look so bad. Papa and Mama came over on the first Sunday and brought her the red leather chair from Papa's study.

And then she bought the car.

It was a convertible, repainted yellow. Although it was an old model, it was tight and clean.

"I'm telling you the truth," the salesman had said. "That car's just like new. Why, you wouldn't believe it, but that car belonged to an old one-legged school teacher! Old maid, she was, and she never learned to drive. During the winters she'd jack it up in the garage and just go out in the morning and let the motor run a few minutes...."

The salesman was cute. Well, hell, there're lots of cute men....

Laura made forty-five dollars a week. She bought dresses on a lay-away plan, plain frocks that suited her figure, and even began payments on a fur coat. On week ends, most week ends, she drove over to see Papa and Mama. At night she drove around town.

Men always whistled at her.

In the convertible, with top down and long hair flying, she was whistle bait. At times she was tempted to make a pick-up, but something inside prevented her.

She read love stories in bed, one after the other, until her eyes burned.

Once, in the summer heat, she went to work wearing nothing but a dress.

It must be psychological.... Exhibitionism, Laura Green thought and fell asleep.

The alarm rang, and she was wide awake without effort. She got out of bed and made coffee, then bathed and dressed.

She drove downtown, without hurrying, and decided to have coffee and a roll.

In the café, seated and waiting for her order, she saw a man eating breakfast with Mr. Halliday. The man was handsome, rumpled and handsome, and he stared at her. Once Mr. Halliday looked up and saw her, and then looked away.

Laura smiled, knowing his embarrassment. He had asked her for a date. Maybe, she thought, I should have gone out with him. His wife must be out of town.

She could feel the young man's eyes on her, burning into her, as she paid her bill and left the café.

Chapter Seven

Martha Halliday slept late.

The plane trip had been tiring, and last night had been more tiring. She had heard her husband get up, go to the bathroom and become sick, and later heard the clatter of pots and pans in the kitchen.

Once, but only once, she considered getting up and having coffee with Ben, but it wasn't hard to decide against it. After all, when one is considering divorce, it isn't wise to get too chummy with your husband.

And Martha Halliday was considering divorce.

Those two nights with Richard Feltz had been, well, heavenly, and her conscience didn't bother her a bit. She wasn't worried about Ben finding out, either, even though he *had* stared at Richard a bit peculiarly at the airport.

Not that I have decided to get a divorce, she thought. Not really. I'll consider it, but not decide for a while. Not until Richard earns more money....

And, she thought, that's just being sensible. After all, Ben *is* wealthy. (Not rich, in Martha's mind, but wealthy.) I *have* been accustomed to money, a great deal of money, and Richard is only a manager of something at Johnson Tool. If he *really* gets to be a vice-president, like he said, well....

Martha slept late. And, after sleeping late, she stayed in bed and considered.

After all, she thought, I have grounds for a divorce. I have a reason. Ben and his precious Nora, sweet precious Nora, have been carrying on an affair for goodness knows how long. A fool could see it.

But, she thought, I have been unfaithful.

Yes, she thought, but not until those two nights with Richard. All these years I have been faithful to Ben, and if he had been faithful to me, well....

Martha Halliday got up, let her gown slide to the floor in a heap, and then went to the bathroom for a shower.

Later, in a robe, but barefoot, she went to the kitchen and warmed the coffee Ben had left in the pot.

No servants. And Ben filthy rich—wealthy. But, then, a woman came to clean.

Two cups of coffee, and starting on a third with the first cigarette of the day. And, only then, did she dare think of the odd proposal of Richard's, made on the plane.

He must have been drunk—he must have been!

"Why sweat it all out?" he'd asked. "Why be conventional? Why don't we go away together, to Mexico or Brazil?"

"But that takes money," she had said.

"Forty thousand dollars would last a long time in Mexico or Brazil."

"Richard!" she had said. "You don't have forty thousand dollars!"

"No," he said, "but I could get it. And you could get a few thousand yourself."

"Well, I must say...."

"Don't be coy, Martha!" His words were sharp. "You could get a few thousand! Ten, say. That'd make fifty thousand in all, and with fifty thousand...."

"You're joking."

"No, I'm not. There's always a forty-thousand-dollar packet in the company safe! Been there for years. The old man keeps it for an emergency. You see, back during the depression, the old man lost a lot of money when the banks failed. Since then he's kept this forty thousand in the safe."

"You mean you'd steal?"

"For you."

"Richard!" She was shocked, but pleased.

"I was joking," he said.

"Of course you were."

But was he?

Smoking and drinking coffee, in broad daylight, Martha wasn't so sure. Suddenly, in a spurt of energy, she snubbed out her cigarette and left the kitchen.

She had considered and now she was sure. She would drop Richard. It had been madness, all of it. A delightful madness, to be sure, but a madness.

Ben was wealthy. Security. Plenty of money and security. No love, no passion.

She smiled and thought, Love and passion can be found.

She heard a noise in the front part of the house and knew it was Ben.

"Where on earth have you been?" she asked.

"Went for a walk."

"What a way to dress! Want some coffee?"

"No, thanks. Had coffee."

He went to the phone and dialed a number. In a moment she heard him talking to Chief Bronson.

Something about putting a man named Willa Ree on the police force.

What a name! she thought. Willa is a girl's name. And Ree, well....

Later, at lunch, she made small talk about her trip.

"How's your mother?" Ben asked.

"Fine. She's coming out sometime in the fall."

"That's good. Say, who was that guy got off the plane ahead of you last night? Works for Johnson Tool, I think."

She almost gasped. Could he know something?

"Oh," she said, "you mean that Feltz man. Richard Feltz, I think."

His face brightened. "That's it," he said.

"I sat by him on the plane," she ventured, "and he told me an interesting thing."

"Uh?"

"His boss, old Johnson, keeps forty thousand dollars in the company safe all the time. Mr. Feltz said that back during the depression the old man lost some money in the banks, and so now he keeps the money in a package in the safe. In case there's another depression, or something."

"Fool thing to do," Ben grunted. "Some burglar'll hear about it some day."

"That's what I told Richard—Mr. Feltz."

"Uh," Ben grunted.

Nora called after lunch, and had to hear all about the trip. And, then, after having said good-by once, she said, "Martha, why don't you and Ben drop over tonight?"

"Why, I'd like to."

"Ben's probably tired of us, though. He was over last night for drinks and dinner." Nora hung up.

Martha slammed the receiver on the hook. "Damn her!" she said. And she meant Nora.

Chapter Eight

Willa Ree finished his breakfast and ordered more coffee and a pack of cigarettes. He sat in the booth and watched the customers come and go. The sun looked hot outside, but it was still cool inside the café.

A newsboy came in with papers under his arm. Ree bought one, giving the boy the dime he'd had when he hit town.

The sun was up, way up, and big and glary and blinding when he went outside.

Most of the stores were open. A few cars were parked at the curb. Men leaned against parking meters and watched other men sweep off the walks in front of stores. A heavy truck, loaded with pipe, meshed its gears and groaned along the street. A lone Negro pushed a broom along the curb, stooping now and again to scoop up dirt and glass and paper and deposit them in a wheelbarrow.

A typical boom town, like so many others. Made to order.

Buildings squatty and cheap, fronted with stucco and garish with neon. A courthouse, old as time, and tired, with grass green under planted elms. An oasis where old men gathered to chew tobacco and whittle and spit.

A gang of roughnecks, wearing safety helmets and driller's boots, climbed aboard a truck, dinner pails clattering.

Willa Ree paid three dollars for a white shirt, and one dollar for a tie. His pants, from the bundle, were cleaned and pressed while he had his shoes shined. He changed clothes in the tailor's rest room.

He got a shave and a haircut.

"Where's the City Hall?" he asked the barber.

"West two blocks. New brick building next on the corner. You can't miss it."

Cars lined the curb now, and the walks were crowded. The hum of traffic was loud and strident. There was a small crowd knotted around the broken plate-glass window of a jewelry store.

The City Hall wasn't large, but it was neat and modern and expensive-looking. Three girls worked behind a long counter in the main office.

"You wanta pay your water bill?" a little blonde asked, posing behind advertised breasts.

"I want to see the chief of police," Ree said.

"Through that door," the blonde pointed.

A fat desk sergeant looked up. He was bald, and his eyes were buggy. His cheeks and wrinkled chin looked pasty white beneath black bristles.

"The Chief in?"

The sergeant looked at a clock on the wall.

"It might be a while yet."

"Thanks."

He left the Hall and walked along a street, past a church, two liquor stores, a laundry, a bakery, and a score of small stores. He walked slowly, stopping to look in shop windows, and whistling softly all the while. Once, while looking in a shop window, he took a wrist watch from his pocket and strapped it on his wrist.

The sign said: "AJAX PRINTERS—Stationers and Publishers."

It was a small shop. An old man, stooped and wrinkled and slow, peered through horn-rimmed glasses that threatened to slide off the end of his nose.

"I need some cards, Pop."

The old man pointed at a pencil and paper.

Willa Ree wrote:

"WILLA REE Private Investigator Los Angeles, California"

"How many?" the old man asked.

"How much for a hundred?"

"Two dollars."

"O.K. If you can get on them right now."

"Come back in an hour. Give them a chance to dry."

"Make it a nice, classy job."

The old man snorted. "For two dollars?"

"The workman is worthy of his hire."

"Come back in an hour."

Two hours later, Willa Ree again entered the City Hall. The blonde with the breasts smiled. Ree smiled.

The chief was not in uniform. He wore gray gabardine slacks and a gray gabardine shirt. He sat in a swivel chair, rancher-type hat, Stetson but not ten gallon, creased expertly, no doubt, between two cans of tomatoes. His feet, booted, were on the desk. His hair was sparse and gray at the temples, his face lined and tired.

Ree flipped a card on the desk, pulled up a metal folding chair, and sat down. He lit a cigarette.

"Have a seat," the chief said. "My name's Bronson."

"I'm Willa Ree."

Bronson sighed, pulled his feet off the desk, and looked at the card.

"Baloney!" he said.

"How do you know?"

"It doesn't matter. I guess you've had experience."

"Yeah."

"You want a job."

"Yeah."

"You're hired."

"Just like that?"

"Just like that. Halliday said you'd see me."

"Halliday?"

"You know."

"I had breakfast with a Halliday. So who does that make me?"

"That makes you a dectective lieutenant, I reckon. At least, that's what Halliday said. He gives the orders." Bronson seemed puzzled.

"What is he? The mayor?"

"More. He's on the council, runs it. Didn't he tell you anything?"

"No."

"Then, how does he know... you'll do the work he wants done?"

"Oh. He wants some work done. Well, maybe he's a judge of character."

"Maybe so, but that doesn't give you anything to brag about."

"That kind of work?"

"That kind. I wouldn't touch it."

"Well, I'll touch it for you—if it's good."

"Not for me," Bronson said. "For Halliday."

"You're not allergic to money?"

"That kind of money." Seeing the look on Ree's face, he said, "Don't worry. Halliday knows how I feel. I tell him to his face what I say to his back."

"I'm sure you do," Ree said, and meant it.

Bronson sucked on a toothpick.

"What is it?" Ree asked. "Tramps on a strike? Pimps won't pay off? Or is Halliday selling protection?"

"I wouldn't know."

"That means I should ask Halliday."

"That's right." Bronson said flatly.

"Tell me," Ree said, "tell me why you stay."

"It's a living."

Bronson pressed a buzzer, and the fat sergeant appeared.

"Where's Swing?" Bronson asked.

"He comes on this afternoon," the sergeant said.

"Is Wesley out there?"

"Yeah."

"Send him in."

The sergeant left the office. Bronson turned to Ree. "Wesley's the present captain of police." He smiled faintly. "The council has been talking about a detective squad or vice squad lately, and Wesley was half promised the job. He'll love you."

"I'll bet."

Willa Ree stood up when Wesley entered.

Wesley looked like a model captain of police. He loved his uniform. Big, brown, and handsome, with squared features and surprising wavy blonde hair.

"You want me, Chief?"

"Yeah." Bronson sighed again. "This is Willa Ree. He's the new detective lieutenant." He raised his hand as Wesley started to speak. "It's not my idea. It's orders."

Wesley flushed, started again to speak, and stared at Willa Ree. Then he turned and left the room.

"You two will get along fine," Bronson said wryly.

"Like brothers."

"Well, that's your funeral."

"You're not very tactful."

"Why should I be?" Bronson asked. "He's a good man. Can't get rich on a captain's pay."

"Does a detective lieutenant's job pay better?"

"Let's just say a detective lieutenant in charge of vice—and other things—would have more opportunity, than a captain of police."

"Well," Ree said, "I should worry. Things are moving too fast for me, but I'll ride it and see where I land. What's the next step?"

"See Halliday," Bronson said. "That's what I'd do. See Halliday."

Chapter Nine

The way Willa Ree figured it, Halliday would get in touch with him, give him the layout.

The day passed, but Halliday made no effort to make contact.

Maybe, he decided, it would be best to go see Halliday. But, then again, it might be better to wait for Halliday to make the first move.

Yes. Better for Halliday to *ask* him to take over—well, whatever it is Halliday needed taken over.

Bronson told him of a place to stay. Ma Ferguson's boardinghouse. It was a big, rambling, two-story frame house, not too far from downtown, and comfortable enough.

"I'll call the old lady for you," Bronson offered. "Tell her you're coming by."

"Thanks."

"You've got to have a place to stay, and it's not easy to find anything decent."

"Appreciate it."

Bronson made the call, and one of the patrol cops drove him by. Ma Ferguson was fat, big and jolly and fat, wrinkled and three-chinned fat, with faded blonde hair which lay about her head in tightly plastered curls.

"Twenty-five a week," Ma said. "Breakfast at seven, lunch at twelve sharp, and supper at six."

"Good enough, Mrs. Ferguson."

"Ma to my people, Willie."

"It's Willa. W-i-l-l-a."

"O.K. Mine's M-a, M-a, Ma."

"O.K., Ma. I hope you'll trust me a few days, until I can get an advance on my salary."

"I trust everybody," Ma said, laughing. "Way I look at it, this world can stand a little more trust."

"I'll appreciate it to my dying day." His eyes laughed.

In his room, oddly restless, he forced himself to lie down. Once relaxed, he fell asleep, and Ma had to come in and shake him at six.

"Supper," she said. "You must be dead."

"Deader than I thought, Ma." He got up and stretched. "And I could use a meal."

"You come on out and eat, and then you come back and take a warm bath and go to bed. Best thing in the world for you."

"I'll do that."

There were twenty boarders. Some school teachers and some oil company clerks, but they paid him little attention. He ate, smoked, and went back to his room.

At breakfast it was different. Talk flowed freely, and he realized that now he was accepted as one of the family.

He walked to the Hall, greeted the girls in the front office, and went in to work.

Only, there was no work.

The sergeant ignored him, as did Bronson when he came in, and Ree spent the first day reading tattered magazines.

On the second day, bored and angry, he went back to the fire house and shot pool.

Wesley was in and out of the office, never speaking, and the uniformed police had little to say.

Well, what the hell, money's money, and I'm getting paid for sitting.

So I'll sit.

The days passed, and still Halliday hadn't made contact.

Two weeks passed—weeks of boredom. He drew his first pay check, went to the movies to escape the heat, and shot pool in the fire house. And, on Monday of the third week, he bought a hammer and saw.

It was Friday of the third week that he worked late. The sun had set when he left the Hall.

Wesley was waiting on the front steps.

"How about some coffee, Wesley?"

"No, thanks."

"Come on. I want to talk to you."

"I said no. Thanks."

"Listen!" Ree made his words sharp. "No kidding! I want to talk to you."

Wesley shrugged his shoulders and followed him across the street to the Aztec.

"Listen," Ree said when they had their coffee. "I know you figure you got a dirty deal."

Wesley lifted his eyebrows and poured sugar in his coffee, stirred, and reached for a cigarette.

"Can't say that I blame you," Ree said. "If you knew the facts, though, you'd understand." He pulled one of his cards from his pocket and said, "Look at that."

He was thinking. If the chump falls for this, he's dumber than I think....

But Wesley looked at the card and handed it back, saying, "If you're a private detective from California, why do you come here and take the job I'd been promised?"

"I'll explain."

"Anybody can get cards printed."

"Sure, if they wanted them," Ree admitted, thinking, The guy's not so dumb, so I'll have to play smart.

"You see, Wesley," he said, "I've been working on a case. A big case. Dope, mostly, but some burglary. The trail starts in Los Angeles, but I've traced it this far. That's why I was given your job—so I'd have authority to work in this state and crack down without going through a lot of red tape."

Wesley's laugh was explosive.

"So why didn't the Los Angeles force send one of their own men?" he asked. "You must take me for a chump, Ree."

"No, but you're sounding like one."

Wesley frowned. "You think I'm sucker enough to believe that a private detective would be put on the job? Hell! The Los Angeles force wouldn't even know you were alive!"

Willa Ree sipped his coffee and thought, so I put my foot in it. Why couldn't I keep my big mouth shut?

"Listen, Wesley," he said, "you can take it or leave it."

"I leave it. Anyway, why should I worry? I got a raise."

"More coffee?"

"No, thanks."

"Well, I've got to go, then. I've got a date."

"Anybody I know?" Wesley asked.

"The blonde over at the Hall."

"Arlene?"

"Right."

"That's my girl, Ree." Wesley got up and walked out.

Ree went uptown and stood on the corner, wondering why he'd lied to Wesley about the girl.

Well, why not call the girl? She'd go a long way, probably.

He called the girl.

"Sorry," she said. "Make it another night. I've got a date."

"Wesley?"

"How did you know?"

"Wesley. Will you tell Wesley I said I'm a great kidder?"

"Why?"

"He'll bring it up, and you just say I'm a great kidder."

"If you say so."

He went to a show, bought a bag of popcorn, and realized he had a dime left.

Here he was. Working for peanuts, and time was slipping by.

The show was a Western, but he forced himself to see it through. Even the comedy.

It was ten o'clock when he entered his room and switched on the light. Without hurrying, he wrapped the saw and hammer he'd bought in a newspaper, switched off the light and left the room.

It was ten-thirty when he turned down the alley that passed behind the boardinghouse, but now he had a coiled rubber garden hose over his left arm, taken from Ma Ferguson's back yard.

Ten forty-five when he entered the alley leading past the backs of downtown stores, and ten forty-seven when he stopped behind Frady's Hardware.

From his pocket he pulled heavy twine, and in a moment he had the hammer and saw hanging from a loop around his neck. He fitted the coiled hose over his left shoulder and began to climb a drain pipe. Without trouble he gained the roof.

On hands and knees he began to work.

The roof was covered with tarred paper, and he used the hammer claws to scrape away a patch. He swore, gleefully, when he saw the boards beneath. They were nailed in short lengths, toed-in at the beams, and he had no trouble prying a board loose. He began sawing.

At eleven, on the dot, he was crouched at the front of the building's roof, hidden by the stucco parapet, and listening to the footsteps on the sidewalk.

Two night-walking cops—Johnson and Cowles.

He couldn't see them, but he had checked the board carefully and had become familiar with the names and routines of all the cops.

One of them stopped to light a cigarette, while the other tried the door.

They walked on down the street slowly, and Willa Ree went back to his sawing.

It took ten minutes more to finish the hole in the roof, and after that it was easy. He tied the hose around an exposed beam, retied the hammer and saw to the looped twine and hung them around his neck. He slid down the hose, feeling with his feet for ceiling beams, for he knew the ceiling would not support his weight.

Standing on beams, he felt the ceiling. Sheet rock, as he'd guessed.

With the hammer, he knocked a hole in the sheet rock, and then began work with the saw. It was a snap.

He lowered the hose through the second hole, looped his tools around his neck again, and went down hand over hand.

There was a night light at the front of the building, and for a long minute he lay flat on the floor, peering at the plate glass windows at the front. Satisfied, he got up and walked to the cash register. He hit "no sale."

There was money in the register and some checks.

He laughed aloud.

For a moment, a short moment, he hesitated over the checks, but then he shrugged and stuck them in his pocket with the money. He didn't bother to close the register.

There was a safe in a small private office, but he made no attempt to crack it. But, damn it, he thought, I should have learned about safes.

He searched the office, but had no luck.

Glancing at his watch, he stood before the safe, and then sat down in the swivel chair before a desk. He lit a cigarette, leaned back, and smoked it to a short stub.

Willa Ree snubbed out the cigarette in a tray made in the shape of an auto tire.

A rack of tools covered the rear wall, and he stuck the saw on a rack with other saws. The hammer he stuck in his pocket with the cord. No use worrying about fingerprints on the saw. He'd looked at those saws, handled them, and had purchased one in this very store.

There was a window at the rear of the building, but he decided to climb the hose. It would be better to replace the hose in Ma Ferguson's back yard. She might read a newspaper account of the robbery, miss the hose, and tip the police.

It was easy. Hand over hand he climbed the hose, found a handhold, and was on the roof again. He pulled the hose up, coiled it, and slung it over his shoulder. A minute later, he was sliding down the drain pipe.

In his room, the hose back in place near the faucet in the rear yard, he counted the money. Two hundred and thirty-six dollars and a pocket full of change. Easy money.

With the checks carefully folded and placed in his billfold, he went to bed. He felt good.

And he slept soundly.

There was hell to pay at the Hall.

Chief Bronson, reporting early, wasn't happy. The night shift took a raking.

"Any ideas?" Ree asked.

But Bronson didn't know where to start. He blustered. A laugh tickled Willa Ree's throat, showed in his eyes, but he choked it down.

Bronson saw the beginning of the laugh and turned red. "O.K., Ree," he said. "You're the detective around here. Suppose you take over on this thing!"

"All right."

"You've been sitting around here for weeks, so now's as good a time as any to show what you can do!"

"All right!"

Bronson went into his office and closed the door.

Ree took a squad car and drove around town alone.

It was his first chance to see much of the town, and what he saw wasn't new.

The sum and total of all the boom towns in the world, of the past and present and future. Fifty thousand people jammed into space meant for five thousand. Honky-tonks and liquor stores, churches and tin-built night clubs, side by side, or facing across streets. A modern swimming pool across the street from a tent town. Unpaved streets running into fancy boulevards. Families in shacks, with limousines at the door. Derricks edging into the city limits. And, across the tracks, The Flats.

It was a sun-scorched town, with few trees for protection, and even the trees were alien to the land. In winter, the old timers said, the town was separated from the north pole by nothing but a barbed wire fence, and in summer not even an umbrella protected it from the scorching fires of hell.

Squat and stark it stood, ugly and scattered and temporary, a shack town of tin buildings with false stuccoed fronts. Its better buildings, in the center, the very center, were of brick, but they were old, square and dirty.

The town was flanked by honky-tonks, on all roads entering it or leaving it, side by side with junk yards and service stations.

Pipe, thousands and thousands of lengths of pipe, were stacked in endless stacks in small net-fenced yards, behind honky-tonks and service stations, beside derelict warehouses and shabby trucking firms.

For this was an oil town.

One railroad served the town, but it was an east-west link and busy. Highways ribboned four ways, long and undulating, like a snake, wriggling across the flat land that looked flat but was really a land of swells, like the sea. The highways were of asphalt, shiny by day and glistening by carlight at night. Travelers could be fooled by these highways by looking ahead into the distance and seeing water that wasn't there, or trees that weren't there, or houses and towns that weren't there.

There were fifty thousand people in Breton.

Few had planned to stay, but they stayed, held by the hope of oil, promise of oil, the fickle goddess of oil.

There were seventy liquor stores in Breton, and twenty churches.

The venereal rate was high, Bronson had said, especially among the young and in The Flats.

The courthouse was surrounded by transplanted elms. The City Hall, too new and bare and modern, looked out of place. A fire house joined the City Hall, and the jail, always full, was on the second of its two stories. There were two newspapers in Breton—The Telegraph, a daily, and the semiweekly Traveler.

Ree drove to The Flats.

A Negro youth shuffled down the middle of the dusty street, and Ree coasted to a stop beside him and said, "Get in."

The youth gasped, started to speak, but Ree opened the car door. The boy got in.

"You're in trouble, son."

"But I ain't done nothin' at all, Captin!"

"Shut up."

"But I ain't...."

"Shut up."

The boy's mouth slacked open. He began to tremble.

Willa Ree drove out of town, taking his time, humming under his breath and ignoring the boy. The last honky-tonk and service station faded behind. Flat land stretched away to the horizon, studded with derricks, sprinkled with sage and sand and washed by the sun. A dirt road intersected the highway, and Ree turned and drove fast for a mile. Both sides of the road were fenced. A rotting coyote was draped over the fence, and grinning steer skulls sat atop posts. First a jack, and then a road runner, darted from the ditches and disappeared into the sage.

"You're in trouble, son," Ree said softly, stopping the car.

"But I ain't done a single thing, Captin," the boy moaned.

"Get out."

"What you aimin' to do?"

"Get out, now."

"But I swear I ain't done nothin'," the boy said. "Not *nothin'*, Captin! I swear I...."

"I said get out!"

The boy moaned.

Ree got out of the car, circled behind it, and opened the door on the boy's side.

The boy got out and stood trembling.

Willa Ree smiled.

The boy tried to smile, but only his lips moved. Willa Ree hit him with his right hand, and blood poured from the boy's nose. He staggered, but didn't fall.

"I ain't done..."

With his left, Ree hit the boy in the stomach. The boy's breath left him with a grunting sigh, and he doubled over. A right caught him on the jaw and stretched him on the ground.

Willa Ree began to kick, but not too hard.

When the boy stopped squirming, Ree bent over and opened an eyelid. White showed.

Taking his billfold from his pocket, Ree removed the checks he'd taken from the hardware store. He stuck them in the Negro boy's shirt pocket, buttoned the flap, and straightened up and found a cigarette.

The boy opened his eyes and began to cry. Willa Ree took the cigarette from his lips and stuck it between the boy's lips.

"Get up and get in the car, now," he said.

The boy dug with his elbows, grunted his way to his knees, caught hold of the car door and stood up. Ree helped him get inside, closed the door, lit another cigarette, and then got in.

"You're in trouble, son," he said.

"Yessuh."

The boy cried softly, rubbing his eyes with a sleeve.

"So what have you got to lose, son?" Ree asked the boy.

He drove fast on the way back to town, parked the car at the side of the Hall, and helped the boy inside.

Bronson had seen him from the office window and was waiting.

"Think we've got our man, Chief," Willa Ree said.

"What happened to him?"

"Resisted arrest."

"I'll bet."

"Well, I had a tip on this boy and I think he's the one."

"It's not right," Bronson said. "Beating up on a kid like that, I mean. If a cop wants to fight and act brave, why don't he pick somebody his own size?"

"I do sometimes."

"I'd like to see it! Why is it that cops think they have to beat up on drunks and Negro boys?"

Willa Ree shrugged his shoulders.

"What makes you think this boy pulled the job?" Bronson asked.

"A tip."

Willa Ree searched the boy's pockets, saving the shirt pocket until last. He grunted when he found the checks.

"Guess that ties it up," he said.

"Well," Bronson said after he'd looked at the checks.

"Book him and see if he'll tell where he hid the money."

"O.K."

"And don't beat it out of him, either."

"You're the chief. Anyway, I wouldn't beat a guy in jail. A guy hasn't got a chance to defend himself in jail."

"Does he out of jail?"

"Well," Willa Ree said. "I don't carry a gun."

Chapter Ten

Laura Green saw Willa Ree many times before he noticed her.

In the morning, or after lunch, every day, she saw him going down the walk to the Hall. He looked more prosperous than he had that morning in the café, for now he wore tailored gabardines and hand-stitched cowboy boots. His walk was arrogant, flauntingly arrogant, or conceited, or something, and she despised it and him for it, but still she was attracted.

The attraction was a challenge and it angered her.

He couldn't call himself handsome, and yet he could.

Instinct prompted her to appear cold and aloof. She began to go to work early, parking near City Hall and waiting for Ree to walk past. She smoked, sat in the convertible and smoked, pretending not to see him, but still she felt his eyes strip the dress from her body. And, still, he did not speak.

Sure of himself, she thought. Taking his time.

And then, one day, he spoke.

She nodded, coolly, curtly.

After that, he spoke every day. And every day she nodded, eyes veiled and disinterested and cool and mocking.

On one day, a hot day, she ate lunch early and went to sit in the car. Her breath came dry and hard and her dress stuck to her body with a gritty feeling, and she opened the car door for air.

Time passed, but no Willa Ree passed, or perhaps he had eaten an early lunch.

Perspiration covered her body, and she straightened her legs, her feet hanging out the door. There were no passers, no cars, no sound but the sound of the wind, and she lifted her dress above her knees and stretched her legs, let her head fall back and closed her eyes.

When she opened her eyes, he was standing before the car door, staring. Then he smiled.

She slid her dress down.

"It's hot," he said.

She smiled and nodded.

"Where do you live?"

"Thirty-three West Seventh," she said.

"I'll be there at eight."

"I won't be there."

"You will be."

"But I won't."

His voice was soft. "You'd better be there."

A threat? But, how a threat?

"I don't fool around with little old policemen," she said.

"I'm not a little old policeman," he said. "I'm a detective, and you are Laura Green and your father is a preacher. What's more, you're on the make for me."

Shock made her gasp. "Well, of all the...." She turned angry red.

And then she laughed in his face.

He slapped her—hard.

His face swam before her eyes. His lips were moving, but rage thundered in her ears and blotted out the sound of his voice.

"Leave me alone," she whispered.

"I will," he said. And he walked away, whistling.

She got out of the car. He had stopped on the walk.

"I'll see you at eight," he said.

Later, at work, she blamed herself. She'd been too obvious. And she shouldn't have had her legs out like that and dress up.

Maybe, she thought, he was just showing off. Maybe he's nice, after you get to know him. Maybe he'll take me out to dinner, and later to a show, and then, maybe, he'll kiss me a little... and be nice.

On the way home, though, she wondered if she wanted him to be nice.

She planned how to act, how to talk, what to say. She would be dignified, aloof.

Apologize for the legs and the dress and the laugh. Take the blame, for after all, she'd provoked him. Maybe he'd apologize, too.

She bought a bottle of liquor after work, went home and ate a sandwich, tidied up the living room. What to wear?

After her bath she fixed her hair and nails, and, after a moment's hesitation, slipped into a negligee.

She laughed and thought, Now how the devil do you figure on being cool and aloof and dignified in a negligee?

And he'd been like—what? A little boy, she thought, a spoiled little boy, selfish little boy....

He knew her name and where she worked and where she came from. She had long, brown hair, and she was tall, beautifully tall, and she had the legs.

Once he'd seen her wearing a thin dress without a slip, and he heard that men often followed her for blocks.

She drove a convertible, and every day she parked near City Hall and smoked a while before going in to her work.

He thought of her often.

At night, in his room, he thought of her walking down the street, hips swaying, legs flashing as her heels click-clicked on the pavement. Her legs were golden-honey colored, and when he thought of her, at night in his room, he could see the flashing of the legs as she click-clicked down the walk.

Sometimes, at night in his room, a tight feeling of desire knotted his throat, and, lying on his bed, the pillow made a sounding board that made the throbbing of blood in his throat audible, throbbingly audible.

At night, in his room, the thought of her was tantalizing, so that sleep wouldn't come, and he would lie on his bed and close his eyes to make her appear with tanned golden legs flashing. On these nights, with gritted teeth and mind ordered to stop thinking, he'd succeed in pushing the vision away, only to have it return when he became drowsy and forgot to guard whatever it is that retains the photographic images of tanned golden legs flashing.

That girl, he told himself, is the girl I'll marry.... Like hell, like hell, like hell I will....

He saw her sitting near the Hall each morning, and after lunch. She'd be in the car, smoking, and each day he'd speak and each day she'd nod.

There'd been no rain in June, and July was hot and dry. The earth was hard packed and cracked, and the wind was a constant howling, mournful thing that swished dust through the streets of the town. Lawns withered and yellowed, and planted trees, carefully pruned and nurtured, drooped thirstily. Ranchers came to town to stand on the streets or sit in the hotel lobby, speaking little, squinting at the sky. The sun became a white hot tormentor, coming up hot in the morning and growing hotter and hotter as the hours passed.

Ree didn't care.

Ree had a good idea what was expected of him now. The town was ripe, dead and juicy ripe, and he was ready for the plucking. When Halliday, if Halliday, gave the word, he'd pick the town clean.

Now, though Bronson remained cool, Ree reported for duty at eight. Gradually, subtly, he began to set up a detective detail. Wesley avoided him, as did a few members of the force, but he did his work and ignored Wesley.

On most days he drove around the town, dropped in at honky tonks and pool halls, drank beer and swapped gossip, and little by little, piece by piece, he began to weave the fabric of the town.

And, one day, he walked down the street and saw Laura Green sitting in her car, with the door open, legs sprawled out, feet sticking out the door.

He started.

She must have felt his eyes, because she sat up, smoothed down her dress and crossed her legs.

"It's hot," he said.

He'd asked where she lived, and she had told him.

"I'll be there at eight," he said.

"I won't be there," she had replied. And he had been fresh, smart, too fast. She laughed in his face and he had slapped her.

And, at eight, he took a cab to the address she'd given. It was a garage apartment, and he climbed to the steps and knocked.

Footsteps inside.

The door opened and she stood silhouetted by the light, her body outlined beneath the negligee.

"Are you going to ask me in?"

"Come in."

He sat down on the couch, propped his feet in a red leather chair, and smoked.

She went into the kitchen, and he heard the clinking of glasses, the clicking of ice cubes.

She brought the drinks on a tray.

"Not poisoned?"

"Drink and see," she said.

"Good," he said.

"I hope you choke."

"You don't, not really. Why do you talk like that, anyway? You're not fooling me."

"No?"

"What're you trying to do? Live recklessly?"

"Maybe."

"Trying to convince me that you're fast enough to handle me?"

"Maybe."

He put his drink on the table and stood up.

She shrank back, slid into a red leather chair, and he had to pull her up, his arms tight around her, his mouth seeking hers.

She pushed him away.

He was breathing hard, but so was she.

"Afraid?" he asked.

"Yes."

"You want me to kiss you."

"Yes."

He leaned over and kissed her cheek, her hair, the back of her neck. Her head fell back and he kissed her lips gently.

Her arms went around his neck, and now his kiss was savage and demanding. Her lips tightened, trembled, parted.

He picked her up and carried her to the couch.

And, in the early morning hours, he went home, shaken.

Drop her, he told himself. She's a trap, a man trap.

He couldn't sleep.

She had cried. He had held her close, for she needed holding close. His murmured words had soothed her, and she had slept.

She was like a child. And, yet, so unlike a child.

More woman than he had ever known, ever hoped to know, ever wanted to know.

"I love you," she'd said. "I love you so much, and it hurts."

"I'm glad," he said. "But love shouldn't hurt."

"My kind does, though," she said. And she had gone to sleep.

Time became nothing to Laura, was unheeded, uncounted.

To Ree, it passed slowly.

Laura worked, and the hours were filled with thoughts of Willa Ree.

He was tender, gentle, possessive.

The days passed, and the nights passed, but the nights passed faster than the days, for he was with her at night and gone with the morning, so that days became times between nights, commas and dashes, the turning of pages.

The days and nights passed, and then they ran together, molded themselves to the weeks, with no separating points and no intervals.

Love, she thought, is not this, for this is not love—or is it—and if it is love for me it might not be love for him, so don't love.

Even in her dreams, sleep dreams or day dreams, she couldn't picture herself as Willa Ree's wife. Or, rather, she couldn't picture him as her husband. Somehow, he didn't fit into the picture.

His name was in the papers, now, and people talked about him. He made traffic speeches before clubs and school children, speeches about dope and vice, talked over the radio, submitted articles to the paper.

"The guy's a comer," someone said.

"The guy's trying to be chief of police," someone said.

The days passed slowly to Willa Ree, for the town was ripe and Halliday might never have existed, for no word came.

Maybe, he thought, maybe I should tap the graft for myself. Maybe Halliday isn't connected.

Bronson, finally, drew into a shell and allowed him to run the detective squad as he saw fit. He was assigned three rookie cops and Sergeant Swing, and he was efficient.

He received invitations to speak before clubs, and he talked about organized crime. The clubs ate it up. He was invited to speak over the radio once a week, and accepted, and the paper asked him to submit a series of articles.

They ran his picture in the daily Telegraph, but the semiweekly Traveler reported his speeches in tongue-in-cheek style.

Still, the town was ripe for a plucking, and it seemed that Halliday wasn't going to call.

And, then, Halliday called.

"Ree," he said, "how about coming up to my house for dinner tonight?"

"Why, I'd like to."

"Good. I want you to meet Sam Byrd. How about eight o'clock?"

"That'd be fine."

"Good. Be expecting you, then."

And, for the rest of the day, he felt good. The time had come.

He drove around town, strangely exhilarated and confident, and the town looked like his town, felt like his town, smelled like his town.

Even the gas smell was different.

"I'll pick you like a ripe grape," he said. "Like a ripe grape, and I'll squeeze you dry."

Chapter Eleven

Ben called Nora. "What're you and Sam doing tonight?"

"The usual, Ben," Nora said. "Sam'll swill beer until he's groggy, and then he'll switch to liquor. Then he'll pass out and I'll read a book."

"Well, bring him over to the house early, before he has a chance to take a drink, and have supper with us. There'll be a fellow there I'd like you to meet."

"Oh, who is he?"

"Willa Ree."

"Oh. Well, we'd love to."

"And, Nora—"

"Don't worry, Ben. I'll be quiet as a little mouse."

"As a little cat, you mean."

"Don't call me a cat, Ben, or I might claw you."

"Some day," he said, "some sweet day, I'm going to let you claw me all you want."

"I'm looking forward to it. What time shall we come over?"

"About eight?"

"Eight'll be fine. Good-by, Ben."

"'By, Nora."

Well, he'd put his foot in it, with eyes wide open, too. All this time's passed and Nora hasn't squealed to Martha, but tonight, sure as shooting, it'll come out. It'll come out in that sly way women have of saying things, telling things, tattling things, with catlike digs.

Well, to hell with it.

He called Martha.

"But, Ben!" she protested. "I'd planned on seeing a movie tonight."

"This is important, Martha," he said.

"What's so important about a little police detective?"

"Politics, honey."

"Graft, you mean."

"What was that?"

"I'm sorry, Ben."

"That was a hell of a thing to say to your own husband!"

"I'm sorry, Ben."

"So that's what you think? That's what you really think?"

"I said I was sorry, Ben."

"You couldn't be sorry if you meant it. And you meant it!"

"I just said it, Ben. Just kidding, like."

"Where did you ever hear anything like that?"

"I haven't heard anything like that! Now, for crying out loud, will you drop it?"

"O.K."

"What time did you set for supper?"

"Eight o'clock."

"Cocktails before?"

"Yes. You know Sam Byrd. He'll be shaking like a rag unless he gets oiled up a little."

Martha hung up.

He didn't feel like working. It was hot, even with the air conditioner going, and he went to the drugstore for a Coke. The soda jerk was a girl, tiny and blonde and high schoolish, but she had sweet little round breasts under a low-cut blouse, and she bent over the counter, wiping it, and he looked.

Leaving the drugstore, he went up the street, walking aimlessly, until he decided to drop in on Sam Byrd.

"He's in his office," Sam's secretary said. "I think he's locked his door."

"The sot'll be too drunk to unlock it by quitting time," he said. "I'll see what I can do." He knocked.

"Who is it?"

The words were muffled, but not thick, only muffled by the door.

"Open up, Sam. It's Ben."

Not footsteps, but shufflings, and clumsy rattlings at the door, and then the door swung open and Sam Byrd stood, glass in hand, smiling foolishly and said, "Oh, h'lo, Ben."

"Starting a little early, aren't you?"

"Early, late, no matter."

"Well, I might as well have one."

He went across to the small box and got ice, watching Sam out of the corner of his eye as he mixed a drink.

"Don't hit it too heavy, Sam. You and Nora are coming over to the house for supper. Want you to meet this Willa Ree."

"He's the new stooge?"

"Stooge isn't a very good word, Sam."

Byrd waved a hand. "Don't try to make it sound good, Ben. No use. Bronson won't play ball. Oh, don't look surprised—I know what's going on! Everybody knows it. Sheriff Messner was telling me yesterday that you were trying to take everything under the police department's wing. And he doesn't like it, Ben."

"No, but he'll take it."

"That county bunch could make things rough if they got mad."

"I think I know what I'm doing." Ben took a sip of his drink, grimaced, and lit a cigarette.

"Arthur Fry's a pretty powerful man," Sam Byrd said. "And you know as well as I do that Messner's a tool for Fry."

"You've got it hind part forward," Halliday said. "Fry's got Messner to thank for getting elected county attorney in the first place. And in the second place, Fry hasn't got the guts to front anything. No, Sam, take it from me, Messner's the brains over at county, and he's smart enough to let me have my way about things."

"Things!" Sam Byrd laughed.

"Well, what do you want me to say?"

"Graft!"

"All right, damnit! Graft! And now I know where Martha gets that word!"

"I've not...."

"No, maybe not! But you cry on Nora's shoulder and Nora cries to Martha! Now, you listen to me, Sam! You're in this thing just as much as I am, and mister, you've got dollars in the bank to show for it!"

Sam Byrd sat down on the desk, put the glass down, jiggled it and turned it and twisted it.

"Yeah," he said. "Yeah. But— Well, it's not been from, well, graft. Before, it's been business."

A slow smile, amused but cold, too, skimmed the surface of Halliday's face.

"Business, you said. Yes, I guess it was. At least, we can call it business. But I know and you know different."

"Yeah. All right, Ben, have it your way. I don't like it, but then I haven't liked any of it. You said Fry was Messner's tool. Well, I guess I'm your tool."

"Tool? You, Sam? A tool's something you use. How do I use you?"

"As a front, Ben."

Halliday pursed his lips and cocked his head. "You're smarter than I thought," he said, "so I might as well admit it. Only, I'm not obvious about it, Sam. I don't let you lead the way like Messner does Fry."

"Oh, you're smart enough," Sam Byrd said. "Even I know that."

"What's bothering you, anyway?" Halliday asked. "Does your conscience hurt?"

"Yes, I guess it does," Sam Byrd said, indecision in his voice. "I guess it's my conscience. I don't know for sure, you see, because it's been a long long time since I inspected it. In fact, I didn't think I had one any more. I know a man can't make a lot of money and stay strictly honest, you see, but in business—real business and not politics—it's all right as long as you use business methods. Ethics, I guess you'd call it."

"Politics is no different."

"Yes it is, Ben. You know it is. A man in business can make money honestly—but you can't make an honest dime in politics. Except a salary, and we don't even get a salary. We're supposed to devote our time to the public good, and that's worse than it would be if we were getting paid, you see, because the public trusts us. We're supposed to be community leaders; the people look up to us."

"What do you want to do—resign?"

"I'd like to. Yes, I'd like to resign."

"I can't let you do it."

"Why not?"

"Publicity," Halliday said. "And you know what happens when you get publicity. People start asking questions. They get curious."

"I could say that business keeps me too busy. I could say my health is bad."

"That would be all right, Sam. But, the truth is, Bronson is going to resign one of these days. If you quit he'll quit too, hoping that it'll cause people to ask questions. And he's the man to talk if he's given a halfway chance."

Sam Byrd poured liquor over the ice in his glass. His hands trembled, his chin trembled, and he drank the whisky off in one big gulping gulp.

"Then stay out of the graft, Ben," he said. There was a pleading note in his voice. "If I can't quit, then, for crying out loud, Ben, don't make things any dirtier than they are. It was bad enough before. We took kickbacks! We took pay-offs on bidding for every damned thing the city bought! We took surplus goods from the government for ourselves!"

"Let that bother your conscience, then," Halliday said. "But, be reasonable, Sam! Don't let it bother you if we take money from tramps and pimps and gamblers and bookies!"

"It's graft!"

"Graft it is, but it's expected! We've got to have gamblers and bookies and pimps and all the rest! You know why, Sam? Well, I'll tell you why! Because the people want them, that's why! The people want them or they wouldn't be around! All right, what would happen if we ran them out to town? Do you know, Sam? I'll tell you what'd happen! The people would raise hell, that's what they'd do! You know who'd be the only happy people if we ran them out of town? The preachers, that's who!"

"I wouldn't say...."

"No, you wouldn't! But it's true, just the same."

"So what of it? It'd be the right thing to do, wouldn't it?"

"No it wouldn't, Sam! They help make this town. Find any live-wire town and you'll find pimps and tramps and gamblers and bookies and all the rest. And something else, Sam. They're *regulated* in every town! They pay off in every town! They help pay guys like us! They help pay underpaid policemen and county attorneys and city councilmen!"

"Regulated is a good word, Ben. A good word for graft."

"Call it anything you want. All I'm saying is that society has a certain element it can't do without, and that element expects to pay off. It might just as well be us doing the collecting. Don't you know the people know what's going on?"

"Cut that out, Ben! You don't believe what you're saying any more than I do! If you do, you're a bigger fool than I thought—or you're just trying to salve your conscience."

Halliday's voice trembled. "Listen, Sam," he said, "Not so long ago, not so dammed long ago..." he paused and pointed a shaky finger. "You can remember not so long ago when you had a two-bit place, and that was mortgaged up to your neck!" The finger became a menacing spear. "I took you practically out of the gutter, Sam Byrd! You'd have been broke in a month and you know it. Oh, you took my help, Sam. You got on your feet and, don't you ever forget it, you were damned glad to run for council when I gave the word!" He stopped speaking, ran a hand over his face, and breathed hard. "I didn't hear anything about your conscience when you first started making money, Sam! For two long years you took dollar for dollar along with me. You built this place and stocked it, and you've got plenty dollars where the others came from! Now, tell me this!" He shouted, and the finger speared out. "Why has your conscience started hurting you all of a sudden?"

Sam Byrd was sober. He splashed more liquor in his glass and drank it like medicine. "Maybe you're right, Ben," he said quietly. "Maybe I waited too long to yell."

"Yeah, too damned long. Know what I think?"

"I'd like to know."

"I think you're plain scared."

"You wouldn't be far wrong."

"What scared you?" And then Halliday added hastily, "Oh, I know you've been scared all along, Sam, but not this scared! What's thrown such a scare into you?"

Sam Byrd sniffed, held both hands palm up and stared at them. "I don't know. It's not just one thing, but a lot of things, and I don't know what they all add up to. Nora, for one thing. We used to be happy, but lately— since the money, Ben—things have changed. That scared me. For another thing, it's been too easy. Just too damned easy! Things have never been easy for me, and this easy money scares me. I've never been lucky before, Ben, and I have a feeling this luck might not be luck at all."

"You don't even make sense!"

"Maybe not."

"About Nora—know whose fault that is? Yours, Sam! You started drinking, and then you started swilling! You started soaking yourself in alcohol. That's about all you do these days!"

"I'm not as hard as you are. That's why I want to quit now, while I'm ahead."

"Two more years. You've got to stick with me two more years."

Sam Byrd slammed his glass on the desk. "Why?" he shouted. "For more filthy money? Haven't you got more money than you can count? Must you rob tramps and pimps of what little they make? How much money do you want, anyway? And what the hell good is it going to do you?"

"Maybe it's not the money."

"It has to be the money."

"Maybe I crave power."

Sam Byrd's laugh was scornful. "Money's power!"

"Maybe so. Anyway, we'll take this up another time. You'd better go home and dress for dinner."

"O.K. See you tonight."

Ree bought a new suit. He had promised Bronson he'd buy a uniform, but he'd decided against it.

"Why should I look like a uniformed dummy?" he asked. "Anyway, a detective should be in plain clothes."

"You won't fool anybody with plain clothes," Bronson pointed out. "Your picture's been in the paper and you've blabbed speeches to anybody that'd listen."

"My badge is enough," Ree said. "And I think you're jealous."

"You could have bought a uniform for what that fancy badge cost," Bronson said. "And I'll never be jealous of men like you."

"This badge has class," Ree snapped.

"Well, you promised to buy a uniform," Bronson said.

"Oh, forget it. Or take your complaints to Halliday."

"I've decided Halliday wouldn't miss you if I fired you," Bronson said. "I've about decided Halliday forgot all about you, or made other plans or something."

"Try it and see," Willa Ree grinned. "Tonight, my friend, I dine at the Halliday home."

"Trouble starts, then," Bronson said. "And I'd about convinced myself I'd misjudged the man."

"There won't be any trouble, Chief. Everything's going to work smooth as silk."

"We won't discuss it!" Bronson said sharply. "Keep all that to yourself!"

"You brought it up."

He bought a new suit, had it altered and pressed, and then went home to dress. He dressed with care.

Martha met him at the door.

"Come in, Mr. Ree," she said, and felt his eyes slide over her body.

"In all due respect for your husband, Mrs. Halliday, I didn't expect to see such a beautiful woman as his wife."

She laughed lightly and said, "I want you to meet Mr. Byrd and Mrs. Byrd, Mr. Ree. And you know my husband, of course."

Sam Byrd extended his hand, and Ree stepped forward to clasp it. He bowed slightly to Nora and then shook hands with Halliday. "It's very kind of you to have me here," he said.

"Not at all, Ree," Halliday said. "In fact, I wish to apologize for not having you out earlier."

"Quite all right. I know you've been busy."

"Would you like a drink?" Martha asked.

"Please."

Nora sat at the piano, idly pecking, her drink on a small end table, and he moved to one side of the piano, leaning slightly, and watched as she played.

"Do you play, Mr. Ree?"

"A very little."

He thought her beautiful, more beautiful than Martha, but he saw her eyes were on Halliday. He wondered if Martha wanted Sam Byrd, but a second look at Byrd was enough to discount the thought.

Nora might be fun, but Martha was more interesting.

He watched Byrd, secretly, and wondered if Halliday was cultivating him or if Byrd and Halliday were connected. Byrd had been drinking heavily, and was still drinking. His eyes were glazed and he smiled foolishly.

Nora took her drink across the room, and Ree sat down at the piano.

He began to play not boogie-woogie or modern classics, but fragments from *"Lucia di Laminermoor"* and *"La Bohème."*

"Play some Viennese waltzes," Martha said.

He smiled and played. The corner of his eye caught Martha's uplifted eyebrow, aimed at Halliday, and saw Halliday's shrugged puzzlement.

A maid appeared at the doorway, and he stopped playing.

"Supper," the maid said.

Halliday asked questions as they ate. "Where were you born, Ree?"

"Hattiesburg, Mississippi," he lied.

"*I thought* you talked like a Southerner!" Martha said.

"Have you had a lot of experience as a policeman?" Nora asked.

"Several years."

The questions kept coming.

Veiled questions, leading questions, but he lied and twisted and doped, naming places he'd seen, could describe, but giving no pattern they could stitch together for a whole.

After supper, over coffee, Halliday steered the talk toward city politics.

"You'll find this a wild town, Ree, a wild town. Most of our population blew in here during the past couple of years, after they hit oil, and transients are flooding the town still. There's fast money here, and the fast money is drawing the riffraff. We've got enough prostitutes to serve a town ten times our size, and the same thing goes for gambling and book-making and all the rest."

"That happens to boom towns."

"Yes, I suppose so. Anyway, it creates quite a problem, made worse by the fact that Chief Bronson's getting old and doesn't know how to handle the toughs and the riffraff. All he knows is that he should arrest people for double parking and speeding. Small-town stuff, you see, and this town is big business now."

"If that's true, Mr. Halliday, why does the council keep Bronson on as chief?"

"Because he's an old timer, Ree, and we'd make the voters mad if we let him go. Understand, I'm telling you this in the strictest confidence."

Ree laughed. "There's no love lost between Bronson and me, Mr. Halliday. He didn't like taking me on at all. Wesley is his fair-haired boy."

Martha asked him to play again, but he begged off, and at ten o'clock he asked her if he might call a cab.

"Must you go so soon?"

"I'm afraid so, Mrs. Halliday. I still have a lot of work ahead of me, and I need my rest."

"I'll show you the phone."

The phone was in a hallway, off the dining room, and it was half dark there.

She stood beside him, her body brushing his shoulder. "You must come again," she whispered. "I'll call you."

"Do that."

Halliday saw him to the door. "Drop by my office some day this week, Ree," he said. "We'll have a nice, long talk."

"I'll do that, Mr. Halliday."

Willa Ree got out of the cab in front of Ma Ferguson's boardinghouse, but he didn't go inside.

As soon as the red glow of the cab disappeared, he started walking.

Twenty minutes later he circled to the back of a service station.

He took a glass cutter from his pocket and went to work.

Ten minutes later he was walking through town. There was a roll of bills in his pocket.

Eighty-seven dollars.

He whistled.

Enough to pay for the new suit.

Laura Green was asleep. She had dreamed, and in her dream she had been happy, for she was in Willa Ree's, arms.

But the dream had gone, Ree had gone, and she reached out her arms in search of him.

And then there was a knocking sound, a knock-knock-knocking sound, and she fought up out of sleep and realized that someone was at the door.

She went to the door and opened it, and only when the night air touched her body did she realize she wore no gown.

It was Ree!

"Where've you been?" she asked. "You were supposed to have come tonight."

"It's tonight and I'm here."

"What time is it?"

"Eleven-thirty."

"Well, that's a heck of a time to—"

But he took her in his arms and cut off her words with a kiss.

Her body was warm, her breasts firm and full as they pressed into his chest, pressed deeply into his chest.

His lips were eager and seeking, but her lips were demanding, pulling at his senses, until he was lost in a deep dark, with the only reality the warm softness of her lips.

Her hands were in his hair, pulling, and he drew her to him, closely to him, and more closely to him, his hands sliding and stroking the satiny smooth hot curves and hollows of her back.

He picked her up, still buried in her kiss, and stumbled his way into the bedroom.

After a while, a long while, he went to sleep.

He went to sleep, but his body didn't relax. Once, when she dozed, he began grinding his teeth, and she laid her hand on his face. It was wet with sweat.

She put her arms around him and held him tight. Once, twice, he cried out.

Chapter Twelve

The sun scorched a calendar path across July and dawned in August with wind-seared heat.

Ree called Halliday.

Ben Halliday's secretary told him, "Mr. Halliday's out of town."

"When'll he be back?"

"Is this Mr. Ree?"

"Yes."

"He said you might call. I'm afraid he'll be out of town three or four days. Maybe longer."

"Oh, I see. Well, I'll call again."

"I'll tell him you called."

"Thanks."

Well, he could wait if Halliday could.

Bronson called him into his office in the afternoon.

"Well, have you and Halliday made some little plans?"

"You said you didn't want to hear about any of our plans."

"So I did. Forget it."

"Well, you asked a question, Chief, and the answer is no."

Bronson gave his head a side twist and raised his shoulders and eyebrows. "Well, Ree," he said, "I know it's coming, and I hate to see it. To be perfectly frank, I don't know a hell of a lot about this business. Oh, I guess," and he paused to consider, "that I handled this town all right when it was small. But this oil hit and everybody and their dog moved here, and it's getting out of hand. Now, Sheriff Messner is a better sheriff than I am a police chief. That is to say, he is in a way, though— Well, you can form your own opinion of Messner. Anyway, I was about to say that you've got a flair for this kind of work, and it's a shame that you can't see your way clear to steer away from Halliday. You could go places in this business, Ree."

"How far?"

"Maybe, well, maybe to a big town. Some day."

"Police work is too slow, Chief. And, anyway, it's political. You have to pull the wires, Chief."

"You're right," Bronson said heavily. "And I'm an example. I'm an example because I won't play ball, and my job's safe just as long as it suits Halliday. I don't mind telling you, because Halliday knows how I feel. And because I don't care any more."

Bronson left the office. "I'm going home," he said. "I'm going home and read a book about poultry."

Ree called Laura.

"It's about time, society boy," she said. "You've been in the papers and on the radio, but you haven't been coming around often enough. And I see by the paper that you've been to some fancy dinners."

"They call it supper."

"Well, that's better than dinner. Anything that makes me sick, it's these corn-pone boys with honey and social ambition. Only mostly it's the wife that gets the society bug, and I can always tell when the bug bites, because then they start saying dinner instead of supper."

"You're just class conscious."

"Maybe. Are you coming over tonight?"

"Bright and early. Order a steak and some beer."

"Well, your tastes haven't changed. See you about eight."

He hung up and dialed Halliday's home number.

"Halliday residence." He almost didn't recognize the voice, the soft slurred woman's voice.

"Hello. This is Willa Ree."

"I recognized the ring," she said, "and about time, too."

"How are you, Mrs. Halliday? Are there burglars in your pantry? Are your jewels missing?"

"Not my jewels, Ree. My husband."

"Well, that's more interesting. There's nothing that interests me more than the wife of a husband who is missing."

"Tell me," she said, "would you like to have dinner at my house?"

"Dinner?"

She laughed. "Supper."

"I'd like having supper with you. What time?"

"Eight o'clock."

"Then I'll see you at eight."

But he was late—deliberately late.

He waited until eight-thirty before calling a cab, and then cautiously got out a block from the Halliday home and walked the rest of the way.

A dim light glowed in the Halliday living room.

He pressed the buzzer.

Martha opened the door, anger in her eyes and in the taut lines of her face. "You walked?"

"One block," he said, handing her his hat.

She was furious. "That was rather silly, don't you think? The neighbors would have thought nothing of a cab, but...."

"You mean it was suggestive," he said.

She shrugged. "It doesn't matter."

He helped mix drinks, and they drank, and the anger left her eyes. She relaxed.

"So you've never dared have a friend out while your husband was away."

"I've never cared to have a friend out when my husband was away."

She wore a white gown, simply cut, of some soft material, the neckline low, not immodestly low, but low, and trim over the hips and flowing about her ankles. Her hair was up, and her neck was beautiful, unadorned and smooth and creamy, and the soft light in the dining room complimented and complemented, bringing out lights in her hair and in her enormous eyes.

They had two drinks. She had prepared a Mexican dish, which she served with beer, and he laughed inwardly at the contrast between the softly lighted dining room and its beautifully laid table and the dish she served.

She chattered of this and that, of a plane trip she'd made, and, quite suddenly, she was talking about forty thousand dollars.

"... and so the Old Man doesn't believe in banks," she was saying. "Oh, he deals with banks and buys bonds and that sort of thing, but he keeps forty thousand dollars in a package in the company safe."

"Who was that again?"

"Old Man Johnson. You know. The Johnson Tool Company."

"Does he advertise the fact?"

She laughed. "Oh, no, not exactly. A friend of mine told me about it. Old Johnson lost money when the banks failed during the depression, you see, and now he keeps a reserve in his safe."

"You seem to be well informed," he said.

"About many things, Mr. Ree."

The conquest was no conquest, but surrender—on both sides.

He played the piano, at random, and then she was in his arms, leading him to the bedroom. "That bed," she said pointing.

Her gown fell about her feet, in a shimmering puddle, and she stepped out of her shoes.

"This is Ben's bed," she said.

She helped him undress and hung his clothes up neatly.

He took her in his arms then.

Her lips were prim and hard and cold.

Tonight, he thought, I'll have no alibi. After all, I can't say I spent the evening in Ben Halliday's bed.

His own bed.

He chose a liquor store, entering through a rear window after cutting a hole in the glass and reaching through to unlock it.

A town full of clay pigeons.

The haul amounted to three hundred and forty-six dollars. And some change.

What I need, he thought, is a car. If I ran a business, he told himself, I'd be damned if I'd leave my money in the register for anybody with guts enough to climb through a window. If I stay in this town long enough, he wrote on the blackboard of his mind, I'll be too rich to count my money. Every little town, he thought, is a potential customer of mine. I wonder, he wondered, how long it'll take the people in this town to get wise.

He left the building, circled around it, and hit the sidewalk. No hurry. Whistling softly, enjoying the feel of rustling money in his pocket, he passed by the store he'd robbed.

A man's footsteps clicked out of the darkness, and a man's bulky outline loomed in front of him.

"Hello, Ree," the man said.

He peered.

It was Wesley.

"Well, Wesley, are you out late or up early?"

"Both."

"Well, come on downtown and we'll find some coffee."

"No, thanks, I've got some business up this way."

"Take it easy."

He walked on down the street, chiding himself for allowing himself to be seen so near the burglarized store.

My friend, Wesley, he told himself, is nobody's fool. He'll be able to add two and two. But, a comforting thought, the guy won't be able to prove a thing. Not only that, but he won't have the guts to make an accusation against me, not without proof, at least.

Whistling softly again, he walked faster, until he saw the café where Halliday had found him when he first hit the town. He went inside and drank coffee, enjoying the stillness, forgetting the store and Wesley and thinking only of the night with Martha in Ben Halliday's own bed.

He shook with silent laughter.

When he'd finished his second cup of coffee, and dawn was breaking outside, he decided to go see Laura.

Laura, he knew, would be furious. He wondered if she'd cooked the steaks.

He walked, and the sun was coming up when he rattled the handle of her door.

Laura was furious. She cried. She was furious, and she cried, and she stormed and cursed and ordered him from the house.

Two steaks, cold and ugly and silly-looking, rested on a platter in the kitchen.

"We'll warm them and have them for breakfast," he said. "And don't feel stood up and unloved and hurt, honey, because I wouldn't have stayed away if there'd been anything I could have done about it. I wanted to call you, but there wasn't any phone where I was."

"Don't hand me that!"

"Listen, honey," he said, "I'm a policeman. If you married me, see, you'd be like a doctor's wife. Alone at night, half the time. I never know when something's going to break, you see, and I have to go when anything does break."

They had the steaks for breakfast.

He showered and left the house, whistling.

Chapter Thirteen

Willa Ree bought two suits, three pairs of slacks, six shirts, a hat, and four ties. He paid cash.

The clerk handed him his change, and a voice said, "You're flush."

Wesley.

"Hello, Wesley."

"I said you're flush."

"I save my money."

"Another store was knocked off last night."

"I got the report."

"You must have been investigating when I met last night."

"That was this morning."

"Night, morning. It was still dark."

"No, I wasn't investigating."

"Well, I've been investigating, Ree." Wesley's voice was soft and drawly. "Say, you're quite a dresser."

"Clothes make the man." Willa Ree kept his voice low, disinterested, as if he had half heard Wesley's small talk.

"You never wear a uniform, I notice. You look more like a sheriff than a cop."

"Never liked uniforms." And to the clerk, he said, "Send these suits to the cleaners for me, will you?"

"Cup of coffee?" Wesley asked.

"Yeah, I guess so."

They went to a small café and drank beer instead of coffee. Wesley traced a moist pattern on the table, idly tracing spilled beer with his finger.

"You know, Ree, you don't fool me a bit."

"No? What makes you think I'm trying to fool you?"

"Well, for one thing, you handed me that bunk about being a private detective from California. You might be from California, my friend, but I know that detective business was a bunch of crap."

"You told me once."

"Well, I'm telling you again." Wesley leaned back in the booth, stuck his feet out in the aisle, and sipped at his beer. "You're pulling these jobs we had lately."

"I'm wondering whether to laugh or make you swallow that bottle."

"You'd better laugh."

"You could take your suspicions to the Chief."

"I have."

"Then it's up to the Chief. And you can forget it."

"No." Wesley shook his head. "No, Bronson wasn't in the least surprised. He said to arrest you—when I get the proof."

Ree threw his head back and laughed.

Wesley blushed. "You might be laughing on the other side of your face one of these days, Ree," he warned, his voice trembling with anger.

"I hope you're around to see it, Wesley. I really hope you're around to see it."

"I'll be around."

"Don't be too sure. Listen, and get this straight, chum! Your pal is on his way out! Even he knows that! The council keeps Bronson for a front, and that's all. And something else. Bronson's front is getting a little thin."

Wesley slammed change on the table and left. Ree finished his beer.

The work was routine. For days he worked in the office, ignored by Bronson and scowled at by Wesley. He took Laura to the movies twice, but didn't see her again for a week.

When he did call, on a Sunday afternoon, she pouted. Then she slammed into the bathroom and showered, taking her time, a long time.

Willa Ree took off his shoes and stretched out on the couch. "What's the matter with you?" he asked when, draped in a towel, she emerged from the bathroom.

She flounced over to the dressing table and sat down. Her hands worked at her hair, swiftly and surely. She stuck bobby pins in her mouth.

"You'll chip your teeth opening those things," he warned. "Come on and spill it. What's the matter?"

She shrugged her shoulders, opened another pin with her teeth.

The towel slipped, exposing a breast and her back.

"You're getting fat," he said. "I never did care for fat women."

"That's not what they tell me!" she gritted.

"Tell you what?"

"They tell me you're after every woman in town!"

"Just stay the way you are, honey," he teased, "and I won't even notice any other woman in town, no matter how they wiggle."

"Don't be cute!"

"Now, listen! Either tell me what you heard or shut up!"

She gave her hair a final pat, peered into the mirror, and whirled around. "What about Martha Halliday?"

He whistled. "What have you heard about Martha Halliday?"

"I heard she's on the make for you and that you make easy!"

"All men make easy, honey, but you don't have to worry about Martha Halliday."

"Who's worried?"

"Well, you sound worried."

"Listen, you no-good bum! I can get any man in this town, and don't you forget it! And you needn't think I'm going to sit here keeping the home fires burning while you go sniffing around every woman in town!"

"Take it easy."

"Take it easy, hell! I heard you spent most of a night with Martha Halliday! That makes a fool out of me and I'm not going to stand for it!"

"I said take it easy."

She walked toward the couch, forgetting to hold the towel, and it slipped away and fell to the floor. She stood above him.

"Get to hell out of here!" she raged. "Go to Martha Halliday and every other worn-out tramp in town for all I care!" She stamped her foot.

He clasped both her legs in his arms and pulled. She fell forward across him, hitting and kicking and scratching.

They wrestled to the floor. She clawed his face, and the blood came.

Finally she stopped fighting and said, "You don't have to go chasing around town," she murmured. "I can supply the demand."

The sun was sinking, but was still hot, and the air had an acrid gunpowdery taste. Along the street, in the yards, men and women held garden hoses from which feeble streams of water squirted at withering lawns.

A jalopy, minus a top, clattered slowly down the street, loaded down with boys and girls in blue jeans and sweat shirts. The girls waved, standing up to display taut young breasts beneath tightly fitted shirts.

A squad car, siren sounding, whizzed past, throwing dust in fast-falling clouds.

A line of trucks, loaded heavily with racked lengths of pipe, rumbled toward the fields.

A woman holding the hand of a toddling boy baby looked up and down the street before crossing.

Somewhere, not far, a man called his son. "Jim-meeee! Oh, Jim-mee-ee!"

Willa Ree stood on the steps of Ma Ferguson's boardinghouse. In his pocket was a screwdriver, and he carried a paperwrapped hammer in his hand.

He walked slowly along the street, toward the town, speaking to newspaper-reading men on doorsteps and front porches.

In town, at the coffee shop, he had a sandwich and bottle of beer. He listened to drillers talk about women and oil wells. The sandwich was tasteless, but the beer was cold.

Night had fallen and the street lights and neons flooded the town in toobright varicolored patterns, misty and swimmy, and the sky was a pale blob without visible stars.

He left the café and sauntered up the street, pausing to look at the window displays. A cool wind came from somewhere in the west, carrying with it some sand and dust.

He turned right, passed the post office, and left the city lights behind. Two blocks, and he ducked into a dark alley beside Johnson's grocery store.

The window he wanted was at the rear of the building. There wasn't even a screen over it. Well, the chumps were asking for it.

Whistling soundlessly, he went to work. He took the screwdriver from his pocket and stuck it under the window. He heaved. The window wasn't locked.

It didn't seem right, but maybe some clerk was careless. Either that, or it had been jimmied before, which wasn't likely. But it was a possibility.

Carefully, very carefully, he grasped the window and pushed it up. It squeaked a little. He held it with one hand and used the other to pull himself up. It was awkward, and he was puffing when he managed to shimmy through. The window squeaked slightly when he let it down.

For a long while he stood. Suddenly, he realized that he was silhouetted against the window. He dropped to his hands and knees, moved to one side, and waited. He heard nothing.

It took several minutes to locate the small business office. The door was closed. He tried the knob, hesitated, and pushed the door open.

A man was on his knees before the small office safe. He was spotlighted by a flashlight lying on the floor.

Ree's hand went to his coat pocket. The man's eyes, white and shiny and stary, were steady. He didn't blink.

Ree stood frozen, staring, unmoving.

The man lifted his hands, slowly and carefully. "Just don't get excited and shoot," he said. His voice was low, steady, calm.

Ree closed the door behind him. "You can take your hands down."

The man stood up. He was small, stooped, old. His head was bald and he had the face of a turkey gobbler. "You're a cop, aint'cha?"

"That's right."

The man nodded in satisfaction. "Thought I seen you in uniform around town."

"Wrong," Willa Ree said. "I never wear a uniform."

"No matter," the man grunted. "All cops look like cops."

"I guess so."

The man grinned, his teeth shining in the light of the flash. "Got yourself a setup, huh?"

"That's right."

The man shifted nervously. "This thing's ready to blow."

Ree kept his hand in his coat pocket.

The man cleared his throat. "Well, what's the score?"

"You want a partner?" Ree asked.

The man grunted scornfully. "Looks like I got no choice. If I say no, all you gotta do is shoot me and take the money. It'll look like I had a partner what was greedy."

"I could take you in," Ree said.

The little man's knuckle went to his mouth and he snickered soundlessly. "You didn't come here after me," he said, "so you ain't going to take me in."

"No, I'm not going to take you in. I'll take you for a partner and we'll clean up. I'll case the joints. You blow the safes."

"Fifty-fifty?"

"Fifty-fifty."

"O.K. Better step outside while I blow this one."

Ree closed the door behind him and went to the back to prop open the rear window. He'd started back to the office when he heard the explosion. It wasn't as loud as he'd expected.

The old man was cleaning out the safe, stuffing the loot into a canvas bag.

There was a lot of dust, an acrid smell, some smoky twirly stuff.

"Let's get outa here," the little man said.

Ree was first through the window and he helped the old man through. "What's your name?" he gasped.

"Baldy. Just Baldy."

"O.K., Baldy. Let's go to my room."

Baldy shrugged. "Well, I guess it ain't a trap. If you want me, you got me. I ain't got no gun."

"Neither have I."

"You ain't packing a gun?"

"No gun."

"In that case, then, just oblige me by putting up your hands."

There was a .45 in Baldy's right hand. Willa Ree put up his hands.

"You're making a mistake, Baldy. Stick with me and we'll pick up every loose dollar in this town."

"Don't know if I can trust you. A cop turned bad ain't usually very trustworthy."

"Maybe I'm a good bad-turned cop."

"Could be."

Ree's hand snaked out for the gun. The old man stood transfixed, staring at the gun that had been taken from him. Willa Ree felt sweat pop out on his face, felt his hand tremble.

"I still want you for a partner, Baldy."

The old man laughed shakily. "Well, in that case, you got one. Never was one to argue with a gun. Now let's get to hell away from here."

Ree whistled a gay little tune as they walked. He felt like dancing a jig. "How long you been in town?" he asked.

"A week."

"Got a place to stay?"

"Yeah."

"Cops bothered you?"

"No. I got a union card and I wear good clothes. I stay clean. And I always manage to have a little money in my pocket. I don't get drunk and I don't fool around with women."

"Where's your room?"

"At my sister's house out on the edge of town."

They avoided the lighted streets, walked slowly. Ree whistled his crazy little jig tune.

"You're brand new on the force, ain't you?" Baldy asked.

"Yes."

"Can you blow a safe?"

"No."

"Got a record?"

"No."

"But you got everything figured out, eh?"

"That's right."

"How was you aimin' to crack that safe back there?"

"I wasn't planning to crack it. I'd have taken any loose money lying around."

The little man chuckled. "Bet you forgot to look in the cash register."

"Wouldn't have been any use, Baldy. You took the easy money first."

Baldy clucked his tongue in cheek. "That's right."

"I've got it all figured out, Baldy. This town is ripe. The city and county setup is rotten. People came here to get their sack full and they're not interested in anything else. Stick with me and we can own the town and the people in it."

"Don't care about owning no town and the people in it. Just so I get the money, that's all I care about."

"We'll get the money first!"

They went around the back way, walking through the dark hall of the boardinghouse, and Ree closed the door of his room before switching on the light. He motioned Baldy to a chair.

Baldy placed the bag on the table.

Ree filled two glasses from the bottle on the bureau.

Baldy emptied the bag, letting the money pile out on the table.

Tens and twenties, rising in a disorderly, conical pile.

"Let's count it," Baldy said.

They counted. Twenty-one hundred dollars.

"I'm going to pay down on a car," Ree said. "Maybe a convertible."

"You going to case me another job?"

"Right away. Drop around Thursday night about this time."

"See you," Baldy said. He stacked his money, slipped a rubber band from his pocket and banded the bills.

Willa Ree had a second drink before he went to bed.

In bed, relaxed, he made plans.

Baldy had been a stroke of luck. Baldy was a tool, one he needed to crack the places with the real money. What he'd been doing was penny ante, child's play, but Baldy would make the same work profitable, with the same risks.

This dumb town, this damned dumb town. Suckers, a bunch of suckers. Fruit on the tree, ready for plucking. Everybody out to fill their sacks and too busy to protect the other fellow's sack. All thinking it can't happen to me. Like lightning and death.

He'd buy a car, a bright red convertible, and let people wonder how he made the money for a car, a bright red convertible.

He'd buy Laura a present.

Something nice.

Chapter Fourteen

Business was bad in August. There was little drilling activity and rough-necks and roustabouts went away to greener pastures, to Oklahoma and east Texas, wherever oil was king.

Ree lined up two jobs a week for Baldy. Sometimes the take wasn't over a grand, sometimes a little less, but now and then the haul was big.

For a while they concentrated on liquor stores, and then they hit a cloth-ing store, a movie house, a grocery, and a department store. They split twenty-five thousand dollars.

The Telegraph wrote editorials.

Halliday called one day. "Take it easy, Ree," he said. "It's getting too damned hot around here."

"I don't know what you mean," he'd said.

"Just take it easy," Halliday said, and hung up.

Halliday didn't know for sure, but he was suspicious.

Baldy began to grumble about the split.

"I do the real work," he said.

"That's right, Baldy. But without me casing for you and giving you pro-tection, you wouldn't have the work to do. You'd have pulled a job or two and skipped town. Right now you'd be a thousand miles away, lying low and spending your money and waiting until things cooled off."

"I was doing all right."

"Like hell."

"O.K.," Baldy said. "If you're so damned smart, why not blow your own jobs?"

"I'll do that, maybe. Things are getting too hot around here anyway. One more job and we'll split up. Only you'll have to skip town."

"Name the job."

"Johnson Tool."

"When?"

"Tomorrow night. It'll be a big haul. They keep the dough in a cracker box. We'll split fifty-fifty and call it quits."

"It's a deal."

"Meet me at my room."

"What time?"

"Ten o'clock. The building won't be hard to crash. It's got heavy doors and bars on the window, but they overlook the restroom in the back. It has a window. It's small, but we can snake through. They thought it was too small to worry about."

"What about alarms?"

"No alarms. The box is simple. It sits in an office that can't be seen from the front."

"Another chump setup," Baldy said. "No watchman?"

"No watchman."

Baldy grunted. "See you tomorrow night."

Willa Ree rode in the patrol car with the young cop, McKelvy.

"I'm nervous," McKelvy said.

"How come?"

"Well, you'd better be nervous, too, because the council is meeting tomorrow. Emergency meeting, they said. Something tells me hell's going to bust loose around here."

"What about?"

"All these robberies. Crime wave, the paper calls it. The Chief's on the spot, and I'll bet he gets the sack."

"Well, that's what newspapers are good for. The Telegraph has been running those editorials every day. They seem to think cops should be psychic or something."

"Yeah," McKelvy sighed.

"The thing is that an oil town's rough. They all are, every last one of them. The drifters and the grifters and the bad babies always like to turn up in an oil town for some fast money. This town's no different, and it's not Bronson's fault."

"Tell that to the council," McKelvy said.

"Maybe I will."

"You'd better lie low and keep quiet," McKelvy advised. "They're liable to shake up the whole damned department."

"Well, I was looking for a job when I found this one."

"So was I, but I got mighty tired looking. This looking for work is tough work, and I don't mean maybe."

"Wonder who'll replace Bronson?"

"Oh, they'll pick up some old codger who stands in good with the old settled element around town—with the ranchers and the businessmen."

"Well, I've seen it happen before."

"Yeah, so have I."

"No use worrying about it, McKelvy. They might not even fire Bronson."

"Maybe not. If we could only get a line on those safecrackers we'd be in."

"Yeah."

The neon sign made a lot of light, but the dim bulb inside the building couldn't compete. Only the front part of the Johnson Tool Company was lighted, and dim forms of shelves and machinery loomed behind the small circle of low watt brilliance.

They went around back.

Willa Ree stood on an apple box and jimmied the window. It came up hard, but it came up and stayed up. He got down off the box and gave Baldy a leg lift. With much grunting and wriggling, the old man disappeared into the darkness.

Ree climbed up, squeezed through head first. It was a tight squeeze.

The door leading into the main building was unlocked.

"They keep a dirty toilet," he told Baldy. "This place smells."

The safe was in an office. Baldy plugged his drill cord into a socket and blew the safe with a rag shot. It was a snap.

Willa Ree waited outside on lookout. He went back to the office and opened the door. "The dough there?" he asked.

Baldy held up a parcel.

"That's good. That's real good, Baldy."

The muscles of his face wouldn't relax. They felt stiff and sore. He tried to smile and the skin around his mouth felt like it would crack.

"What—?" Baldy began.

"Why'd you bring your gun tonight, Baldy?"

"You brought your gun."

"Maybe I knew what you were thinking."

Baldy licked his lips. "Maybe I knew what you were thinking."

They stood, stiff and tense, and stared at each other.

The old man dropped the parcel and went for his gun. His movements were fast, incredibly fast, and his claw-like right hand dipped under his coat.

Willa Ree was faster. The gun barked. He squeezed the trigger, but it seemed an eternity before the hammer fell and the gun barked.

Baldy's hand was under the coat, and then it was coming out, and then the gun appeared and swept up and out.

Willa Ree's gun jumped in his hand again and Baldy's body jerked and twitched and began to crumple. Even as he fell, his gun fired, and Ree flinched as the bullet hit and shattered the glass of the door behind him.

Baldy fell face down, arms outspread, still.

A feeling of loneliness, a feeling of despondency, swept like a cold breeze over Willa Ree. He felt numb and tired. Almost, he felt afraid. And lonely, so all alone lonely.

Baldy had been a friend, or what passed for a friend. But he'd been complaining about the split and he'd been carrying a gun.

Maybe he always carried a gun. Well, why shouldn't he? Fear, if it was fear, was a grasping clammy thing.

Voices, clanging and monotonous, spoke inside his mind. Gotta move fast, move fast, move fast, gotta move fast, move fast.

His pulse was hard and fast, and his breath seemed to sing, wheeze and sing in dreadful and rhythmic cadence, as he picked up the parcel and headed for the back of the building. It took a long time to slide through the window, and, once outside, he could see but dimly. He trotted across a junk-strewn lot and stopped beside a gas meter. His wildly groping hands found the lid of a sunken water shutoff. He lifted the lid and set it aside, falling to his knees and stuffing the parcel in the hole. Swiftly, but quietly, he replaced the lid and hurried back across the lot.

He climbed back through the window, found the iron bar he'd used to jimmy the window on the floor, and he wiped it with his handkerchief. Breathing hard, fighting the voices in his brain, he walked to the front of the building.

Once more he drew his gun from the holster beneath his coat. Facing the back of the building, he fired three times. Glass shattered and tinkled, and he reholstered the gun. He went into the office, where Baldy lay, stepped across the body and picked up the telephone. He dialed police headquarters.

"Drake? Willa Ree. Listen, I'm at the Johnson Tool Company— Yeah, west Main. I got one of the safecrackers but the other one got away. Send out an alarm— What? Yeah, he's dead. I think I might have clipped the other one but I'm not sure. Check with the hospital and all the doctors in the book— Okay, I'll be here." He hung up.

His legs trembled and the muscles jumped. He felt shaky all over, and his stomach was queasy.

He thought— How much money, how much—maybe twenty, maybe forty—Martha Halliday had said forty. But poor old Baldy, the poor poor old guy, maybe I shouldn't have.... Too late for that kind of thinking. Time to act. Stay cool and act. If Baldy'd ever got caught he'd have sung like a phonograph.

Ree sat down on the desk and smoked, keeping his eyes away from Baldy. A feeling of unease followed the thought of his trip across the back lot to hide the money.

Footprints? Doubtful. He shrugged the feeling away. Too dark to follow footprints tonight, and he could move the money before morning. The footprints could be explained away. He could say he'd been looking for the guy, the other guy, the one that got away.

Sirens.... A police car swept into the driveway at the front of the building, its siren screaming and red light blinking. The flood of lights went out, and three figures floated from the car to the front door. He slid off the desk and went to open the door.

Crowley, Wesley, and Johns stood there.

"What's going on here, Ree?" Wesley asked.

"Well, it's not a social gathering."

"What's happened?"

"Safe-cracking job, chum." He was careful to keep his voice under control, fighting against tight anger.

"You got one of them."

"That's right."

Wesley went into the office, switched on a light. He got down on his knees and peered at Baldy.

"Did one get away?"

"Yeah." He didn't know whether to go on answering questions. Maybe he should take charge.

"Know either one of them?" Wesley asked.

"No. Didn't get a good look at the one that got away. Just a fast-moving shadow." He laughed. "I mean fast. I got about three shots at him and might have made a hit, but can't be sure. Caught this little dried up cuss in the office, though. He tried his best to gun me, but I was faster."

"How'd you happen to be here?"

"I was on my way to see my girl."

"Where's she live?"

"What's that got to do with it, Wesley?"

"Maybe a lot. Where's she live, Lieutenant?"

"Thirty-three West Main."

"Her name?"

"Laura Green— What the hell does this mean, Wesley?"

Wesley was taking notes. He didn't look up. "You mean Legs Green."

"Laura Green."

"They call her Legs."

"The name is Laura and you didn't answer my question."

"Look, Ree," Wesley said. "You're off duty. I'm on duty. It's my job, see. So, if you'll just answer my questions—"

"Shoot."

Wesley turned to Johns. "Call the coroner and get an ambulance."

"Want me to call Bronson?" Johns asked.

"No need. He's about finished, anyway."

Johns made the call. Wesley turned to Ree, his eyes betraying his inner excitement.

"Tell us what happened, Lieutenant."

"Well, I was walking by—"

"And saw the men at work?"

Willa Ree suppressed a laugh. "No, Wesley," he said. "With that front light on, it's impossible to see back here from outside. I heard a noise."

"How'd you get in?"

"I tried the front door and then I went around back. They'd jimmied a window. I slipped in and came up front. There were two of them in the office. The safe was open and they were bent over it. The little guy went for his gun and the other one ran. I got the little man and shot at the other."

Wesley scratched at the pad with his pencil. "We'll have a look around."

They found the bar, picked it up carefully with a handkerchief, and examined the window. They forced the back door and surveyed the ground outside.

"Not much chance getting footprint impressions," Wesley said. "The ground's too hard."

"Might look for blood," Johns said.

"No use," Wesley grunted. "Well, not much we can do here. It looks like you had a good night, Ree. Yeah. I'd say you had a good night."

"In what way?"

Wesley shrugged.

"In what way?" Ree asked again.

"I only said you had a good night, Ree. Don't make a federal case out of it."

"Well, if you're hinting at anything, Wesley, why don't you search me?"

"That won't be necessary," Wesley said, stiffly. "You're a lawman."

"Just the same, chum. There are newspapermen present. I think you ought to search me."

"I didn't make any accusations, Ree. You're wearing your feelings on your sleeve."

"Just the same."

Wesley smirked, and did the searching. He did a good job.

"Okay, Ree. You're clean."

Ree's lips trembled, tightened back against his lips.

"I'm going now, Wesley. Since you've taken charge here you can finish the investigation. And be sure to search yourself before you leave."

"You'd better wait until the coroner finishes in there."

"O.K."

He wasn't going to give Wesley anything to think about. Or talk about.

The coroner was in a hurry to get back to bed, and finished his investigation in a few minutes. A reporter and photographer came from the Telegraph. They asked Ree to pose. He obliged.

"You'll be a hero now, Ree," Wesley said.

"I'm going now, Wesley. If it's all right with you?"

"Go ahead. But you won't leave town for a while, will you?"

Willa Ree swung around. He walked up to Wesley. Close. For a breath, a short breath, he stared into the man's face. He smiled pleasantly.

His right hand chopped, side down, and the blow caught Wesley behind the left ear. Wesley slumped to the floor and Willa Ree rolled him over on his back with his foot.

"He'll wake up in a minute, boys," he said. "Maybe he'll want his picture in the paper so he can be a hero."

Johns cleared his throat. "What're our orders?" he asked.

"Look around the back of the building. Better try for prints on the safe. See what you can find out about the dead man, and leave a report on my desk. I'll want it first thing in the morning."

"Yes, sir."

And Willa Ree walked away.

"Hey!" It was the reporter calling. "You want a lift?"

"Thanks."

He directed the boy to Laura's apartment.

"I've gotta hurry back to the office," the kid chattered. "I wouldn't be a bit surprised if we got out an extra."

"Just over one dead safe-cracker?"

"Well, the town's been on its ear for a long time about these burglaries," the boy said. "The paper's been running editorials."

"Yeah. I know."

The boy let him out, and drove away.

Willa Ree tried the door, but it was locked. He rapped.

"Who is it?"

"Open the door."

Laura opened the door. Her hair was up in curlers and she wore a house-coat.

"Any time of the day or night," she said. "Don't bother to call. Let me guess. Let me dress and sit around wondering whether you're coming or not."

He took her in his arms....

He opened his eyes to darkness and felt smothered, hot and smothered and panicky. He lay still and felt the sweat start, felt his heart race and jump and gallop. His hand found warm flesh, and he knew it was Laura and was glad. He threw back the sheet and climbed out of bed, his fumbling fingers touching the table, groping for a cigarette and matches.

The brief flare of the match hurt his eyes.

It was two o'clock. He sat on the edge of the bed, sucked in smoke, and listened to Laura's regular breathing.

She didn't know.

His stomach, suddenly, was a ball of white fire. He went into the bathroom and was sick. He felt better then, and he splashed cold water on his face, the back of his neck.

He looked out the window and saw a man across the street, in the shadows, leaning against a telephone pole.

"Wesley!" he whispered. "The bastard knows."

He dressed fumblingly, and rushed out of the house. He walked toward town, not daring to look back.

The shadow moved away from the post and followed.

Willa Ree walked past the Johnson Tool Company without slacking pace. His footsteps made a brisk clip-clop on the walk, and he heard an echoing clip-clop far in the rear.

An all night café flooded light into the street. A few cars were parked at the curb. He entered and had a cup of coffee. The shadow didn't show.

Wesley would follow him to his room, he was sure. It would be too risky to head back to his money cache now. He cursed, bitterly, to himself.

One suspicious cop on an entire force, and he would get nosey tonight of all nights. He's bucking for Chief, Ree thought, and too bad for me if he gets it, but he won't get it by catching me, the bastard.

He reached the boardinghouse. In his room he flipped on the light, undressed and hung his clothes in the closet. He slid into pajamas and brushed his teeth. Turning off the light, he lay down on the bed.

An hour passed. He wanted a cigarette but didn't dare strike a match, lest Wesley see through the window.

The second hour dragged. Must be getting on toward morning, not much time left.

He fumbled for his clothes and dressed in the dark, and in the dark groped his way down the hall and out the back door. He ducked under a clothesline and vaulted the fence. Instead of going down the alley he cut across yards, and emerged into the street at the far side of the block.

He began to run. For two blocks he ran. Turning left, he walked for one block, turned right and ran as fast as he could. He was puffing hard when he turned down the alley.

In the middle of the alley he climbed a fence and traversed a yard. A dog growled in the darkness, and a heavy weight hit the fence as he gained its top. Wearily, he dropped to the ground and began to trot.

He approached Johnson Tool from the north, crossing a lot and hitting the alley. In case guards had been posted, he dropped to his knees and crawled the alley's length. Once he flattened out on his belly and waited, holding his breath, while a car rolled down the street. For an agonizing moment he thought the car was turning into the alley, but then it was gone and he was wrapped in friendly darkness.

On hands and knees he searched for the lid to the sunken water shutoff box. A tight smile pulled at his lips when his hands hit the lid. He lifted it and thrust both hands into the opening.

The package of money was gone!

Chapter Fifteen

Wesley was in the office when Willa Ree entered. He was smiling, showing teeth. There was a lump on his chin, red and blue tinged. "Good morning, Ree," he said.

The guy was smart. Too smart to be surly over last night's ruckus. Or maybe he was expecting something, planning something.

Ree pointed at the squad room where the entire force stood, backs to wall, waiting.

"Oh, them," Wesley said. "The council is in session and said they had an announcement to make. Said for everybody to wait here except the men in the patrol cars."

Ree grunted.

"They're going to name the new chief," Wesley said.

"And you expect the job."

Wesley showed more teeth. "Well, I might take it. I could retire, though." He winked. "I had a big night with the cards. Made a killing."

"Yeah?"

"Yeah. Guess you could call me a wealthy man."

"I could call you a thieving sonofabitch."

"Pot calling the kettle black, Ree."

"So you made yourself a haul."

"And you did the dirty work, Ree."

The office door opened. It was Morris, the city secretary. "Ree?"

"Yeah."

"They want you in the council room."

"Be right with you."

Ree waited until Morris closed the door before turning back to Wesley.

"Wait for me," he said, "and we'll have a little talk."

Wesley shrugged. "You want to make a proposition, but I'll tell you now I won't be interested. But I'll be here, Chief."

Willa Ree went to the door. "I'm not chief, yet."

"You will be. Last night's job put you over. But I can tear all that down when I get ready. Just remember that, if you've got any bright ideas. You slugged me last night." He fingered the bruise on his chin. "I don't forget easy."

"You wait for me."

Wesley laughed. "Course," he said, "you could say I was well paid for that blow."

Willa Ree went into the council room.

The councilmen sat around a large table, cigars and cigarettes between their fingers or between their lips. The mayor sat at the end of the table, heavy and pompous and prosperous. He introduced the members of the council, as if Willa Ree were a stranger: Halliday, France, Carter, Simpson, Mueller, Byrd.

Byrd looked tired, drawn, hang-overish. Unhappy, maybe. Or scared. His suit was well-cut, expensive, and he wore a flashy diamond. But his hair needed cutting and he could have used a shave. There were shadows under his eyes. He had a tiny black mustache, but his nose stuck out over it like a finger from a fist. He'd been drinking when Willa Ree had seen him last, and now, sober, he looked like another person.

"Ree," the mayor said, "the council has voted you in as the new Chief of Police." He rolled the title off his tongue as if the words were sacred.

"I accept," Willa Ree said, "with pleasure."

The mayor cleared his throat. "The council recommends that you retain Wesley as Captain of Police."

"That's all right with me."

"We feel," the mayor said, "that you have shown qualities of—ah—leadership that—ah—qualify you for—ah—leadership."

"Thank you."

"We—ah—want you to clean this town up, Ree! Too many—ah—burglaries around here lately; though—ah—you seem to have made a beginning, a good—ah—beginning on that already."

"I'll do my best."

"We are all—ah—sure that you will—ah—do your best."

"Thank you."

"Well," the mayor said, "that takes care of everything, then. Congratulations, Ree, and—ah—good luck."

Ree shook hands with the mayor, with each of the councilmen, and left the room. He went directly to the squad room.

"Men," he said, "the council has just named me as chief, replacing Chief Bronson who has—retired. Carry on your duties as before. Wesley is still captain. Dismissed."

They buzzed excitedly as he left the room.

Wesley was waiting in the office. He was smoking, leaning back in the swivel chair with feet on the desk.

"Beat me out of a good job, Ree, and I'll bet they didn't even throw me a bone."

"You're still captain."

Wesley's lips tightened as he watched Ree fumble for a cigarette, strike a match on thumb, and light up.

"We could bury the hatchet," Willa Ree said. "We could organize this town right."

"Maybe."

"Might make some money, real money."

"I'm set for money now. Not that I couldn't use more. Or, I could spill the dope about last night and get your job. Then I could organize things myself. It wouldn't be hard to do, Ree. Just a whisper here and a whisper there in the right places. About you and the dead guy working together."

"You forget something, Wesley. I was searched last night. That reporter saw me searched. Remember?"

"Just horsing," Wesley said. "I was just horsing you."

"Well, since we're going to work together anyway, we might just as well make some money."

"You're so right."

"We'll talk it over tonight."

"Where'll I see you?"

"You got a car?"

"Yeah."

"Well," Willa Ree said, "pick me up out front about nine."

"O.K."

"And now, let's get some work done." He grinned at Wesley and walked into the chief's private office.

He couldn't eat.

That damned Wesley. Damned chiseler, long-nosed chiseler, poking into my business—damn him!

He tried to think.

No use crying over spilled milk, but forty thousand dollars is a hell of a long way from being spilled milk. Wesley could offer to split, at least.

And he wants to work with me. Can I trust him? No. Hell, no.

If he's bad enough to keep the forty grand, he's bad enough to double-cross me later. And he's smart. He was smart enough to figure where I hid the dough, or he followed my tracks, and that makes him too smart to suit me.

But I'll give him a chance. I'll ask him to give me half the dough. If he does, O.K. If he doesn't....

He took a bite of steak, chewed slowly, and drank some coffee.

If he splits—which he probably won't, maybe—I'd better skip. But that would leave him in the driver's seat, with the dough. And he'd send the hounds after me. Anyway, this is my oyster. My own personal in my pocket oyster, and I'm going to suck it dry and spit out the seeds. And no two-bit copper from the sticks is going to scare me off.

He took another bite of steak.

He read the Telegraph in his room. They'd given the police shake-up a three-column spread on page one, and they'd given him a big play.

He threw the paper on the floor.

There was another paper on the bureau, the Traveler.

He picked it up and scanned it. On the second page was an "Around Town" column. And, beneath the column heading, in bold type, was the question: "WHO IS WILLA REE???"

The writer asked the reader questions about Willa Ree.

"Where did Willa Ree come from? What police experience and background has he? Why did he come into town by slow freight?"

The string of burglaries and safe-crackings were traced... dated.

"More burglaries in three months than the town's had in ten years," the article trumpeted.

It bothered him, that article. It would start people thinking, asking questions. Of themselves and others.

The prying bastard, I oughta shove his teeth down his throat is what I oughta do....

It was 8:45 when he slid into his coat and walked briskly toward town, and exactly nine when he reached the Hall. A car swooped around the corner and pulled in to the curb.

"Get in," Wesley said.

"Thanks."

"Where'll we go?"

"You know where my girl lives," Ree said. "You ought to. You stood around that telephone post long enough the other night."

Wesley laughed. "I thought you saw me."

"I'm not blind."

"Want to go there? Your girl's house?"

"Might as well."

"It's all right for her to hear what we're going to talk about?"

"She's all right."

Wesley didn't like it. He drove in the right direction, but he didn't like it. He frowned a little, fidgeted, and threw quick, nervous glances at Ree. "So you got a record," he said.

Willa Ree froze.

Wesley turned a corner and slowed, letting the car idle. "I said you got a record."

"I heard you."

"That's not so good for a chief of police. Not good at all."

"So it's not so good." Ree fought his voice. "So I've got a record. So what?"

"So I know all about it, that's so what."

"Now you know. So we're gonna work together. What difference does it make to you, Wesley?"

Wesley's laugh was dry and sarcastic and mocking. "Well, I'll tell you, Ree. It's good to know things about people. Especially about people you wouldn't trust any farther than you could throw an elephant."

"You mean you'd squeal if I tried to cross you?"

"Sure. And you'd do the same thing. In fact, you'd squeal just to get me out of the way, and—"

"You might do the same thing. Whether I try to cross you or not."

"That's exactly right. If things don't go to suit me, I'll squeal like a stuck pig. I might squeal because I don't like the tone of your voice or the color of your necktie."

"I see."

Wesley stopped the car. There was a light burning in Laura's apartment, but Ree made no move to get out.

"So you got the dough, Wesley. So now we're partners and we split."

Wesley laughed. "I got the dough before we formed the partnership, Ree. You're nuts if you think I'm gonna split with you!"

"I don't think it would be a very good partnership then, Wesley. The dough would stand between us all the way. I think it's mine and you think it's yours, so the only answer is a split. An equal split."

"It's my dough," Wesley said. "That's final."

"You're too ambitious. You might even get in the way of my ambition."

"Meaning?"

"Meaning you're a bastard, Wesley! Meaning you went to a lot of trouble to get my record so I'd be out in the cold! Meaning you'd squeal whether we became partners or not! Meaning, damn you, that you're playing me like a cat does a mouse right now!"

Wesley snickered.

"I'll just take the forty grand," Willa Ree said. "If I trusted you, and if you'd been willing to split, everything would be jake. I could use a partner. But, now, I'll just take the whole roll."

"You going to try to get tough?"

"Just keep your hands on the wheel! I'm no Boy Scout and I'm not bragging, but I'm better at judo and better with my fists than any man you'll ever see! Reach for that gun and you'd be sorry!"

"I won't take this!"

"You'll take it. Where's the dough?"

Wesley snorted, "None of your damned business!"

Ree plucked the keys from the switch and put them in his pocket. Wesley opened the door on his side and got out of the car.

"I'm going back to town, Ree. Leave my car in front of the station."

Ree watched him walk down the street. He lit a cigarette, fished for the keys, and started the motor. Wesley stepped up on the curb when the car pulled up.

"You go on and leave me alone, Ree! I'm warning you!"

"Put away your gun, Wesley. You won't need it."

"You go on away!" Wesley repeated. "Leave my car in front of the station!"

"It's your car. I'll walk." He got out of the car and held out his hand. "Here's your keys."

Wesley reached for the keys with his left hand, grunted when Ree caught it and spun him about. He cursed when he found himself helpless, back turned to Ree and arm pushed up between his shoulder blades.

"Drop the gun," Ree grunted.

"Go to hell!"

"Drop it, Wesley! I can twist your arm off!"

"Go—to—hell!"

Ree applied more pressure, and the gun fell to the pavement. He pushed Wesley from him. "Get in the car, pal."

Then he pulled a handkerchief from his pocket and used it to pick up the gun, saying, "I wouldn't want to get my prints on your gun, now would I, Wesley?"

Wesley was slouched over in the car, head bowed.

"Get under the wheel," Ree ordered. He grinned, because the guy was scared, and showed it. "Drive around the block and stop when I say." He made Wesley start the car, and directed the turns.

"Stop here," he said. "We'll walk back."

Wesley got out of the car and tried to run.

Ree tripped him and the man fell to the pavement, hard.

"Where's the dough, Wesley?"

Silence.

"We could still be partners. I want all the money, but we could still be partners."

"I'll bet you'd kill your mother. Your own mother."

"You're liable to get hurt, chum. Hurt bad. I'm telling you straight, Wesley, you're liable to get hurt so bad you won't recover. All you've got to do is tell me where you hid the money."

"You wouldn't kill me, Ree. Stop clowning."

"I'm going to have that dough! One way or the other I'm going to have it! Understand?"

"You're bluffing."

Wesley got up. Slowly.

"Ree. You're bluffing. You're tough and you can handle me, but you won't go too far. You're too smart."

"Maybe smart enough to know I can go as far as I like."

"You're bluffing, Ree!"

"Care to make a bet? Say, forty thousand dollars?"

"You'll never see a dollar of that money, bud! Not a damned dollar! Know why? Because I know you're bluffing, that's why!"

"Wesley, I thought you were smart. I mean business, and I thought you'd be smart enough to realize it. Haven't you been playing cop long enough to know when a man means business?"

"Long enough to tell a punk when I see one, Ree! And, believe me, you take the cake!"

Willa Ree leaned against the side of the car. Wesley stood before him, hands clenched, breathing hard.

"I'm not waiting much longer," Ree said. "I'll give you about sixty seconds."

"I'll give you two thousand dollars if you'll blow town."

"Time's passing."

"Three thousand dollars, Ree, if you'll get out of town and not come back."

"Ten seconds."

"Ree! I'll give you four thousand—make it five—but you've absolutely got to leave town! Listen, see, you can go a long way on five thousand and there're a lot of towns just as good as this one and you'd have the money to get started. Instead of—"

Willa Ree hit him. With the side of his hand, he hit him. He stuck the handkerchief-wrapped gun in his coat pocket with his right hand and hit Wesley with the left, across the bridge of the nose.

Wesley staggered. He shook his head, and then he rushed, arms flailing wildly.

Willa Ree caught one of the arms, stooped, and sent the man over his back to plop flat on the asphalt of the street.

He waited for Wesley to get his breath and said, "Get up."

Wesley groaned.

Willa Ree kicked him in the ribs, not too hard. "Get up."

"I can't." The words were blurred, thick, mouthy.

Ree kicked him again. "Get up, I said."

Wesley groaned.

Another kick, harder, and Ree snapped, "Get up. Now!"

Wesley scrambled up. He stood with hands palm up, foolishly looking for gravel cuts.

Willa Ree shoved him. "Start walking."

Their progress was slow. Wesley blubbered a bit before switching to blustery threats. "You'll get yours for this, Ree! Tomorrow's another day, and you'll get yours! Tomorrow you'll be up before the county attorney, you cold-blooded bastard! Wait'll I tell him...."

Willa Ree kicked him. Wesley's back arched and he was forced to trot, grotesquely, to keep from falling.

"Keep your mouth shut and keep walking," Ree warned.

"I'll kill you for—" His words ended in a sharp thin cry as Ree rabbit-punched him. He staggered forward, fell to his knees, and shook his head. His breath was raspy.

"Where's the dough?"

"You'll never find it! I'm telling you, you won't find it and this won't get you anywhere!"

A car turned the corner, lights stabbing at the darkness. Willa Ree caught Wesley by the arm and helped him to his feet. He slid an arm around his throat to choke off a yell, but the car passed and Wesley made no attempt to move or call.

"They think you're drunk, Wesley."

The car was gone.

"Get moving," Ree said.

Laura opened the door at his knock. She gasped.

"Accident?"

"Sort of, sweet. This guy is about to have a serious accident."

He pushed Wesley inside and closed the door.

"What's happened?" Laura asked.

Willa Ree backed off. He swished a right to Wesley's chin, and the man crumbled to the floor.

Laura screamed.

"Shut up!"

"But what's he done? Why'd you hit him?"

"None of your business! You sit down over there and be quiet! Stay out of the way!"

The girl bent over Wesley. "You get out of here, Ree! Get out and stay out, you hear? There won't be any rough stuff in my house—"

He backhanded her across the face, saw blood ooze from a split lip. She sat down on the couch, breathing hard. He bent down to look at Wesley and saw the man's eyelids flutter.

"Faking!" He kicked Wesley in the ribs savagely. "Come on, get up!"

Laura came unwound, arms flying and hair flying and hands clawing, but he pushed her away and she fell sprawling on the floor.

Wesley was standing, arms clasped over his belly.

"I'll give you one more chance to talk," Ree said.

Wesley spat.

He caught Wesley's coat, held him close, and belted his fist to the chin. Wesley's legs folded. He was out. Ree let him fall.

"Well," he said, "that's one tough cop—"

The lights brightened blindingly, went out for an instant, came on not so brightly and dimmed. He felt himself stagger and knew the girl had hit him with something.

She had a beer bottle in her hand and she was stalking him. He backed away, hands outthrust, and felt blood trickle on his forehead.

"Put it down, baby," he coaxed. "Put it down or I'll hurt you. Now, I don't want to have to hurt you, sweet, so put it down."

She swung but he backed away, and the bottle struck only his hand.

"Don't do that again, sweet," he said. "Don't do that..."

She swiped at him and he was too slow. The bottle hit his wrist. It hurt like hell, and his hand went numb.

"Get out of here!" the girl said. "Get out or I'll kill you!" Her teeth were clenched, nostrils dilated and fluttery, and her eyes glared through strands of hair.

"I'll go," he said.

"You go now, you thieving murdering coward!"

"Take it easy, now," Ree said. "O.K., take it easy. I'll get out. I said I'd go." He headed for the door, angling away from the girl. "What about him?" he asked, pointing at Wesley.

Her eyes flicked to Wesley and he moved in. She was too slow, and he caught the bottle with one hand, slapped her with the other. The sound of his palm smacked loud against her cheek. He gave her a knuckle, and the force of the blow twisted her head. Again he slapped, and again and again. Anger surged and he hated her, suddenly he hated her, and his hand turned into a fist.

Anger was gone. Fire was ashes and anger was gone. He watched her slump to the floor, half conscious, blubbery and limp.

"Don't try that again, honey," he said. His breath was dry against his throat and he felt tired. "Don't ever do a thing like that again! You don't know what's going on, see, and I can't tell you right now! Just take it easy and I'll make it up to you. You'll see. You just wait and see."

Wesley stirred and moaned.

Ree dug a toe into the man's ribs. "Get up," he said.

Wesley only moaned.

Ree had to kick him again. He kicked until he was tired.

"Open your bright little eyes, Wesley. I know you're awake. Open your eyes and talk, or I'll break every bone in your body!"

"You're wasting your time, Ree." Blood stained Wesley's teeth and dribbled over his chin. "You shouldn't have brought me here, chum, because now you'll have to slow down. She's a witness and she'll talk if you go too far." He laughed, weakly. "She's not what you thought, eh, Ree? Not what—"

Willa Ree caught his coat and pulled him up. He stepped back, allowing the man to stand alone, swaying. He waited until Wesley's eyes came into focus.

Wesley's face was a mess. The nose was flattened and the lips puffed out, cut, and blood came from the tongue or the cheek, and from the lips. More blood dribbled from a gash over the right eye, and from a cut on the right cheek.

"You got anything to tell me, Wesley?"

Wesley spat in his face.

Ree slapped him. Once, twice, backhanded, and again.

"Feel like talking now?"

"You're wasting your time."

Ree slapped again. Wesley's head swiveled, and he staggered.

"You going to talk?"

Swaying, breathing hard, Wesley didn't reply. He looked from Willa Ree to the girl.

He chopped Wesley in the stomach, and Wesley doubled over, retching.

Laura screamed.

Willa Ree walked over to the couch. "I said be quiet, sweet," he said and slapped her.

Wesley sat up, brushing blood off his chin with the back of his hand.

"You get up and wash your face, honey," Ree said to Laura.

She sat up, tossing back her hair and feeling her face with tender fingers!

"You're going to live, honey. Your face is a mess and it'll be worse tomorrow. But you'll live."

"I'll kill you," she said.

His words mocked her. "I don't think so. I might buy you a coat. Or a car. Wesley, our friend here, Wesley, might decide to give me a present so I can buy nice things for you. Isn't that right, Wesley?"

"He'll kill me," Wesley told the girl.

"Oh, no," Ree said. "I'll take you home. Come on, chum. I've had enough exercise for tonight."

"He'll kill me," Wesley said again.

"Come along, Wesley."

Wesley shook his head, slinging small, bright droplets of blood.

"You coming?"

"No," Wesley said. "You go along, Ree. I'll take myself home."

Willa Ree chuckled.

"I couldn't let you do that. You're in no condition to drive and you're not able to walk. Come along and I'll drive you home."

"You'll kill me."

"Don't be silly. I'm no fool."

"Yes, you are, Ree. You're a fool and a killer." Wesley's voice was matter of fact. "You're a sadist and you're nuts, plain nuts."

"Get up."

Wesley shook his head.

Laura spoke. "You go along, Ree. I'll call a cab for him."

"I couldn't let you go to all that trouble, Laura. Besides, the cabbie would wonder what happened to Wesley. In your apartment, too. Why, he might even call the police!"

"I'll risk that."

"Well, it's noble of you, sweet, but I can't let you do it. I just wouldn't feel right about it. No, I think I'd better take Wesley home. After all, I brought him here."

"You go on and leave him alone," Laura said, "or I'll call the police."

"You'll keep your mouth shut, honey! You'll keep your mouth shut and your nose out of my business! You're going to forget everything that happened here tonight! Or do you want me to play rough with you again?"

"You wouldn't dare!"

"Wouldn't I?" He walked across the room and slapped her again, not hard. "Wouldn't I, sweet?"

She rubbed her cheek. "Yes," she whispered. "Yes, you would."

"O.K." He turned to Wesley. "You ready?"

"I told you," Wesley said. "I'm not going. If you're going to kill me you'll have to do it here."

Ree caught him by the hair and pulled. Wesley fought back, weakly and clumsily, but he was pulled to his knees.

"Are you coming, Wesley?"

"No."

"You want it here? You want me to rough Laura up some more?"

"Leave her alone, Ree. Leave the girl alone and I'll go." Wesley turned to the girl. "Shake clear of this guy, girlie. For your own good, shake clear." He staggered to the door, leaned against it.

"Listen," Laura said. "Listen to me, Ree! Tomorrow I'll do some checking up! This man better be around!"

Ree shrugged. He helped Wesley down the steps, across the yard, into the car. Wesley slumped against the door, head back against the cushions, breath coming ragged and fast.

Wesley was scared, scared stiff.

Well, hell, why not? I would be, too, in his shoes. But I wouldn't be in his shoes because no man is big enough to slap me around like that and, anyway, if anyone could or did I'd fess up and give him the money....

"Listen, Ree," Wesley said. "I'll split with you. We'll go along just as we planned and I'll forget about your record and about tonight." He coughed a little. "I can get a doc in to patch me up and I can stay in my room a week or so until I look okay again."

Willa Ree turned right, away from town, away from lights.

"What say, Ree? I did wrong. I know it! We'll split and go on just as we'd planned, see. What say, Ree?"

"O.K. Where's the dough?"

"Pull up."

"Wait a minute. Too crowded here."

He passed the city limit sign, stepped on the gas, and passed the last service station. He passed the cemetery, found a gravel road, pulled down it and stopped the car. Wesley leaned forward and fumbled beneath the dash.

Ree saw the racked gun concealed there.

"Can you turn on the dome light?" Wesley asked.

"Not a chance. The dash light'll have to do. And I see that gun."

"I know you see the gun!"

"Well, just don't try to pull anything." He snatched the gun.

Wesley fumbled with a paper-wrapped package, hands trembling, head bobbing forward in eagerness.

"It's all here, Ree! Just like you put it in the water box! You take half and we'll go ahead like we planned! You'll need help and there's no one else you can trust! Why, you don't even know anybody else that'd work with you and I can do you a lot of good! I know the town, see, and I know where the money is! We can clean up...." His voice faded.

Ree took a cigarette and pushed in the dash lighter. "Smoke a fag, Wesley. Slow down and take a cigarette. It'll settle your nerves."

"Thanks."

Wesley sucked in smoke. He let the package fall in his lap.

"You're going to take it all, Ree." Wesley knew; it was a statement.

Willa Ree inhaled.

"You plan to bump me."

"I can't trust you, Wesley."

Wesley's voice was tired. "Who can you trust?"

Willa Ree stared at the cigarette, turning it and twisting it, watching smoke rise and fade into the darkness.

"You'd burn for it, Ree. There's the girl. She'll talk."

"She won't talk!"

"She'll talk."

"I said she won't!"

"Don't be a fool."

"Maybe she won't be around."

Wesley coughed, cleared his throat. "She'll be around, Ree. I think you've got her in your blood."

"She won't talk."

Wesley sucked at his cigarette. "I know you're going to kill me and I just sit here. I could try for the gun. I could open the door and start running. I could fight you."

"I'd get you."

"I know it."

"You shouldn't have crossed me, Wesley. You should have left that money where you found it."

"I know it."

"You should have known what would happen. I killed one man...."

"I know. And I just sit here. Know something, Ree? Know what scares me more than death?"

"What?"

"Being left out in a pasture where they won't find me. Or under a bridge. Where they won't find me."

"Want another cigarette?"

"Thanks."

Ree drove down the narrow road. The headlights sent a wide swath of white light over the fence posts and skitteringly across clumps of sage and grass and sand.

Ahead was the railroad.

Beside the tracks, on the right, in the pasture, was an abandoned well. He couldn't see it, but he knew it was there.

It was a covered well. The railroad people had built a conical roof over it and enclosed the sides, from bottom of roof to the ground, with net wire so that bums and drunks and kids and dogs wouldn't fall in.

He stopped at the side of the road and listened to the motor sigh to a stop. He cut the lights.

"Don't do it, Ree," Wesley screamed. "Don't do it!"

"Shut up."

"You'll regret it all your life!"

"Maybe I will, but shut up!"

"Ree, please—"

"I'm going to do it and shut up!"

Wesley began to cry. Softly, helplessly, his chest and shoulders heaving. "Get out."

"Don't do it, Ree. Take all the money." Wesley's tone was pleading, whispery and violent and pleading. "I'll leave the country and do anything you want! But, don't oh please for goodness' sake don't do it Ree I beg you don't do it!"

"Get out."

"Don't you have any feeling for crying out loud Ree don't you have any feeling aren't you too smart to kill a man in cold blood and don't you know you can't get away with it you'll burn, so help me I'll rot in hell, Ree, but you'll burn Ree don't you know you'll burn don't you know they'll catch up with you—"

"Get out."

Wesley's scream was spluttery, and his saliva hit Ree in the face.

"Dammit, get out!"

"No... ooo... ooo!" Wesley shrilled, his voice burbling as the high pitched scream trailed off.

Ree pulled the gun with his left hand and half turned. He caught Wesley's shoulder with his right hand.

"Come on and get out, Wesley, and we'll talk it over."

"You're crazy if you think I'm just going to get out and let you kill me in cold blood without even making a try to save myself you crazy fool you—crazy—crazy—crazy fool bastard to think I'll just step out as nice as you please and let you knock me off without even making a fight for it...." He never knew what hit him.

The gun barrel made a sodden thump as it landed.

Wesley slumped and the package fell to the floor of the car and Ree picked it up. He tore off a corner of the wrapping. Stooping, he struck a match. He held the package below the dash level and examined the bills. O.K.

He buttoned the package under his shirt, opened the car door, got out and walked around to open the door on Wesley's side.

He first tried to get his right arm under Wesley's knees, his left under the back. No soap. The man was limp as a dish rag, heavy as lead, stubbornly and passively resistant. He slid and sagged. Minutes passed.

Sweat ran down Willa Ree's face, into his eyes, into his mouth so that he tasted it. The droplets trickled down his back, ticklingly. A breeze came and the sweat was cold.

He grabbed Wesley by the arm and pulled. He grunted when the inert body slid out of the car head first. Wesley was heavy. He grunted from the strain, felt his knees buckle under the weight. There was a fence and barbs stuck and cut and tore. He cursed, half sobbed, staggered back and gathered his strength to lift Wesley higher.

Half tossed, half dropped, the man went over the fence.

The body thwacked to the ground and lay still.

He stumbled back to the car and fumbled with keys, found the right one, unlocked the trunk. He risked a match. There were pliers and he slipped them into his pocket. Leaving the trunk lid open he felt his way back to the fence and climbed through. He stumbled over Wesley, toe digging deep into taut flesh, and fell to his knees. Curious, breath suckingly serious, suddenly, he felt with his hands until he found Wesley's arm. His fingers slid down the arm to the wrist. Pulse weak.

Once more he slid an arm under the unconscious man's knees, the other under the back. Stumbling, staggering, he moved across the pasture. Weeds tangled around his legs. Thorny mesquite branches stabbed and ripped.

Ree thought, Should have gone down the railroad tracks....

A second fence stopped him and Wesley got the barbs. Again he lifted, heaved, tossed, dropped, and heard the body thump to the ground.

There, across the fence, on the railroad right-of-way, was the well, its conical roof silhouetted against a distant oil flare. He stood staring at it, waiting for muscles to stop trembling. In the distance were dim lights of town.

What to do with the car?

Too early to worry about that now. First things first—and maybe last.

He climbed through the fence, staggering across a shallow ditch and walked on shale up the incline leading to the rails.

The well was as he remembered it. He'd seen it but once, and then it was just a well. He'd been with Wesley that day, routine day patrol, and Wesley had pointed it out.

Net wire made a wall at ground level, leading up to the roof's bottom edge. Three feet from ground to roof, plenty of room.

He used the pliers to pull staples from a post, careful not to lose the staples. It was slow work, and once the pliers slipped and he raked his knuckles across the wire.

Removing staples from one post wasn't enough, not enough slack to pull the wire down out of the way, or up. Something held the wire at the bottom. Probably a beam, sunk into the earth.

Ree fumbled in panic, trembling panic, and he forced himself to pause.

Minutes ticked away as he worked at the top of the wire. The staples were hard to grasp, and the pliers slipped loose time after time.

A match, the light from just one match—too risky.

At last there was slack in the wire. In the middle it sagged. Not all the way, but enough.

His hands burned. They were sticky with blood, and sweat stung open wounds. His head throbbed and his mouth was fuzzy dry. He longed for a smoke.

Gravel clattered as he hurried down the embankment, but he didn't care. Who could hear? It was almost finished, almost done, and the bundle of money was inside his shirt.

Barbed wire hit his chest, the barbs digging in. He backed away, stooping to feel along the ground.

There—no. Gone—?

He turned to look at the bulk of the well roof, and then he fought the sudden panic that knotted his insides.

This is the place—the very place—right here—on this spot, he thought. But Wesley was gone.

So the guy had been playing possum all the time. He wasn't even out. Smart. Playing possum and getting carried around like a babe in arms. Smart.

Panicky hands dived into his pockets, and then he smiled at his panic. The keys were there, safe and snug. Well, the smart aleck can't ride. And he can't go far.

Ree tried to think. It was hard to do, because he was scared. Think now—Wesley's hurt, bad hurt, weak and dizzy and scared. What would he do? He knows you can't make a light, and he knows you've got the car keys. So what would he do? Drag himself off and lie low. That's it.

Loose gravel clattered and Ree strained to hear footsteps.

So it's O.K. Just take a little longer, that's all. His foot touched something on the ground. He recoiled and backed away and stood still, mentally blacked out, tired, exhausted.

If I could just take my brain out and rub it, he thought.

His foot went out and touched something—a rock. Moving slowly, on tiptoe, he advanced. Across the shallow ditch, up the incline, he walked. Once he stopped to listen but the sound of clattering gravel was not repeated.

Could have been a rabbit, he thought. Or a coyote. A dog, maybe. Or Wesley.

When it came, out of the dark, he didn't know what had happened. Not at first. One second he was walking along—and then the world caved in. He was on his back, looking at stars. The right side of his face felt numb, crushed, broken.

Must have been a rock.

The fool had thrown a rock.

It seemed he was down for minutes, staring at stars and fighting the creeping darkness that wanted to pull down the curtain behind his eyes. And all the time he knew that Wesley might be moving in, with another rock, maybe. Somehow, somehow it didn't seem important.

Got to move, he thought. The fool's dangerous.

His right arm seemed numb. He thought of the gun and tried to get it, but the right arm seemed numb. Odd. He was lying on it, and stifled a desire to laugh.

Rolling over, off the arm, he got the gun. It came to him then that it would be safer to lie still than to get up. Wesley was on the ground, flat on the ground, and could see him against the sky line if he stood up.

Wesley played possum, so two would be playing the game.

It seemed unreal. Flat on his back, a gun in his hand, everything still and quiet—unreal. Again he had the silly desire to laugh. It bubbled in his chest and moved on up to his throat, but he choked it down.

Wesley wouldn't be feeling like laughing.

You could make book on that.

He heard nothing except the sound of his own breathing and the soft sound of the night wind. Stars were pale in the sky, far off and flickering pale, and even the moon was a fragment of moon, dim and almost transparent.

What am I waiting for?

I've got a gun.

The gun hung heavy in his hand, heavy, heavy, when he rocked to his knees. He surged to his feet and ran in a crouch to the right. He stopped, still in a crouch, and listened. His eyes burned as he scoured the darkness.

There was a swishing noise past his nose. Wesley had thrown and missed. But it would have been too bad if that rock had been an inch to the right—too bad.

He stepped back and stooped lower.

Even as Wesley's shoulder hit his knees, and even as he pitched backward through air, he was glad. The waiting was over, the strain gone, and now it would end.

And Wesley was fighting for his life instead of dying like a mouse in a trap. Now it would end.

His head banged against the gravel and pain thundered and flashed, but he twisted as he fell and kicked out with both legs.

Something squished against his nose.

Wesley's fist. With a rock in it, maybe.

Blood flowed and tasted warm and salty in his mouth. He couldn't see, but he continued to squirm and kick. One of his kicks landed and Wesley cried out.

The guy can't take it. Only he's taken a lot. He's weak.

Wesley's hands were on him, clawing and gouging, but he kicked out again with both feet and both feet landed. The weight of Wesley was gone.

Ree was on his knees, on his feet, and the gun was pointed at the twisting dark blur on the ground, the threshing twisting half seen dark blur on the ground.

He squeezed, one, two, three, four, five times. He missed five times. And Wesley was gone.

Ree was half deafened by the gun's blasts. His ears rang, but still he heard the clattering of Wesley's feet across the gravel along the tracks.

And a train was coming. Its light was an eye, a dim eye that grew brighter and brighter.

And, oddly, there was another light now, a small dim eye of light, directly across the tracks. There was a house over there.

Someone had heard the shots.

Wesley was far down the tracks, a small dark figure impaled in the glare of the train engine's one-eyed light.

The bastard.

Ree stood, safe in darkness, as the train clattered by. He heard a yell, a thin and high pitched and almost unheard yell.

Wesley had swung aboard that freight!

But he'd be back. Wesley would be back, bringing trouble.

He went to the car and got in, relaxed against the cushions and conscious of the pain in his head, his bruised arms and legs and hands.

A cigarette and a drink would taste good, he thought, damned good. There had to be a bottle in the glove compartment—and who keeps gloves in glove compartments and trunks in trunk compartments—and he willed a bottle to be in the glove compartment and there was. He swallowed some of the stuff and laughed because it burned his throat. He held the lighter in the plug and stuck its glowing end to a cigarette.

Screaming nerves became still.

This, he thought, is more like it. But gotta stay cool, stay cool all the time and think. The thing to do is think and use the old brains. Because that's what they're for, to use. Think all the time, all the way, and leave nothing to chance.

Wesley'll be back, so you've gotta think fast.

Are you staying or are you leaving?

He wondered what he should do with the car.

If he knew where Wesley lived he could take the car there. No.

Leave it where it was? Take it to town and park it? No. Blood on the cushions. Undoubtedly, blood on the cushions. With Wesley gone, someone would ask questions. So burn the damned thing.

He had another drink and chased it with smoke. This time the whisky burned his lip, and he felt with his tongue. Split lip. Bet my face is a mess.

He replaced the bottle in the glove compartment. His hand touched paper. It felt like an envelope. He picked it up and stuck it in his hip pocket.

Everything, for some reason, had gone wrong.

Plans whirled in Ree's head, faster and faster. Too fast they came and went, neatly, but too fast. Fear came. He fought it.

He decided it would be silly to burn the car. He'd leave it.

There'd be questions, but he'd leave it.

With a cloth he found in the car pocket he wiped the steering wheel, the door handles, and the car keys and dash. He even wiped the gear shift and cigarette lighter knob. That ought to do it.

He left the car and crossed the fence, stumbled across the pasture, and decided it was impossible to make it in the darkness.

Too many fences, too much sand, too many mesquites and sage clumps and hillocks.

He angled back toward the road, stumbling. There was sand in his shoes. Thorny bushes clutched at his clothing, stabbed at his legs.

Oh, for a cup of coffee! he thought. A cigarette would help, but he had no match.

At the road, exhausted, he sat down to dump the sand from his shoes.

Tired, tired, brain tired and body tired and aching.

His fingers were slow to lace the shoes, and he forced himself to concentrate on the task. Finished, he got up and began to limp toward town.

That damned girl!

Three miles can be a hundred miles, or three steps, or three times the distance to nowhere. Some spooners were parked beside the road, and he had to climb the fence and circle around. Again his shoes filled with sand, and again he had to stop and empty them.

Blisters on his heels, one broken.

That damned girl, and who the hell says I missed the dim dark blur of Wesley purposely or if I missed because I just couldn't hit that twisting dark blur in the darkness, and who says anyway it's hard to kill a man when it's not hard to kill a man at all but hard as hell to kill the things a man knows or feels or leaves in other peoples' minds....

Damn her....

It's no use wishing you could undo a thing. Maybe he should have gone easier with Wesley. Maybe he should have split with Wesley. Because now Wesley's gone, but he'll be back.

A man is what he is and he is the product of other men—I guess.

Oh, hell, oh hell, oh hell.

That damned girl....

Houses loomed before him and he was startled. He tried to think. For the past hour he'd been thinking wrong, confused thoughts, and he told his mind to figure the angles.

The girl first.

He walked faster, almost trotted, avoiding the lighted streets.

It was two-thirty. Not bad. He'd walked faster than he realized.

Plenty of time, he told himself. For what?

Feet wanted to turn toward his room, his room and bed. His body was drained of strength and he was hungry. His strength was gone, replaced with aches and pains. He felt the right side of his face with timid fingers, found a lump, crusted blood, and winced at awakened pain.

What happened? Wesley threw a rock.

There was no sense to this night. No rhyme, no reason, no sense at all. Nothing gained by any of it. Except money.

And it all seemed a nightmare, one of those revolving pin-wheel nightmares that begin nowhere and end never, splits in the middle and goes both ways to bounce like a yo-yo and start over again.

Crazy to think like that—crazy, crazy.

Forty thousand bucks will pay for a lot of nightmares.

But Wesley would be back.

Crazy to think like that—crazy, crazy.

Wesley offered to split.

Yes, but a split means half and a half is only part of all and who wants half when all is all and half is all divided in half....

Crazy, crazy, crazy....

Wesley couldn't be trusted. Wesley tried a double-cross. Wesley wanted it all. And Wesley would be back with a bag of trouble.

He'd have to sack the town and get out.

He shook his head. There were big buildings, bulky and squat and dark, with shiny, dim shiny windows, like dead eyes.

What the heck?

The school!

Feet must have moved fast. A block, two blocks, nearly there. Next block. Her apartment was dark. Well, no wonder. Nearly three.

He stood before the door, but heard no sound. The door was not locked.

His fingers found the light switch. He walked across the room and peered into the bedroom.

She wasn't there.

Panic came from the floor, numbing his feet and shooting up his legs.

She's got to be here!

She thinks you killed Wesley!

And how are you going to prove you didn't?

Now, wait a minute. Don't go off the deep end. What does she know? Plenty. No. Not about the money, and not about Baldy.

She knows nothing, absolutely nothing.

Maybe she got scared. Maybe she spent the night with a friend.

He went to the bathroom and opened the shower curtains, laughing at himself for a fool.

His face stared at him from the mirror above the sink. The bump, the slight cut, the crusted blood with flesh blue-black beneath the blood, was unbelievable. His eyes were red-shot, glary, stary and wild.

He was tired.

It wasn't worth it, he thought. Not worth it. Can't quit.

He muttered it aloud, "Can't quit now."

Can't undo what's done, clock turn back come months and days back again time turn back and start all over. Set the pins up again, in the other alley. Come back before then, come back and backward go. Or let me stop dreaming.

His hands started to work first, and then the rest of him co-operated.

There was blood on his coat, blood on his sleeve, the left sleeve, and on the front. He unbuttoned the coat and his body slid out. He examined his shirt and found a small spot on the cuff. He scrubbed it with a washrag, but it was impossible to wash it away.

He rinsed the rag and scrubbed his face gingerly. It wasn't so bad with the blood gone. The cut was small. The flesh was discolored a bit, but the cut was just small. (What hit you, Ree?) He could put powder over it, a small piece of tape, maybe. (Oh, nothing. Just ran into a door.) He found adhesive and gauze in the medicine chest and applied it over the cut. Swelling'll go away, he thought.

He wet his hair and combed it. His pants were wrinkled, and there were small rents in the legs, but not too bad. His shoes were dusty and he scrubbed them with the rag.

His fingers unbuttoned the shirt and reached for the bundle of money. The brown wrapping was taped. Rubber-stamped on the paper was "Johnson Tool Company."

It occurred to him that he should hide the money. The girl could have gone to the police about last night.

But she wouldn't. She wouldn't. Why not?

If she did—and she might have—they'd be waiting at his room.

It would be awkward if they found the money on him. They might want to know where he'd taken Wesley. Better hide the stuff. But where?

He sat on the edge of a chair and smoked. His eyes touched a cut-glass bottle on a table. Whisky.

He went to the kitchen for a glass.

He had his drink, a quick one, and he thought of a hiding place for the money. He took his time, pausing for deep drags on a cigarette, and up-ended the red leather arm chair. He cut a slit in the lining, underneath, and stuck the money through the slit. In the bathroom he found adhesive tape and used several strips to seal the slit in the lining.

That does it.

Ready to go.

He switched off the bathroom light and left the house. He didn't look back.

But an envelope had fallen from his pocket. It lay, unseen and unmissed, in the middle of the living room floor. The envelope he'd taken from the glove compartment of Wesley's car.

Chapter Sixteen

The whole thing was a nightmare. It all happened too fast.

At first, when she saw Ree standing with Wesley in the doorway, she thought there had been an accident. And things got out of control.

First, Ree had hit Wesley.

When she protested, he slapped her.

She had the feeling that if things would start over again, at the beginning, with Willa Ree and Wesley in the doorway, she could control what happened after. But, this way, things got out of hand. She couldn't handle things.

Everything blurred, went out of focus, and became unreal. She saw Willa Ree kick Wesley. Wesley was on the floor, bloody, bloody. She had to do something!

The beer bottle was on the table, and then it was in her hand. She hit Ree. Now, she thought, things will be as they should be. But, although there was blood on Ree's forehead, he didn't fall.

"Put it down," he said. "I don't want to hurt you."

She heard herself say, "Get out of here."

He said something. He took a step toward the door, and then pointed at Wesley and said something.

She looked at Wesley.

He grabbed the bottle from her hands.

The blow didn't hurt, but the jar blinded her and sent lights streaking behind her eyes. She knew he hit her more than once, she knew it. She dropped to her knees and cried. Things blurred again, until Ree forced her to get up.

"You'll live," he said. His lips kept moving, but she heard nothing.

"I'll kill you," she said.

His lips moved again, as if in pantomime, and there was a smirk on his face. She realized that he had looked that way before, but it was different then. He looked funny with the blood trickling above his eyes, standing there and moving his lips and gesturing with his hands.

"He'll kill me," Wesley said.

She heard that.

"Oh, no," Willa Ree said. "I'll take you home."

But she knew he would kill him, unless— "You go along, Ree. I'll call a cab for him."

Willa Ree refused, as she knew he would.

Time passed and they were gone.

She cried again.

Later, sometime later, she bathed her face with cold water, thinking, I'll be a mess in the morning. She dressed.

It was in her mind to call the police, but she couldn't decide what she would say. If she said that they should arrest the chief of police because he gave the captain of police a beating in my apartment, they'd laugh.

One thing she knew—she couldn't spend the night at home. Ree might return.

She switched off the lights, left the house, and drove across town.

Rita was asleep. She pounded on the door.

"Who is it?"

"Laura. Open up."

Bare feet padding, and then the door opened.

"For crying out loud! What're you doing out at this hour?"

"I'm going to spend the night with you."

Rita switched on the light. "What happened to you?"

"Willa Ree. I'll tell you about it in the morning."

"I'll get some salve for your lip."

She put the salve on her lip, mind racing. The sheriff? Would he do anything? Maybe they're all in it together. What did Ree want from Wesley? What did he want Wesley to tell him?

She slept, but before daylight she was awake.

I've acted like a tramp, and I've taken a tramp's beating. It's my fault, and now I'm soiled....

The sun was rising when she drove across town to her apartment.

He's been back here, she thought. She felt it. At first glance, she saw nothing changed. All was as she left it. And then she saw the envelope.

It was on the floor, and she picked it up. It was addressed to Wesley. It had been opened, and now she opened it again.

Pictures of Ree—front and profile. Hair clipped short and a number across the bottom, right-hand corner—68397642.

She sat down.

Was this what Ree wanted? Couldn't be if he left it behind. It must have fallen from Wesley's pocket when he was lying on the floor.

There was a sheet of paper in the envelope. Ree's record. Armed robbery, three years, she read.

She replaced pictures and papers in the envelope, and slid the envelope beneath the cushions of the couch. And then she had breakfast, dawdled over coffee, and smoked a cigarette. She had a shower and fixed her hair, applied make-up and scowled at the cut lip and bruised face, promised herself she'd get even.

One question burned her mind: Had Ree killed Wesley?

The day was a nightmare, as the night had been. She cleaned house, made plans, discarded plans.

Go to the police? she thought. What could she prove? She could discredit Ree, give him some explaining to do, even reveal that he was an ex-convict. But, what if they knew that?

Go to the city council. What if they knew that? They wouldn't hire a man without checking his background. Would they? Suppose she told them Ree killed Wesley? She didn't know for sure. Wesley could be on the job this morning, for all she knew. They'd want to know why she thought so in the first place. Well, she'd say, he beat Wesley in my apartment. For all I know he killed him later. And Ree is an ex-convict. So? But Ree brought him, Wesley, to the apartment and beat him! Beat him unmercifully! Prove it, they'd say. Show us the body.

No, the police are out, she decided. The sheriff. What about the sheriff? But, so they say, the sheriff's department is worse than the police. And they say the county attorney is a stooge for the sheriff, and both work for that man Halliday.

And something inside her said, Keep your mouth shut, Laura. Keep quiet, keep still, know nothing, do nothing. Wesley may be O.K.

She had a sandwich and glass of milk for lunch, washed the dishes, mopped the kitchen floor, took out the garbage.

She examined her face again, applied more make-up, and left the house.

It was a long day, a hard day. No one asked her if she had run into a door. Her mind was numbed, fuzzy-foggy numb, and she kept seeing Ree's face looming before her, lips moving and twisting and moving. It had been a nightmare, as this day was a long drawn-out nightmare.

But the workday ended, and she drove home. She showered, mixed a drink, and sat on the couch, smoking.

There was a piece of paper on the coffee table—a note.

Her father had written, "Laura, I'm fixing up a new study at the church and the red chair will fit it nicely. Was in town and thought I'd pick it up. Write soon. Your mother has been worried. Dad."

Chapter Seventeen

The cut wasn't so bad, and there was little swelling. The flesh was discolored around the cut, but he'd shaved and used fresh tape over gauze.

Ree combed his hair, patting at a wave with the side of his hand, and went to the closet for the new tan suit.

It was seven-thirty when he left the room and strolled toward the Hall. The sergeant looked up when he entered.

"Mornin', Chief," he said.

"Good morning, Swing. What's new?"

"Not much. Drunks. A Negro for a knifin' job. Wesley's car was found out on a country road."

"Whose car?" he said, and then cursed under his breath.

"Wesley's. He must have hung one on last night. I dunno, though. There's something funny about it. There was blood all over the seat."

"Yeah? What else?"

"That's all."

"Where's Wesley?"

"Hasn't been in. Probably sleeping it off—or maybe he's just sore. He sure wanted to be top dog around here."

"Does he hang them on very often?"

"Two or three times a year."

"Tell him I want to see him the minute he comes in."

"Yes, sir."

"Who's getting the gravy in this town, sergeant?"

"Sir?"

"Who gets the gravy?" Willa Ree repeated. "Who really gets paid off in this town? Who pulls Halliday's strings?"

"Well, I'll tell you," the sergeant said. "I don't know what you're talking about. Now, if I wanted to find out, I'd see the sheriff and the county attorney."

Ree walked to the window and stood looking out. He thought, So, O.K., you punk, be cagy. But maybe I worked too fast.

He said, "Maybe I will, sergeant. In the meanwhile, do what I say and I'll see if I can raise your standard of living."

"I could stand a raise of some kind," the sergeant said.

"Get me a list of the call houses in town and the names of the girls. I want every single girl at the health center for a checkup once a week."

"They're supposed to be doing that now, but...."

"Yeah, I know. They're donating to somebody's favorite charity. You see to it they get a checkup every week. I want the sick ones escorted out of town. You see to that, too."

"O.K."

"No rough stuff. Be gentle, but firm. And get me a list of the bookies and spot their ticker, if they've got one. Ought to have one in a pool hall."

"It's over at the Black Gold."

"O.K. I want the dope on the gamblers. Give me the inside on everything from floating games to the swank spots. The honky-tonks and night clubs must have rooms."

The sergeant snuffed out his cigarette on the sole of his shoe. "You want it sewed up tight, O.K. I'm your boy."

"Don't drop any hints. Don't make any threats. Just do what I told you. Do it yourself or use a flunky you can trust."

"Don't give it a second thought. It's good as done."

Ree started for the door. "Tell Wesley to wait here for me."

He winked at the blonde in the outer office.

"Hey," she called, "what happened to you?"

"Ran into a door."

"Yeah, I'll bet."

He paused. "I'll tell you all about it tonight."

She bent over a ledger, saying, "Eight o'clock."

He went outside, down the steps, whistling.

A car, he told himself, is what you need. A nice, shiny car like Wesley's convertible.

No.

Just a bad dream, and forget it. Today's a new day and nothing happened yesterday. You have the world by the tail, so twist it.

Maybe he could take care of Wesley—when Wesley returned.

He must have known where he was going when he left the Hall, but he was surprised to find himself in front of Halliday's store. It was a good store. Tile front and fancy windows, and cool inside. Air conditioning and thick carpets and classy fixtures and good lighting.

A clerk came bowing and scraping. "May I help you, sir?"

"I want to see Halliday."

The clerk pointed to an office door at the rear.

Ben Halliday was sitting behind a metal desk, reading a paper. He smiled and said, "I was hoping you'd come, Ree. Have a seat. Cigarette?"

"Thanks."

"I was just reading something about you in the paper."

"Telegraph?"

"Traveler."

"Then it probably wasn't complimentary. Who runs that rag, anyway?"

"Couple of kids—brothers. Looks like they're out to make trouble too."

"Wonder what they've got against me and so soon?"

"Not you, Ree. Me—and Sam Byrd. They've been sniping at us for a long time."

"Are they well fixed?"

"No. To tell the truth, they're in a jam. They've been owing the bank for some time. Irvin's been good to them and they've had three or four extensions on their notes."

"And they can't pay?"

"They can't pay."

"Can they borrow anywhere else?"

"Not if Irvin—well—not if Irvin passes the word."

"Then they'll go broke."

"No. Fact is, they've got a good thing. Started with a shirttail full of type and a lot of guts and ran them into a nice business. They've expanded too fast, of course. Had to borrow some money now and then. The fact is, they'd clean up if they got a little backing and entered the daily field. The Telegraph is weak, you see, and these boys print what the people like to read. Not what I like to read, of course, but they've got a good thing if it's properly developed."

"So...."

"So we'll find a way."

"These boys are smart?"

"Sure, they're smart."

"And yet they've been pushing you when they know you tell Irvin what to do."

"Well, they've got courage. They don't like me and, to tell the truth, a lot of people don't like me. You can't make a lot of money, Ree, without making enemies. You know that."

"Who are the two boys?"

"Ed and Cliff Barrick."

"Why don't you freeze them out?"

"Going to. At least, they'll think I'm going to. Irvin's going to demand payment on their notes. Then—we'll see. Maybe they'll listen to reason."

"What's this they wrote about me?"

"Nothing much. Usual line when they're trying to start something. Disorganization of the police force—dissension. They say you and Wesley don't click, and something about a brush you had with him after the Johnson Tool burglary."

"That all?"

"That's all. Nothing much. Don't let it bother you."

"O.K. Listen, Mr. Halliday, I know the setup you want around town. I've been feeling my way, but now I'm ready to get moving. I've taken the first steps, but it'll take a little time to get things sewed up."

Halliday cleared his throat, doodled with a pencil. His pale eyes flicked up and down, up and down, shiny hot. Willa Ree waited, wondering.

"Glad to hear it," Halliday said finally. "Perhaps, though, I'd better explain my position." He cleared his throat again, twiddling with a pencil, and stared hard at Ree.

"Your predecessor, Bronson, was a good man. A good man, but not a good businessman. Now, Ree, I'm a businessman. I'm honest, but I'm a businessman. You know what that means. Some people don't, because they confuse ethics with honesty."

Then he picked up a letter opener and began to clean his nails with the point.

"Ree, it is my belief that things like, well, like vice can't be stamped out. People are people and they're going to play. The world has had prostitution down through the ages, and will always have it."

"I guess you're right."

"Well, I always say that if you can't whip a thing, join it! Make it work for you! Control it!"

"My idea exactly."

"We'll get along fine, Ree. However, you'll have problems to solve."

"The county boys?"

Halliday smiled. "You don't let grass grow under your feet. Yes, you're right. The county boys are controlling our little, shall we say, ah, our little problem. Now, by rights, they shouldn't meddle inside city limits. That's our territory."

"Maybe you'd better tell me a little something about these boys, Mr. Halliday."

"You know the sheriff, Claude Messner?"

"Met him."

"He's serving his second term. Claude used to be chief of police, and he was a good one. Yes, he was a good chief and a good businessman. Knew how to get things organized. Well, when he ran for sheriff and was elected, he took the organization with him. We put Bronson in as chief, but he was never able to break Messner's hold on things. Bronson wasn't a businessman, you see. And he was too strait-laced."

Ree chuckled. "In other words, Messner got the city lined up and then ran for sheriff so he could expand."

"That's about the size of it."

"Tell me more about him. What kind of man is he?"

"Hard," Halliday said. "Messner is a hard man, smart and hard." He paused, musing, his eyes looking at something far away. "One might say he's dangerous. Yes. But what a man to have on your side! If you could control him, that is."

"How do you mean, hard?"

"He's a killer, Ree. He likes to kill. They say he's killed seven men."

"Well, that makes him hard, all right. So much for him. What about the county attorney?"

"Arthur Fry's just a young fellow. A tool in Messner's pay."

"Who else do we play with?"

"Well, there's Byrd, but we stick together, work as a team. And, of course, there's the mayor, but he's a Pooh Bah. Does anything I tell him."

"But he'll get a cut?"

"Well, let's not call it a cut, Ree. This is business, you understand."

"O.K., a dividend."

Halliday smiled warmly. "That's much better."

Ree got up to go and shook hands with Halliday.

"We haven't discussed the percentages," Halliday said.

"That's a good point."

Venetian blinds were drawn over Halliday's eyes. "You take a third, Ree."

Halliday would eat out of his hand—later. For now, a third it was. "That's satisfactory," he said.

"After all, there'll be the sheriff and Fry and Byrd and the mayor out of the other two-thirds."

"And you, Mr. Halliday."

"Naturally. That's all right with you now? If not, let's talk it out now."

"A third will be O.K.," Ree said. "I'll be doing the work and taking the chances."

"That's true, but you'll be getting the lion's share."

"It's O.K.," Ree said again. "Forget it."

"Very well, Ree. We'll get along fine, I think."

Chapter Eighteen

Ree had a letter from Wesley a week later. It was mailed from Houston and said: "I'll be back soon, chum."

That was all. One pregnant sentence.

It was still hot. There were no clouds in the sky, and the sun was a pale blazing blob. Ree left the Hall and walked through town, watching the wind whip the dust into the air. Old newspapers flapped against the curbing, danced across the sidewalk, flattened against store windows, wrapped around light poles. Few people were out, and those who walked were forced to lean against the wind. Men held their hats, and women pressed arms flat against their sides, hands reaching downward over hips in quick, furtive movements, as they tried to prevent skirts from flying upward.

That damned Wesley! Well, there'd be questions, but he did most of the questioning.

Sand stung his face, worked under his collar, gritted into his eyes. He held his mouth closed tightly and breathed through his nose, leaning into the wind and walking rapidly. His tie fluttered over his shoulder and he was forced to pull his hat down again, ducking his head so the wind wouldn't send it swirling.

Some damned country, he thought. Sand and oil and money. And women. He wondered about Laura, wondered if he should call her.

No, he decided. Let her cool off a while longer.

He found Sam Byrd at the Byrd Motor Company. It was a brick building on Eighth Street, a block off Main, with curved plate-glass windows and double doors opening on a showroom. Business offices were lined against a wall, narrow cubicles.

A long-nosed bookkeeper looked up, and Ree asked for Byrd.

Sam Byrd was drunk and comfortable. His muscled arms stuck out of sport-shirt sleeves. His tiny mustache still looked out of place beneath his fat, blue-veined nose. Black eyes stared unwinkingly under bushy brows. He still needed a haircut.

"Come in, Ree." His voice was flat, uninterested, impatient.

"How are you, Mr. Byrd?"

"Busy."

Willa Ree ran the tip of his tongue around the inside of his cheek.

"You've talked to Halliday, Ree, and he runs things. It isn't necessary for us to discuss anything."

"Like that, huh?"

Byrd shuffled papers on his desk and said, "Like that."

Ree felt his muscles draw tight, felt hot blood pounding, but he forced himself to close the office door gently.

Back at the Hall, he rushed through paper work, scanned reports, and helped the sergeant draw up new patrol schedules.

"It'll take a while to get those lists you want," the sergeant said.

"That's O.K."

He strapped on the gun belt and twisted it around so the .38 rested on his hip, far back, holstered muzzle resting in the hip pocket. When his coat was buttoned, the gun didn't show.

"See you later, sergeant."

"Adios."

There were elm trees on the courthouse lawn, and the grass was green and close-cropped. Flowers and shrubbery lined the walks.

The courthouse was a massive stone structure, steepled, with a clock on each of the four sides. Halls and stairs took up most of the space inside, with small offices flanking the halls.

Sheriff Claude Messner looked like a hard man. His face was without expression. He sat with cowboy-booted feet on a desk top and stared. His rancher's hat was pushed to the back of his head, revealing thin black hair. Ree, studying the man's dark eyes and thin, pale lips, decided he could be thirty or fifty.

"Hello, Messner."

"Hello." Messner stood up and extended his hand. Ree was impressed by the man's well-cut gray gabardine suit.

"Thought I'd drop over and chat a bit."

"Glad you did, Ree. Been hearing a lot about you. I should have been over to visit you, but you know how it is. Something always turns up."

Two men entered the room. Deputies. One was old, paunchy, slow-moving, and dirty. The other was young, blondly handsome, athletic, and green as grass. Both wore holstered guns with fancy handles.

"Can we talk in private, Sheriff?" Ree asked.

"Sure," Messner said. He led the way to a cubicle of an office, furnished with one metal desk, two folding chairs, and one hunting calendar on the wall.

Willa Ree sat down. Messner straddled a chair, elbows resting on the chair back.

"What's on your mind, Ree?"

"A horse trade."

"Maybe I don't deal in horses."

"Maybe we won't trade, then. But it seemed like a good idea."

Both spoke slowly, feeling the strain, and their eyes roved the walls of the office as they fought to appear cool, casual.

"If you've got a deal...."

"Sheriff, I've got a deal. To speak plainly, a deal that you'd do well to go for."

"If that's a threat...."

"No threat, Sheriff. Don't jump so fast."

"I know what you're driving at, Ree. You don't have anything to trade with."

"I will have."

"And that's a threat."

"You're too jumpy, Sheriff. If you'll listen without getting your dander up, I think we'll both profit."

"You're cutting in," the sheriff said. His face remained expressionless, his voice calm.

"Do you want to listen?"

Messner fumbled at a shirt pocket, his trembling fingers betraying his anger. He pulled a tobacco sack and papers from the pocket, and rolled a cigarette.

"You're working for Ben Halliday, of course," he said. "I don't work for anybody. Why should I listen?"

"Suit yourself. But work with me and you'll make more money. Work by yourself and I'll cut the ground out from under you."

A flush, dull and ugly, began at the top of Messner's shirt collar and crept upward. He took one last, deep puff at his cigarette and threw it on the floor.

"Sheriff," Ree said, "I'll run every tramp in town across the county line. And that's not all I can do."

Messner stood, one hand trembling near the big .45 on his hip.

"Just relax and take it easy," Ree said. "Don't get tough with me. I'm telling you just in case you're curious—I can make you eat that gun." For long seconds he thought the sheriff was going to jump him.

"Just don't talk to me like that," Messner said, at last. His voice trembled and his face went chalky white.

"O.K. Only, don't act like I'm a pip squeak like Bronson. I don't push anybody around—unless I have to. And I don't like to be pushed around. You had the town sewed up, but now it's a partnership."

"So you run the girls out of town, Ree. So I'd bring them back."

"You'd never make money that way, Sheriff. Besides, if it comes to that, I'll take a few statements from the girls. The town wouldn't like to hear the tramps have been paying you."

"And where would that get you?"

"It wouldn't hurt me. Might even leave the field open."

"All right," Messner said, "let's hear your proposition."

"What're you nicking the girls?"

"Ten per cent."

"And half of that goes to the county attorney?"

"Fry only gets three per cent."

"Then here's my deal. Turn the girls over to me. Keep your hands off. I'll take twenty-five per cent from them, and you'll still get ten. That'll leave you seven per cent after you pay Fry—the same thing you're getting now. I'll have to give—somebody—half of mine, so we'll be about even in the long run."

"How do I stand to gain by that setup?"

"I'll bring in more girls. With all the small hotels and tourist courts, this town can take care of a lot of girls. So you'll make more money."

"Sounds O.K. If you do what you say."

"I will. Now, suppose we get this gambling thing under control, too."

"Now, just a minute!"

"Listen, Messner," Ree said, holding his hand up, palm outward. "I know you're nicking them. Ten to one they're paying a fee to operate, and you're getting a small part of the take. You're missing out on the floating games. They won't pay off because you're county and they know you're not going to make raids inside the city limits. That leaves you with the honky-tonk games at the edge of town—chicken feed!"

"Maybe, but—"

"We can make them pay a percentage. You handle the business outside the city limits and I'll handle the town. We'll split fifty-fifty."

Messner took off his hat and scrubbed his hand through his hair. He pitched the hat on the desk and hooked his thumbs under his belt, standing stiff and spraddle-legged.

"Got any more ideas?"

Willa Ree stepped on his cigarette. "A few, but it'll take a while to develop them."

"You can't touch liquor licenses," Messner said. "That's handled higher up and there're too many fingers in that pie. The city boys have got building permits and garbage and paving out of your reach, so that doesn't leave much."

"We'll get along. There's bound to be some dope and a hot-car ring."

"And bookies."

Ree rubbed his nose. "O.K., bookies. Have you been nicking them?"

"Couldn't handle it. They're paying higher up—state, maybe."

"I'll handle it. Fifty-fifty?"

"Right. But Halliday'll raise hell if he finds out we're collecting without splitting."

Willa Ree let his hand fall on the door knob. "Do you think anybody's working dope here?"

Messner was studying the calendar on the wall. "O.K., Ree. Fifty-fifty on that, too. Only, we've got to be careful."

"We'll be careful."

"And Ree?"

"Yeah?"

"Be careful. You talk hard. That kind of talk might work with me once— if it's to my advantage to listen. But not twice. I'll do business with you on a strict business basis, but be careful. I'm allergic to hard talk."

"We don't have to like each other."

"So long."

"Yeah."

Ree's back prickled as he left the office.

Mean, Messner was. A mean bastard. Ree had the feeling that Messner would have been on him like a dog on a bone if he'd backed down an inch.

As he stepped into the glaring sunlight he saw the old Negro woman. She was thin, stooped, with deep-lined wrinkles covering her face, for all the world the spitting image of an aged simian. Krinkly gray hair frizzled her head, and she was crying.

"No, suh, please, suh," she was mumbling. "They can't hang my boy! They ain't goan to hang my boy, no! He's a good boy. Yas, foah God he's a good boy! Yes!"

The deputy, the young one with the blonde good looks, was leaning against the door.

"That's right, mammy. I told you we'd hang him next time he got in trouble."

The old woman's body shook and trembled as she sobbed. "No, suh, please! They ain't goan hang my baby! He's my baby boy, yas, and he's good!"

Ree put his hand on the deputy's shoulder. "Tell the woman you're not going to bother her boy, Blondie. Tell her you were playing a joke."

"You go to hell!"

"I'll count three, Blondie. And keep your hand away from your gun if you don't want to eat it. What the heck you star toters think you are—movie cowboys?"

The big boy's hand clawed above the .45. "I'm telling you, Blondie," Ree warned, "I'm carrying a gun." His hand dipped under his coat at the hip and flashed up with the gun. He waved it under the deputy's nose and slid it back into the holster.

He began to count. "One."

The deputy curled his lips, face flushed, and gritted his teeth.

"Two."

The old Negro woman sobbed softly.

"Three."

The big deputy swung first, a wild hay-maker, and he grunted as Ree's left came across. Blood streamed from his nose.

The rest was easy. Ree chopped him down and walked away, noting that a crowd had gathered.

Why'd I do that? he asked himself. The word'll get around.

An old mammy, for crying out loud!

It was a long day. A dozen times he caught himself reaching for the telephone, ready to call Laura.

At five o'clock he ate and went home. He showered, shaved, and dressed, but it was only six o'clock when he finished. Now, with surprising suddenness, he was sleepy. There was a gritty feel to his eyes and a weighty, tired feeling in his bones. He'd go now.

Waiting for a cab, he decided how to act. He'd be gentle, make love, promise marriage—anything—to get her back.

Something delayed the cab. Irritated, he walked to the curb to wait. For the first time he noticed that the wind was gone, and with it, the sand.

The sun was low in the west, the slant of its rays orange-tinging the scattered clouds. It was almost cool, but the air was heavy with gas fumes from the fields.

A battered cab whirled around the corner and pulled in at the curb. He snapped the address to the driver and sat forward in the seat without relaxing, thinking, She'll be madder'n the devil. Shouldn't have hit her. A woman scorned is a hell on wheels.

The cab pulled up, and he stepped out.

"That'll be fifty cents," the cabby said.

He flipped the coin and trotted up the steps. He opened the door, and knew she wasn't there. The apartment felt empty, and it was.

And the leather chair was gone.

She'd found the dough!

But why should she move the chair? He had to have that money!

He had to fight to control his breathing, and his body seemed paralyzed. He had to will his limbs to move. The chair wasn't in the small bedroom. It was silly, he realized, but he looked in the closets and in the bathroom.

The front door opened. Laura? Cops? Laura.

"It's you," she said. Her face was bruised. One eye was puffed, and her lip was cut.

"Yeah. Look, honey...."

"What did you do with him?"

"Threw him in the clink," he said, not meaning to say that.

"Wesley—in jail?"

"Yeah."

"Why?" (She didn't believe it.)

"Why in hell do you think I beat him up in the first place? The guy was taking graft! We've been watching him." He knew she didn't believe it, but she wanted to.

"How'll he look to the public if he's in jail?"

"They won't know it. He'll leave town. Later we'll announce he resigned." He was confident now. He had her.

"Look, honey," he went on, voice low, apologetic. "I'm sorry about hitting you. It was instinct. I was out on my feet and didn't know what I was doing. And, after all, you did hit me with that damned bottle and things went black, sort of."

"Why did you bring him here?"

"That was a mistake. I meant to take him out of town, see. You can't work a guy over in jail. Well, we were driving by and he jumped out of the car. Another car came by, so I just ducked in here when I caught him."

"Where is he now?"

"In the jug, like I said."

"What'll he do when you let him out?"

"Head for Mexico, or California. We can't prosecute, because it'd give the department a black eye."

"Maybe he'll cause trouble."

"He can't afford to."

"I guess you're telling the truth," she said. "I don't know."

"Drop it for now. It doesn't matter to me whether you believe me or not." She tossed her head and sulked.

"I'm sorry I hit you, baby," he said. "Like I said, when you hit me with that bottle, I just hit out of instinct."

"I'll make coffee," she said.

He walked nervously from kitchen to living room.

"Where's the chair?" he asked.

"Papa took it for his study."

She must have noticed the expression on his face.

"Why?" she asked, when she noticed the expression on his face.

"Well, hell!" he said. "It was my favorite chair."

She laughed. "There are plenty of chairs. Sit down. Coffee'll be ready in a minute."

So there goes my dough, my slice of life. Wouldn't Wesley laugh? Wouldn't Baldy laugh?

"Only a good-for-nothing coward would kick a man like you kicked Wesley!"

"What?"

"I said only a good-for-nothing coward would kick a man like you kicked Wesley!"

"He had it coming."

"Maybe. But I thought you were a man."

"I thought I proved that." He said, grinning.

"Now I believe all I ever heard about cops!"

"Some cops are good and some are bad."

"You're bad."

"No, just in between."

"Then I'd hate to see a bad one."

"You saw one—Wesley. He was taking graft. We couldn't punish him by law, because we'd only make the people think all of us took graft. So, I punished him. Even at that, he got off light."

She went to the kitchen for coffee.

"Where did you say your folks are living?" he called.

"Rockford." She came out of the kitchen, carrying pot and cups on a tray.

"What denomination is your dad, anyway?"

"Methodist."

"His church right in Rockford?"

She poured coffee and said, "Edge of town."

"This study he's fixing up—is it in the church or in his home?"

Her hand jiggled his cup. "Church. Why?"

"Just wondered. I've never gone with a preacher's daughter before. What say we run over there one day and meet your folks?"

"I'd like that."

He finished his coffee and glanced at his watch. "Well, I've got some business." He reached for her hand. "Listen, honey. I'm not good at talking, especially apologizing. Anyway, I'd rather lose an arm than hurt you. Honest, it was reflex that made me hit you."

"What made you talk like you did?"

"I don't know. Believe me, will you?"

"It's all right," she said. "After all, I hit you, too."

He fingered his scalp. "So you did. Pretty damned hard, too." He bent over, kissed her cheek. "Say, I dropped back by here that night. You were gone."

"I spent the night with Rita. I was upset."

"See you tomorrow night."

"Night."

He closed the door gently.

Chapter Nineteen

Cliff Barrick made a tour of the town, and the town was wide open.

Every honky-tonk had a game going, and some of the better ones had plush rooms complete with tables and wheels.

He dropped a few dollars and went back to the office to write his column.

"The town is wide open," he wrote. "City and county officials are closing their eyes to open gambling, and that can mean but one thing.

"Graft.

"Gambling itself, open or not, is bad enough. When honky-tonks can invest money for elaborate rooms in a town where gambling of any form is illegal, it means that the law is not feared. Gambling begets graft and attracts hoodlums.

"Somebody's getting paid off."

Two day later he ran the column and waited for something to happen.

One minister dared speak from the pulpit.

Barrick talked to the minister, a young and earnest man.

"There's little we can do," the Reverend Howard said. "We can preach about it and hope the people will listen, but I can't get any backing from the other ministers."

"Have you tried?"

"I called them all to a special meeting last night. I was the only one present."

"What had you planned to do?"

"Well, I thought if the ministers called on the sheriff and the police, they'd listen. That's what I told the other ministers when I called them to come to the meeting."

Barrick laughed bitterly. "I'm disillusioned."

"You mustn't be. Ministers are just like everybody else—most of them. They have to make a living. Security has come to mean a great deal to them, and you see few who are willing to take a firm position on a, shall we say, a political matter."

"Well," Barrick said, "I guess it's more my job, anyway."

"We can keep trying," the Reverend Howard said. "We can try and hope and pray."

Chapter Twenty

It was forty miles to Rockford.

Ree wanted to go at once, but was afraid to ride a bus. Tomorrow he'd have a car. The city furnished a car for the chief, or would furnish a car. He'd insisted, and tomorrow it would be delivered. Tomorrow night, then, he'd go.

He was tired.

If, he decided, he had the forty thousand, he'd go to Europe. Or to South America, or Mexico, and buy a ranch. Get married.

He walked along, head down and shoulders sagging, thinking. He had to get that money. Here he was, walking, living like a cop on a cop's salary because to do otherwise would make people talk, wonder where he got the money. If he had that forty thousand—and Baldy's share of what they'd taken—he'd go to Europe, or South America, or Mexico. Maybe Australia.

Baldy hid his share of the money before he—died. Ree wondered where.

In his room, in underwear, he had a drink and tried to read the paper.

A knock on the door.

"Chief Ree?" the landlady said.

"Yes?"

"Telephone."

"O.K. Thanks."

He slid into his slacks, donned a shirt, and wondered who wanted him on the phone. Laura, maybe. He padded into the hall, barefooted, and picked up the receiver.

"Hello."

"Ree?"

"Yes."

"This is Ben Halliday. Like to have a little talk with you."

Now what? Had Wesley returned? Halliday had said only yesterday that Wesley must have gone on a binge because he didn't get the job as chief. His hand, on the receiver, trembled. Maybe, he thought.

"Sure thing. When?" he asked.

"Right now, if you're not tied up. I'll drive over and pick you up."

"O.K. I'll be ready."

Maybe Wesley was back, blowing the whistle, or threatening. Well, maybe he could take care of Wesley.

Halliday's car pulled up as he reached the curb.

"Evening, Ree."

"Evening."

He circled the car and entered, sat tensely as Halliday drove.

"Sorry to bother you, Ree, but something's come up I thought you ought to know about."

"Yeah?"

"Yeah." Halliday sighed. "It's the Barrick boys."

"Barrick?"

"You know. They run the Traveler."

"Oh! The punks that put out that rag! What's the matter? Have they written something nasty again? Have I robbed a bank or something?"

"Well—"

"Anyway, I thought the pressure was going on those boys."

"They raked up some money somewhere. They've been prying down at the Hall all day. Morris, he's the city clerk you know, says they've been talking to his secretaries. They even asked him a lot of questions. I don't know who else they talked to."

"About what?"

"Paving contracts, for one thing. Building permits, liquor licenses, garbage. They've been checking everything."

Ree choked back laughter. "That doesn't trouble me."

"No. Not directly. But this will. I have a friend—a woman—on the south side. She runs a house. Well, she tells me those boys have been to see her. Tried to get her to talk."

"She doesn't have anything to talk about—yet. We haven't collected a dime."

"No, guess not. But she knows by now that you'll collect, not the sheriff. And those boys have wind of it or they wouldn't have gone down there."

"The sheriff, maybe. The sheriff did some talking out of school."

"Maybe so, but it could have been one of the madams."

"Why should they talk? Messner clipped them and they didn't squeal."

"Man!" Halliday said. "Messner was taking his cut, but you've raised the ante! How do I know? Messner told me! And I know that Sergeant Swing is your contact man, too, and that he's passed the word to the girls. Well, do you think the girls are happy? Do you think they're going to pay off with a smile?"

"No, I guess not."

"Of course not! They're sore! Sore as hell! And those Barrick boys are smart enough to get a hint of what's happening. They're smart enough to stir up the girls while they're mad!"

"A whore wouldn't make much of a witness."

"She wouldn't have to! Wake up, man! People will believe what they read in the papers, and they're not going to sit around and wait for a public hearing before they act! They'll kick you out faster than you can think! Where'd you be then? Where'd I be?"

"You'd be out too."

"That's right, and I don't want that."

"Well, what's the answer? What do you want?"

"Throw a scare into the Barrick boys! Buy them if you can't scare them! If they won't play ball, discredit both of them!"

"How?"

"That's your problem! Just do it!"

"Now, wait—"

"Wait hell! You've been clumsy as a virgin about this whole damned thing! I thought you had brains and I risked a good set-up in the hope that you'd make it better! Instead, you've about frigged the whole business!"

"You want a frame! All right, you'll get a frame! Those boys are not going to scare or sell, or they'd have gone under before this!"

Halliday didn't answer. He drove Ree home and drove away with a curt good night.

Ree went inside and had a drink, a stiff one, and fought down bitter bile tasting rage.

Halliday, with a tramp for a friend, and scared. The bastard must have a mama whore tipping him off, because he knew the whole score.

Well, trouble, bound to come, had come,

If he just had his hands on that forty grand!

He slept soundly.

Sergeant Swing was admiring the new car when he got to the Hall.

"Wish I was a chief," the sergeant said.

"Stick with me and you'll have something better than this."

The car had two-way radio. On the door, stenciled in gold letters, were the words:

Breton Police Department
Chief of Police

"That's me, sergeant."

Ree spent the day in the office, but he couldn't keep his thoughts away from the red leather chair. He grinned at the thought of Laura Green's father sitting on forty thousand dollars.

Once he heard someone outside saying, "Those Barrick boys are out for blood."

He asked Swing how the prostitutes had taken the news he'd passed.

"They were mad as hell," Swing said. "The bookies and gamblers said nothing at all. But the cats blew their tops."

"Let them rave."

"I can't stop them."

"Did you tell them you'd do the collecting?"

"Yeah. That O.K.?"

"O.K., but figure a safe place and a safe way. Can't take any chances."

"You're not wolfing! Those Barrick boys are nosing around already. They've got wind of something."

"So I heard."

"I thought I'd rent a room in some joint on the south side," Swing said. "I can set up a dummy office and do my collecting at night."

"Let somebody else rent the place. And stay away from it except on collection nights."

"O.K."

Ree wondered about the Barrick boys, if they were tough and smart. What do they want? Money. Everybody wants money. Halliday said they were on a shoe string, in debt, so they could use money. Maybe, he thought, that was the answer. The boys needed money. They had been smart enough to know there was a vice pay-off, and smart enough to get the tramps mad. So maybe they meant to get part of the take.

"Sergeant?"

"Yes, sir?"

"Where's this Traveler rag?"

"Ten blocks north on main and two blocks left. You can't miss it."

"Thanks."

The new car smelled of baked paint, drove well, and it felt good to drive it.

Ten blocks north on main and two blocks left. Frame building, not large, needing paint. There was a sign across the front, a couple of cars parked at the curb. The windows were cracked and dirty.

Ree pushed against the rickety door and went inside. The front office was clean. Machinery clanked somewhere in the rear.

A woman leaned over the counter.

"May I help you?"

"I'd like to see the Barrick boys."

"Ed Barrick is in," the woman said. "If you'll wait a moment."

There were a couple of tables with typewriters, a few chairs, and a desk piled high with ledgers, copy paper, proofs and books. The walls were painted blue, but the floors were of rough pine.

The woman returned. "Mr. Barrick will be with you in just a moment. You're Willa Ree, aren't you?"

"That's right." He smiled.

"I'm Clara Speed," she said. "Society editor, reporter, classified ad chief, janitor, chief cook, and bottle washer."

"Do you set the type?"

"I never learned, thank goodness!"

"They must keep you busy."

"All the time, day and night."

Ed Barrick appeared, hesitated at the door.

Ree advanced, hand extended, smiling. "I'm Willa Ree."

"Yes, I know. I'm Ed Barrick. My brother's out just now."

Ree sized him up as Barrick led the way to his small office. The man was rangy, with sandy hair, wide blunt face and rusty freckles. His brows were bushy, eyes light blue, and he had big ears. He was gangly and embarrassed. There was ink on his hands, black smudges on his shirt sleeves.

The office was poorly lighted. One desk and two chairs, a calendar on the wall.

"Have a seat," Barrick said. "I guess you really want to see my brother, but maybe I can help you."

"I've never met your brother."

"Well, he really runs this rag. I help out, but he's the newspaperman."

"I thought you were partners."

"We are. It's just that Cliff knows the business and I'm just learning."

"Well," Ree said, "I'm going to lay my cards on the table. I have it pretty straight that you boys need money. They tell me you have a good thing here, but that you need capital."

He paused.

Barrick frowned, cleared his throat, drummed his fingers on the desk top.

"I think I can get the money for you, Barrick."

"On what terms?" The guy was no dope, but he needed dough.

"You'd have to incorporate, I suppose. The men I deal with are businessmen."

"They'd want fifty-one per cent of the stock, I suppose."

"That's right." Lay it on the line, give it to him straight. He waited.

Barrick drummed the desk top with nervous, fluttery fingers.

"Mr. Ree," he said, "that would give your—associates—complete control. Financial and editorial."

"They won't be hard to do business with. They'd be reasonable. They'd probably give you boys a free rein. After all, they're not newspapermen."

"I'm speaking for my brother when I speak for myself," the Barrick boy said. "We've been offered plenty of deals like that, Mr. Ree. Some of them say they know a good thing when they see it and that they're ready to toss in the money to make it go. But they always want fifty-one per cent. None of them would dream of taking forty-nine. It's fifty-one or nothing."

"Well, what do you care?" Ree asked. "You'd have a real newspaper. You'd make money."

"Sure, we know that. But we won't do it, Mr. Ree. We won't do it because we'll make it anyway, eventually. We're growing. Someday we'll get the backing without any strings attached."

"My associates are prominent, Barrick. They can help you a great deal."

"Yeah, I know. Halliday, Byrd, hizzoner the mayor, Sheriff Messner, Fry."

"Well, in that case...." Ree hesitated.

"Thanks just the same."

"Maybe you'd like to talk it over with your brother."

"I'll tell him you were here, Mr. Ree. But his answer will be the same as mine. A bit more emphatic, perhaps."

"Just one thing then, Barrick. Be a little more careful about your facts before you spout off in print."

Barrick drummed his fingers on the desk top and didn't answer.

Ree left the building, wondering what to do next. Barrick, despite his calmness, had been mad as hell. He and his brother would go out for blood now, and it was time to move fast.

He drove back to the Hall.

Sergeant Swing looked up from his papers. "See Barrick?"

"Saw Ed Barrick. He wouldn't listen to reason."

"Won't play, huh?"

"No."

"What're you going to do?"

"Fix his wagon."

"When?"

"Tonight."

"You figured out how?"

Ree plopped in the swivel chair, put his feet on the desk and lit a cigarette. He held it between his fingers and watched the smoke curl upward. "What would you suggest?"

Swing leaned forward. "Burn 'em out?"

"Too obvious. Besides, they've probably got insurance enough to put them back into business. Then they'd have the sympathy of the whole damned town."

"Not if you made it look like they did it."

Ree chewed on it a moment. "No," he decided. "We'll save that one."

"Then what?"

"We've got to put the boys in a bad light. See to it that it's publicized."

Swing scratched under his arm and waited.

"I think," Ree said, "that we'll follow this Ed Barrick after he quits work."

"O.K.," Swing said. "So long as there's no rough stuff."

"There won't be."

"O.K."

Swing drove, and they parked a block from the Traveler office at six o'clock.

"How do we know he hasn't quit for the day?" Ree asked.

"I know," Swing said. "He'll leave the building in a little while and go have a beer at the café on the corner. Then he'll go downtown to eat."

"I hope you're right."

"Like I said, I know."

They waited. A man walked past, a young man with broad shoulders, black and wavy hair, good features.

"That's Cliff Barrick," Swing said.

"Ed's brother? They don't favor."

"No. Cliff's the smart one. About half tough. Been around a lot. He was on some paper in New York before the war."

"He in service?"

"Yeah. Paratroops, I think. Got some medals. His folks used to have a ranch around here, but lost it during the depression."

They watched Cliff Barrick enter the Traveler building. Ed Barrick left the building a few minutes later. He nodded when he passed the car.

"We'll let him have a beer first," Ree said.

Five minutes passed.

"Let's go."

"No rough stuff," Swing said.

"No rough stuff."

"What'll I do?"

"Just watch."

"O.K."

Ed Barrick was seated at the counter, drinking beer from a bottle and smoking. He didn't look up.

Ree took the stool next to him, swung his foot and felt his toe hit Barrick's leg, hard.

"Hey, what—?"

Ree threw his hand out, swept an ash tray into the boy's lap and pushed the bottle of beer off the counter. Barrick slid off the stool facing Ree, his eyes asking questions beneath a furrowed brow.

Ree stood up fast and brought his right knee up into the boy's belly.

Barrick doubled over and Ree clubbed him behind the ear.

The waitress screamed.

A cook rushed through a rear door, shouting. Ree saw Swing standing, mouth agape, near the door.

"Take this drunk to jail, sergeant," Ree said.

"But he wasn't—" the waitress said.

"Yes, he was, sister. He caused trouble down the street a few minutes ago."

Swing lifted Barrick. The boy was groggy, and sagged in the sergeant's arms.

"Take him away, Swing," Ree said. "Bring the car back. I think I'll have a beer."

The cook stood in the doorway of the kitchen, an angry frown on his face. The waitress was sullen. Ree drank his beer and wondered if he'd made a mistake.

He was relieved when Swing returned. "I'll take you by your place," he said.

"O.K."

They went to the car and Ree slid under the wheel.

"What's the matter, Swing?"

"I think maybe you bit off more than you can chew."

"Why, Swing," Ree said, lifting his eyebrows in mock surprise. "The man was drunk and disorderly! And he started a fight with a police officer."

"Well, maybe you know what you're doing. That waitress knows better, though. And I don't see why you had to get so rough. The kid's still sick."

"He'll get over it."

"Yeah, but his brother won't."

"What do you mean by that?"

"I mean, turn left at the next corner, that Cliff Barrick's going to be damned mad. Ed's his little brother and they're thicker'n two peas in a pod. That guy will be out to get you any way he can! He'll be breathing down your neck before morning!"

"Well, maybe I'll have to cool off big brother."

"Maybe so. You're handy with your fists. And your knees. But you'll find Cliff a hell of a lot harder to handle than Ed was. In fact, if you hadn't caught Ed by surprise..."

Ree laughed. "Don't underestimate me, sergeant. That was child's play."

"White house on the corner."

"O.K."

"This is home," Swing said. "Better come in and meet the little woman."

"No, thanks. I've got a date. See you tomorrow."

"Right. I wouldn't miss tomorrow. Only, do me a favor."

"What?"

"Show up early. Cliff Barrick is going to raise hell in the morning, and I don't want to be the one to say good morning to him."

"I'll be there. Good night."

"Good night."

Chapter Twenty-one

Ree drove into Rockford at seven o'clock by the courthouse clock. A wind had come up and clouds were forming. As he pulled into the curb and stopped, splattering drops of rain began to fall. He rolled up the windows and ducked across the walk, entered a café, and ordered a steak.

He started to ask the waitress the location of the church, but decided against it. She might remember.

He went to the telephone behind the counter and speared the directory hanging from a nail.

The church was at 111 Macklin Street.

"Where is Macklin Street?" he asked the waitress when she brought the steak.

"Macklin Street? It's—I think it's—I'm not sure, but I think it's near the edge of town on the south side. I'll ask Abe. What'll you drink?"

"Coffee."

She brought his coffee and then walked to the rear and talked to the cook through the serving window.

"Yeah," she said when Ree paid his bill. "You go south on this street for eight blocks. There'll be a signal light there, and you turn right. Go three blocks and you'll hit Macklin Street. It's a short street, Abe says."

"Fine. Thanks a lot."

"Welcome. Come again."

He ran to the car, but the rain was peppering down and he was half wet before he got the door open. Things smelled wet and fresh. For a moment he sat still, listening to the drum of rain on the car top, enjoying the feeling of security and isolation.

Street and store lights had been turned on. Neon glowed half bright in the rain. Cars swished by, and a rolling peal of thunder jarred and rumbled.

Things couldn't be better, for the rain would keep people inside for a while. He only hoped Preacher Green would stay away from his study this one night.

It was a cinch, finding the church, and the plain brick building was dark and lonely. He circled the block twice and parked the car a hundred yards from the church.

The front door was unlocked. Somebody inside? Or did they leave church doors unlocked all the time?

Maybe they did. Who'd want to steal anything from a church? And what? A piano, maybe?

Closing the door behind him, he stood and listened. It was pitch dark. He heard nothing but rain drops on the roof.

He struck a match. He was in a vestibule, with double doors in front of him. Locked.

He worked on the hinges with his pocket knife, hoping to loosen the screws. He gave up when his knife blade snapped.

Nothing for it but to try a window. He went outside.

Rain was falling in sheets now, soaking his clothes and trickling down his collar. His feet squished water inside his shoes, and the earth near the walls was soggy.

He was cold.

All the windows were fastened. Break one? It wouldn't be hard, and the rain would drown out the noise. Shouldn't do that—not to a church window.

For a breath, a long breath, he thought about it.

And what's a church window? he decided. After Baldy.

A car, lights probing dimly at sheets of rain, passed swishingly.

He decided to try the back of the building.

His feet hit something, and he half stumbled on concrete steps.

There was a door at the top of the steps. It was unlocked. Again he stood inside, in darkness, listening to the rain on the roof.

He felt water trickle down his body, down his legs, inside his clothing.

He'd turn on the lights, he decided.

He reached out in the darkness, found the door and let his hands explore the wall beside it. The switch. Light. He was in the study. A desk, with typewriter, bookcase, and chair.

The red chair.

He wanted to laugh, thinking, if that preacher knew he'd been sitting on forty thousand dollars!

Whistling soundlessly, one eye on the door, he turned over the chair.

The tape had been torn away!

Laura! Not so dumb Laura! She'd played him for a sucker.

He raged from the room, stumbled across the churchyard, and drove away. The rain fell steadily, but he ignored it as he sent the car hurtling over the slick pavement. Once, when he passed a truck, the car went into a slide. He almost lost control.

Not until he passed the city limit sign did he let up on the gas.

Laura had the money, forty thousand bucks.

To hell with the money as money—but it was wrapped in the Johnson Tool wrapper. That wrapper could burn him—if Laura decided to talk.

And he'd hit Laura that night, so she'd be out to get even.

Laura's apartment was dark. The door wasn't locked, and he went inside. She wasn't there. He went back to the car.

The scared feeling was gone, but he was cold and tired.

It was good to shuck out of the wet clothes and slide into bed. Flat on his back, he tensed his muscles and let them relax. But he couldn't sleep.

He couldn't sleep, but he couldn't stay awake. For a time he was half awake and half asleep.

Someone knocked at the door.

Or, maybe he imagined it.

"Ree?"

Someone knocking, someone calling, close but far away.

"Ree?"

"Who is it?"

Wide awake now.

"Swing."

"Come on in, sergeant."

He fumbled on the table until he found the bed lamp, and then sat up in bed and blinked at the light.

"What's the matter?"

"Plenty, Ree. All hell's to pay!"

Wesley's back, spouting off. Maybe he went to the papers.

But no, couldn't be.

Not yet.

Maybe Laura had talked.

"What is it, Swing?"

"It's that Barrick kid! He's in the hospital!"

"Why?"

"You busted something or something, or ruptured him! When you let him have it with your knee, I guess. Anyway, he's at the hospital."

"Aw, hell! He's faking!"

"No, he's not! Ree, he's not! He's unconscious and they're going to operate!"

"Guess I'd better go down there then."

"Yeah, you better had! There'll be hell to pay when Cliff Barrick gets down there!"

Ree dressed, taking his time. He wanted to ask Swing if the doctors had expressed concern at the boy's condition, but he decided not to show concern himself.

Swing was nervous. Scared.

"Calm down," Ree said. "If the guy hadn't resisted arrest he wouldn't be hurt."

"Yeah," Swing said. "Yeah, that's right."

"Don't forget it."

"I won't, but—"

"But what?"

"That waitress. And the cook."

"They won't talk."

They went to the car. The rain had stopped. On the way to the hospital, Ree spoke once.

"The waitress and cook didn't see how I started it."

Sergeant Swing grunted.

Cliff Barrick was in the waiting room. He was sitting on a wicker couch, a cigarette burning to long ash between his fingers, legs stretched out. His eyes sought Ree's, locked and held.

He didn't speak, didn't move.

A nurse was seated at a desk.

"What about Barrick?" Ree asked.

"He's in surgery," the nurse said.

"How is he? How bad is he?"

"I'm sorry. You'll have to speak to the doctor."

Ree sat down and motioned Swing to a seat. The nurse shuffled papers.

Five minutes.

Ten.

Barrick snubbed out a cigarette, leaned back and folded his arms across his chest. Swing shifted in his seat, crossed his feet, picked at his nails.

Cliff Barrick stared at the wall. Ree eyed Barrick. A nurse entered the room, spoke to the nurse at the door, and went out again.

"Mr. Barrick?" the nurse at the desk called.

"Yes." Barrick walked across the room.

"You may see your brother now."

Barrick turned to Ree. "See you later," he said. His voice was soft.

The nurse led him down the hall.

Swing cleared his throat. Ree lit a cigarette.

Five minutes, six, seven.

The nurse returned.

"How is he?" Swing asked.

"As well as could be expected," she said. "Under the circumstances."

"That's good," Swing said.

Five minutes.

A man came through the front door. He was a big man. His gray hair was close-cropped, his cheek bones high, his mouth wide and lips thick. He spoke to the nurse in a low voice.

"They're expecting you," the nurse said.

The two disappeared down the hallway.

"Who was that?" Ree asked.

"That was Hurly Barrett," Swing said. "He's a lawyer."

Trouble.

"I guess Barrick will want to sue," Ree said.

Swing laughed nervously. "They can't get blood out of a turnip."

"Maybe they'll sue the city."

"Maybe."

"That'll be a shade rough."

"We'll lose our jobs," Swing said.

"Maybe."

"Maybe you can do something."

"What?"

"Well," Swing said, "apologize. Pay the hospital bill."

Ree laughed. "That would be an admission of guilt, Swing. Anyway, they wouldn't listen. Kick a guy in the crotch and go in and apologize to him while he's still in the hospital and he might not be in a receptive frame of mind. Maybe they won't sue. They're just mad now. Later on they'll change their minds and hit us some other way."

"You hope!"

"Yeah."

The lawyer and Cliff Barrick came into the room. The lawyer was doing the talking.

"I'll check at the café," he said.

Barrick stopped, but the lawyer went outside.

"Ree," Barrick said. "You're Willa Ree?"

"That's right."

Barrick slid his eyes up and down Ree's body. "We're about the same size," he said. "Would you have the guts to fight?"

Ree's laugh was honest. He was amused.

"Now?"

"Now."

"This isn't the time and place, son."

"What would you consider the time and place?"

"Well, that's a trade secret. I always pick my time and place."

"So I know. Tell me. Why'd you jump my brother?"

"He jumped me. He was drunk and disorderly."

"That's a lie, Ree, and you know it." Barrick didn't raise his voice. He seemed sure of himself. "You know it and you know I know it. He didn't have time to get drunk."

"Run along, Barrick. Talk to your lawyer."

"You're sure this isn't the time and place?"

"I'd like to oblige you."

Barrick's lip curled. "You're not tied."

"Run along home, Barrick."

"Is there any name you particularly dislike, Ree? Yellow? Bastard? Coward? Pimp?"

Ree's laughter caused the nurse to look up, frowning.

"Barrick, it's going to hurt me when I do have to take you."

"Try not to let it hurt too much. I'll try to be as unpleasant as I can. Sure you wouldn't like to step outside with me?"

"Sorry."

Barrick puckered his lips.

Spit squirted against Ree's face, and rage was a seething bitter bubbling tide within him. He threw back his chair and went to his feet, but Swing's hand was on his shoulder.

"Not here, Ree! Not now! That's what he wants!"

Ree turned away.

"Some other time, Barrick," he said.

Barrick hadn't even taken his hands from his pockets. "Maybe you'd like to go back there and fight my brother, Ree. He's conscious now."

"Good night," Ree said.

"Good night, you yellow-bellied bastard."

Ree followed Swing outside.

"He's a tough cookie," Swing said.

"Well, he talks tough."

"He's tough, or he wouldn't talk like that."

"I guess you're right. Anyway, I'll get a chance to find out soon enough."

"You'd better dodge him," Swing said. "You'd better listen to me and dodge him. You'd have been ruined if you'd fought him tonight."

"Yeah, but he was asking for it."

"Sure, he was asking for it! He wanted it! He'd have had your ass in a sling if you'd hit him!"

"I guess so."

"Well, no matter. You're in enough trouble as it is. Halliday's going to be madder'n a puppy with the piles when he hears about this. The guy don't like any kind of direct action, and this was too damned direct! And it backfired!"

"Swing, I'll tell you what you do. First thing in the morning you get down to the Telegraph office and tell them Ed Barrick was arrested for being drunk and disorderly. Might as well say he resisted arrest, too."

"Will they print it? After all, Barrick was a newspaper man, and those guys stick together. Even if they're rivals."

"The Barricks are a thorn in the Telegraph's side. They'll print it."

"Just the same, I think you're nuts! I think you'd be better off to drop this whole thing where it is."

"Don't be a fool, Swing! I'd be glad to drop it! But do you think the Barricks will forget it? Hell, they'll print their story all over their paper tomorrow! I've got to beat them to the punch."

"Maybe so."

"I know so. If I drop it now, it'll show I'm afraid and in the wrong. Barrick will have to appear before the judge and pay his fine like anybody else. Then he can howl all he wants—or try to sue, if he wants to."

"You think he'll pay a fine? Why, man, he'll fight!"

"What with? It takes money to fight! Anyway, let him fight! His name will be mud!"

"He's been here longer than you have, Ree. His family was well thought of."

"We'll spread enough rumors to ruin him."

Swing spread his hands. "You're the boss. But I say you ought to drop it here and now."

"You give the story to the Telegraph."

"O.K."

Chapter Twenty-two

Someone was pounding on the door. Again? It was dark, still dark.
Was it the same night as last night, or another night?
"For crying out loud!"
He didn't know whether he said it or thought it, but someone in the hallway muttered something.
"Who is it?"
"Swing. Open the door."
There was a foul fuzzy taste in his mouth and his eyes burned. He kicked back the sheet and went to the door. The floor was cool to his feet, and his body prickled with cold.
Swing was a dark blob in the doorway.
"What is it now, Swing?"
"Turn on a light."
He found the switch. "What time is it?"
"Five o'clock." Swing closed the door behind him.
"Well, hell!"
"Halliday's down at the Hall and spittin' fire. He said for you to get down there."
Ree dressed.
Halliday was standing on the steps of the Hall, his cigar glowing, his hat pulled low.
"About time!" he grunted. "Come on inside."
Ree followed him up the steps, through the door, into the council room.
"All right, Ree," Halliday said. "I'm aware that you tried to fix things your way. We'll let that go—for the moment. But Barrick's going to sue the city, and we may all be ruined. Tell me what happened in the café."
Ree sat down on a table.
"The man was drunk," he said. "We went in for coffee and I took the stool next to him. He stood up and took a swing at me, and I got him in the crotch with my knee as I stood up. I was surprised, see. Startled. I remember swinging on him, more in reflex than anything else, and he went down."
Halliday's eyes didn't believe it.
But that didn't matter.
"Tell me," Halliday said, "tell me who saw it."
"Swing saw it. The waitress might have had her back turned, but I'm not

sure."

"Anybody else in there at the time?"

"No customers. The cook came running out after it was all over."

"All right! I suggest you get to that waitress and make sure she didn't see it. Or make sure she saw it like it happened. *Or like you say it happened!* I'll see that the Telegraph prints it our way and I'll cover some of the other angles. I can't keep Cliff Barrick quiet, but I may keep him from getting this thing into court. After all, Ree, you acted in self defense."

"That's right."

"There'll be a stink," Halliday said. "Even if he doesn't sue, Cliff Barrick will spread it all over that rag of his. And, too, you had the guy thrown in the can when he needed medical attention. That's bad on the face of it."

"Yeah, Barrick can go to town on that one."

Halliday pursed his lips. "He can make it rough."

"Maybe not."

Halliday stared, shrugged.

"Maybe you have an idea. If so, don't tell me about it. I'm sticking by you now because I don't have a choice. That's the only reason. From now on, when you play rough you're playing by yourself."

"O.K."

Halliday got up. "It's going to take some hard work to fix this, Ree. I hope you'll remember that the next time you feel like hitting somebody."

"I'll remember."

"It's easier to fight with your brains than your fists, son."

"Sometimes."

"All the time! The brainy boys get to the top fastest. Just remember that."

"Right."

"We'll talk more about this later," Halliday said.

"I've got a job to do. See you."

Ree left with Swing.

"You're lucky," Swing said.

"Lucky. I'm lucky, he says."

"Yeah, lucky. Halliday can fix this thing, and you're lucky to have him around."

"He can't do anything else, Swing. If I go down I'll take him with me. He knows that."

"That wouldn't be playing it square, Ree. It's not his fault, any of this mess, and it wouldn't be right to drag him down with you."

"Listen, bud, I'm looking out for number one!"

"So I see."

"That's the only way to get anywhere. Look out for number one! You say I'm lucky to have Halliday around. Well, did you ever stop to think I might have picked him? Think I went into this thing blind?"

"You played the angles."

"I played the angles! If you play in the big leagues you've got to have somebody to play interference."

"What am I? More interference?"

"You'll get yours."

"I intend to."

Ree drove to the café, parked at the curb. The place was well lighted, and he could see the waitress busy at the coffee urn.

They went inside.

"Coffee'll be ready in a—"

"We'll wait," Ree said.

"So it's you," the girl whispered.

Short black hair, cute freckles, three cornered eyes. Full lips, trim figure.

Cute.

Ripe.

For plucking.

"What's your name?" Ree asked.

The girl stared.

"I'm Willa Ree."

"I know."

"What's your name?"

"Barbara."

"Barbara which?"

"Barbara Locke."

"You saw what happened here last night?"

"No."

"You didn't see it?"

"I had my back turned."

"You didn't see Barrick hit me when I sat down?"

"No."

"There's a mirror, Barbara."

"I wasn't looking! Anyway, it all happened so fast it was sorta like a blur, kind of! I was stacking cups! I wasn't paying any attention, please, and I don't want anything to do with it, not any of it, and please leave me alone, please!"

"Did you know Ed Barrick?"

"I knew his name. He came by for beer nearly every day."

"Would five hundred dollars make you remember anything?"

The girl picked up two cups and went to the coffee urn. She filled the cups and placed them on saucers.

Her hands trembled.

"Cream?" she asked.

"Never mind."

Swing cleared his throat. "I'll take cream."

"Could you use five hundred dollars, Barbara?" Ree persisted.

"Yes."

It was a whisper.

Her breasts, tight against the once starched now limp white front of her uniform, rose and fell, rose and fell.

She spilled the cream.

"I'm sorry," she said. "I'll get some more."

"Never mind," Ree said.

"What do you want?" she asked.

"That it's worth five hundred dollars to me if you can remember Barrick was drunk last night—and if you can remember seeing him take a swing at me when I sat down."

"Oh."

"Look—" Swing began, but Ree stopped him with a wave of his hand.

The girl looked back at the kitchen, at the door.

"I'll—do it," she said.

"Fine! They'll ask you some questions, but don't worry about it. All you have to do is say Barrick came in here drunk. Say he staggered when he walked. Say his voice was thick when he asked for beer. Say I came in and took a seat and that Barrick said he wouldn't sit by a lousy cop."

"But he didn't—"

"He called me a lousy cop outside, on the street, before he came in."

"Oh."

"You say he said that in here, though, and that he stood up and took a swing at me. Tell them I tried to dodge back and that my knee hit him. Then say I got to my feet and hit him with my fist."

"Is that all?"

"You saw the rest. He fell and Swing helped him up and took him out."

"Yes."

"I'll give you two hundred now and the rest when it's over. All right?"

"All right."

He took two one-hundred dollar bills from his billfold and slid them into her hand.

"Thank you," she whispered.

"Thank *you!*"

Swing didn't speak until they got out of the car in front of the Hall.

"Think you can trust her?" he asked.

"Well, it's more money than she ever dreamed of getting at one time."

"Yeah, I know. But Barrick's lawyer may cross her up. She's just a kid!"

"She's taken the money. Anyway, I'll work on her a little. And that'll be a pleasure."

Pounds was on the desk. He nodded.

"Anything on the fire?" Ree asked.

"Drunks."

They listened to the dispatcher droning instructions to a squad car until the staticky answers got on their nerves. Ree called Swing into his office.

"I've got coffee on the hot plate," Pounds called.

"I'll get some," Swing said.

Pounds poured black coffee into thick mugs, black and strong and hot, and went back to his work.

"Now, then," Ree said, "tell me how our business is stacking up."

"They pay off tonight, the tramps," Swing said. "I'm making them shell out every week."

"What about gambling?"

"That all narrowed down to one man."

"One man runs all these dives?"

"And all the floaters. He rents the places and hires his help on percentage. He's got hookups with the big boys out on the coast or in the Midwest, they say."

"Who is he?"

"Fellow named Parnell. Milt Parnell. And he's tough."

"Have you talked to him?"

"Yeah."

"What'd he say?"

"He laughed. Said he'd talk to you—maybe. Said he likes Sheriff Messner, but he might talk to you."

"O.K. What about the bookies?"

"They wouldn't talk. Some connections. You bluff Parnell and you've got it all in the bag. But I don't know. This Parnell is pretty sure of himself."

"We might have to get tough with him."

"He might bring an army of goons out here."

"They wouldn't get far in this country."

"Maybe not, but you'd be working against somebody here in town. Parnell's paying somebody. Maybe just the sheriff, maybe Halliday, the whole council and the mayor for all I know. Anyway, he damned sure wasn't scared of me—I'll tell you that right now!"

"Messner must be giving him the O.K. If Parnell is representing the syndicate, they're paying off. They don't take chances. They've learned it's cheaper to pay their way than to fight their way."

"You want I should make you an appointment with Parnell?"

"Might as well, I guess."

"He's big town, Ree, and tough. You want to watch your step."

"Well, I'm not a native of this burg, either."

Pounds stuck his head through the door. "Chief, Mr. Halliday wants to see you in the council room."

"Thanks. Come along, Swing."

"He didn't ask for me."

"Doesn't matter. Come along."

Swing followed, reluctantly.

Halliday looked tired. There were new circles under his eyes. He needed a shave.

"Well, boys," he said. "I've been busy."

"So have we," Ree replied. "I talked to the waitress. She saw it like I told you."

"Good! That's a break!"

"Do we need a break? Is it that bad?"

"Well, we can use it. It's going to be a big help. After all, we'd be in a hell of a jam if the waitress told a different story."

"Right."

"I've seen Arthur Fry and he's agreed to help squelch it—if the waitress tells it like you did. He'll talk to Barrick, try to discourage him. And he'll talk to Barrick's lawyer, and make him an offer."

"And what about the newspaper?"

"S. P. Barney is the best friend I have," Halliday said. "Besides, he doesn't exactly love the Barrick boys. I got S. P. out of bed and he's agreed to soft-pedal the whole thing. He'll slant it our way as much as possible."

"That about fixes things, then."

Halliday shook his head. "There's still Cliff Barrick. He's got a newspaper to print things in, and he'll print plenty. He's got a lot of friends. I know him well enough to know he's going to splash this thing. He may try to get this thing before a grand jury."

"Can he do it?"

"He might. We can squelch it if he does—Fry would have to present it and the jury'll follow his recommendations on the matter. I can see to that, because the district clerk'll know who I want on the jury. But, the point is that you're ruined if it goes that far. Even if you're not indicted, you're ruined. And I'll be hurt. Hurt bad."

"I can see that."

"Pity you couldn't have seen it last night before all this started. But that's water under the bridge for the time being. What it narrows down to, Ree, is this: Cliff Barrick has got to be hushed up. And I don't mean violence!"

"Then how would you suggest?"

"I don't know."

"I can't reason with him, and I can't scare him, so it looks like he won't shut up unless I kill him."

Halliday looked up, startled. His face flushed. He opened his mouth to speak, closed it, and slammed his fist on the table.

"Don't ever say a thing like that to me again!"

He shouted it.

Ree laughed.

"Don't get so excited, Halliday. It was just my way of saying I can't stop Barrick from printing his paper."

"Sorry," Halliday said. "I just want you to know I won't be a party to violence."

"Understood."

"When does Barrick's paper come out?" Ree asked.

"He'll get out an extra on this thing if I know him," Halliday answered.

"Maybe I can stop that, anyway."

"How?"

"Well, if I can find him he'll jump me sure as shootin', and we can haul him in for assaulting an officer and resisting arrest."

"Too risky," Halliday said. "There might be witnesses, and he might kill you. Or you might kill him. No, I don't want you two clashing. We'll have to think of something else."

"He won't kill me, and I sure as hell won't kill him."

"What makes you think he'll jump you, Ree? He's no fool."

"No, he's no fool, but he's mad. He hates my guts. Swing and a nurse at the hospital saw him trying to start trouble with me last night. He used what you could call abusive language. He made threats."

"And he spit in your face," Swing said.

"And he spit in my face."

"In that case," Halliday said, "my advice is to find him. At once."

"Where?"

"Newspaper office, on the streets, at home. How should I know? Just find him."

"Come on," Swing said. "He'll be on the street or in a café. We'll find him."

Halliday stopped them at the door. "Be as tactful as humanly possible," he said. "And remember, he's not to be hurt."

"Just mussed up a little," Ree said. "That's all."

Ree grinned at Swing's mocking mutter, "Be as tactful as is humanly possible," as they left the Hall.

"That's what the man said!"

"It's too late for tact!"

"Look who's talking now," Ree laughed.

"Well, I don't say the guy should be harmed. You're the one started all this, but it's gone too far!"

"What would you suggest?"

"Someone's calling you," Swing said, pausing.

It was Pounds, on the Hall steps, yelling and motioning.

They went back.

"Telephone," Pounds said. "I thought I'd better stop you."

"Is that all?"

"Well, I—"

"Never mind. Thanks."

Ree picked up the receiver.

"Is this the chief of police?" a woman's voice said. An old woman's voice.

"Yes, it is."

"This is Mrs. Larrimore." The old voice cracked and quavered.

"What can I do for you, Mrs. Larrimore?"

"I'm calling about Mr. Lemuelson's things. I want to know what I should do with them."

"Lemuelson?"

"Yes, Mr. Lemuelson. I had to rent the room, you see. Not that he ever stayed here, that is, but he had his things here, you know, and now I don't know what to do with them."

"I'm afraid I don't understand."

"Well, I have to rent the room, you see. Though I did intend to wait until the end of the month because his rent was paid until the first, you know, and it wouldn't be right to rent it to anyone else before that time. Don't you agree?"

"I don't know. I don't—"

"Well, I just want to know what to do with his things. Mr. Barrick took the diary, of course, but I guess you know all about that because he said you told him to take it."

"No."

"I beg your pardon?"

"Did you say diary?" Ree asked, his voice thin and high.

"Yes. Yes, I did."

He began to sweat. A drop trickled along the side of his nose.

Somebody pulling his leg, maybe.

Barrick.

Barrick had cooked up this deal, but it wouldn't get him anywhere.

"Did you say Mr. Barrick took the diary?"

"Yes, he said you told him it would be all right. Of course, if I did wrong—"

"Cliff Barrick?"

"Yes, that nice boy with the newspaper. Was it all right?"

"I don't know. I don't know what this is all about. Who was this Lemuelson?"

"Oh! You surely know! This is Chief Ree, isn't it?"

"Yes, but I don't know any Lemuelson."

"But, Mr. Ree, you're the one. Well, you shot—Mr. Lemuelson."

Baldy! Diary? Baldy's diary? Ree thought wildly.

"Mr. Ree?" The old voice was evil, whispery evil and mocking. "Are you there, Mr. Ree?"

"Yes, I'm still here. I'm sorry, Mrs. Larrimore. I understand now, of course. It's just that I didn't know Baldy's real name."

"I see, Mr. Ree. And what am I to do with his things?"

"Hold on to them. I'll be there to examine them today."

"Did I do right about the diary? Letting Mr. Barrick have it, I mean?"

"I'm afraid not, Mrs. Larrimore. He didn't have my permission."

"But he said—"

"It isn't your fault, Mrs. Larrimore." Butter up to her. Soft soap the old crow.

"Don't worry about it," he said. "Now, if you'll give me your address?"

"Oh, I forgot. You'll have to excuse me, Mr. Ree."

"Quite all right."

"It's at the end of Oak Street. You cross the railroad track and turn left, and it's the last house on the road. I'm off the pavement out here—in the country, really. But you can find it, I'm sure. You go right along beside the railroad track until you reach the old covered well, and the white house with the red roof is my place."

Well, covered well, but no old oaken bucket the moss covered bucket but the well where he'd intended to dump Wesley's body.

The phone was hot to his hand, hot to his ear, and his breath came in gasps.

Diary?

Well, hell.

"Mr. Ree?"

It wasn't true.

"Yes, Mrs. Larrimore. I just wrote down the directions. I'll see you sometime today."

"All right, Mr. Ree. Good-by."

"Good-by."

Hands, stop trembling.

He found Swing in the car. He slid under the wheel and let his head rest on the back of the seat.

"Ree," Swing said, "I was just thinking."

"What?"

"I was just wondering what's happened to Wesley."

"What?"

"I was just wondering what happened to the bastard. Left his room, left his clothes, left town. Why?"

"Maybe he's on a binge."

"Maybe. But he wouldn't be likely to leave town. He never has. And they found his car with blood on the seat."

"He probably had a fight. Or nose bleed. He'll show up."

"Maybe so."

"To hell with Wesley! We've got to find Barrick! Where'll we look?"

"His office, probably."

"Why there?"

"Well, he's mad, madder'n all hell, and he'll be moody and mean feeling. He'll sit down at a typewriter and froth, that's what he'll do."

"If he's at his office we're too late. Once he sits down to a typewriter we're sunk."

"He may be in a bar."

"Let's look around."

Ree rubbed his eyes and fingered the stubble on his chin.

Tired, tired, tired.

Tired, and time to blow, far away.

"Ree!"

"What?"

"Look coming down the street!"

It was Barrick.

"It's him!"

"Yeah."

"Right in our hands," Ree said. "I thought he was smarter'n that!"

"Why? It's a civilized country, or supposed to be. He doesn't know—"

"What?"

"Never mind."

Barrick passed the car without seeing them. They watched him go up the Hall steps, pause at the door, and then go inside. They followed.

Barrick was talking to Pounds. They could see him through the glass door. He turned his head. His head came up, and he saw Ree. Swing saw it first, and threw himself to the floor. Barrick had a gun. He could have shot through the glass, but he chose to open the door.

Ree grabbed at the gun on his hip, fumbled.

Barrick opened the door slowly.

Ree crouched as Barrick's gun came up, tugged at his own .38. Barrick's gun came up, and Ree beat him to it. He fired.

The roar was deafening.

Barrick's gun fell to the floor. His right hand went over, quite slowly, to clutch at his left shoulder.

"I could have killed him," Ree said to the echoing vacuum.

Barrick walked forward.

"Why didn't you shoot?" Ree asked.

Barrick smiled. "I decided that wasn't the way I wanted it."

Ree waved his gun. "Get back."

Barrick's left arm dangled. He moved his right hand away from his shoulder and looked at the blood.

Ree looked at the hand, Barrick's hand. He saw it turn into a fist, veined and hairy, grow bigger and bigger.

It exploded in his face.

"The bastard hit me!"

He was sitting on the floor, shaking his head, spitting blood. Barrick's blurred figure was there, and Ree raised his gun, but something slammed at his hand and the gun clattered away.

Pain came from nowhere to splatter in his face. Guess the bastard's kicked me, he thought.

And then he couldn't see at all, couldn't feel at all nor hear at all.

Then he could see again. Someone was helping him to his feet. Blood was flowing from his nose, and his lips burned.

"Take me home," he said.

His voice was thick, blood thick and hoarse.

"I want to clean up," he said.

Barrick was seated on a bench, his face drawn white and twisted. Pounds and Swing bent over him.

Halliday was standing by the outer door, his hand on the knob.

Ree laughed.

Swing looked up. "What'll we do with Barrick?"

"Take him to the hospital," Ree said. "Put a man on him. Don't let him see anybody or call anybody."

Barrick looked up. "Call my office," he said. "Tell them I'll be away for a while." He tried to laugh. "Maybe you'd better call my lawyer."

"Call an ambulance," Ree said. "The guy's bleeding."

Blood stained Barrick's shirt, oozed between the fingers of his clutching right hand.

"You'd better get out of town, Ree. You'd better go and get down on your knees, or get out of town in a hurry."

Ree turned away. He bumped into Halliday on the way out.

Chapter Twenty-three

Things were piling up. Luck had been on his side, so far, but things were piling up.

Of course, Baldy's diary might not mean a thing. Funny to think of Baldy keeping a diary—and funny Baldy would rent a room at the edge of town, so far from town.

Things piling up—and that Barrick punk!

He had a shower as soon as his nose stopped bleeding, and then shaved. His lips were puffed and a couple of teeth were loose and sore. Then he dressed and returned to the office.

"Halliday said call him at his home," Pounds said.

Halliday must have been waiting by the phone, for he answered immediately. "Ree?"

"Yeah."

"I saw Arthur Fry again, and he's been up to talk to the waitress. Her story substantiates yours in every way."

"Does that end it, then?"

"Unless someone stirs up a stink."

"Good."

"Ree, I've been meaning to ask you. Where in hell is Wesley?"

"They say he's on a big drunk," Ree said. "Somebody found his car out at the edge of town."

"Well, I guess that finishes Wesley, then," Halliday said. "He's done it before, but I warned him. Guess we'll just have to jump Swing up to captain."

"That's what I'd recommend."

"See to it, then. I'll see you later. By the way, how's business?"

"Good," Ree said. "I've been intending to tell you, but things kept piling up. Anyway, our plan will show dividends tonight."

"Tonight, eh? Fine, fine! See you later." He hung up.

Things piling up....

Ree's insides felt tight and coiled, like a spring begging for release.

And he thought, time to blow, go away, come again some other day, time to blow, far away and long ago, to hell away, gone. Time to grab that forty grand and blow.

His lips hurt, his nose hurt, his head hurt. He put his head in his hands and tried to think. How long before they'd know? What's in Baldy's diary?

Nothing! But where is it now? Cliff Barrick has it— If he has it, there's nothing in it, or he'd have used it before now. That's it! That makes sense. But—what about Laura? Does she have the forty grand? And will she talk? That wrapper has Johnson Tool printed on it. She knows I must have taken it. Will she talk? No. She knows. She must know, and she hasn't talked. She's had plenty of time, and she hasn't talked. But she could change her mind.... She won't talk. If she has the money, she'll keep it. She'll try to keep it, but she won't talk. She'd have to be tamed—again.

"A lady to see you, Chief."

Ree hadn't heard Pounds enter and he started at his voice. "Send her in."

The woman was fat and she waddled. Her face was red and creased, and she had a black mustache, sparsely mottled, above her upper lip.

"What can I do for you?"

"I'm Mrs. Coker," she said. "I'm Wesley's landlady." She giggled. "He's like a son to me."

What was she trying to say? Had Wesley returned? The spring, that spring inside him, slipped and threatened to unwind.

The woman continued to speak. Her silly lips moved. Sweat, droplets of sweat, clung to the hairs on her upper lip.

"...so I got worried," she was saying. "He left without a word and didn't take any clothes, but when I went in there this morning his dresser drawers were open and clothes were strewn around, and I don't know whether he's been back or if someone burglarized his room, you see."

Wesley was back in town—somewhere in town!

"It must have been Wesley," he said. "He's been out of town on a case, an important case, you see, and he didn't have time to pick up any clothes."

"But why should he slip in like that?"

The old bat, the damned old bat, he thought, but he said, "He may have passed through town in a hurry, or he may have tailed—trailed—someone here. But, at any rate, he'll call me today."

"Oh." The woman frowned. "Well," she said, "it was sort of funny and I was in town and thought I'd drop by. How long will he be gone, do you think?"

"He may show up today, or it may be a week."

"Well, I guess I can wait on the rent."

He reached for his wallet.

"I'll be glad to pay his rent, Mrs. Coker."

She tittered. "That won't be necessary, unless you'd rather. I guess Wesley can pay you back."

"Of course. How much is it?"

"Forty dollars a month."

Ree fumbled through the bills in his wallet, hoping the woman wouldn't notice his trembling fingers. "Here you are, Mrs. Coker."

"Thank you, I'm sure." She waddled out.

And now he had no time to waste, no time at all. Wesley had returned. Right now he was in town, somewhere in town, holed up in a tourist court or at a hotel or in the home of a friend, biding his time, waiting it out.

Ree shrugged.

Well, he'd have to wait and see. Maybe he could deal with Wesley. Maybe Wesley wouldn't spill the beans until he'd tried making a deal. Wesley would want the forty thousand. He wouldn't spill a thing until he'd tried getting his claws on that money.

Ree went into the outer office and said, "I'm going out for a beer, Pounds. Be back after a while."

"So early, Chief?"

"I need it. I feel like I've been run through a sausage grinder."

"You look it."

Ree rubbed his fingers across his lips. "Does it look so bad?"

"Nah, I was just kidding. It's puffed up a bit, but it doesn't look so bad."

"I'll be back in a little while. Oh, I almost forgot. Swing is moving up to captain in Wesley's place. You'll take Swing's job. Arrange the shifts and make the assignments."

"Gosh," Pounds said. "What about Wesley?"

"The crud hasn't considered the department, so he's out."

"Good riddance."

Ree flipped a butt at a cuspidor. "Yeah," he said. "Good riddance."

He went over to Main street and ducked into a pool hall. The place was crowded, smoky, stale with wet tobacco drowned in pools of table-top beer, smelly with a urine smell, acrid and evil. Foursomes played dominoes or cards, and pool addicts humped over tables.

Ree shouldered his way to the bar and ordered a beer.

A hand fell on his shoulder. Messner, he thought, turning.

"Hello, Sheriff," he said.

"Hello, Ree. Had a little trouble, I hear."

"Too damned much."

"Trouble always comes in bunches," the sheriff said. "How's business?"

"Looks good. We'll know tonight."

"How come you got rough with my deputy, Ree?" Messner's stare was direct. Ree, for a moment, was puzzled, and then he remembered the big deputy and the old Negro woman.

"Oh, that," he said. "Guess I owe the boy an apology. He was baiting an old woman and it rubbed me the wrong way."

"It was a Negro woman," the sheriff said.

"Yeah."

Messner's face was expressionless as he stared at his beer. "Say, Ree, there's something screwy happened."

"Yeah?"

"Yeah. We found Wesley's car out at the edge of town. Blood all over the seat. Where is Wesley, anyway?"

"Wesley's on a hell of a drunk, the boys tell me."

"Yeah?"

"Yeah. He flipped his lid when I made chief instead of him. Man, he blew his top! Said he'd been on the force a long time and that I was a johnny-come-lately. They say he really blew his stack to Halliday."

"That's news to me. I hadn't heard."

"So long, Messner."

"So long, Ree." The sheriff walked away. Ree watched him go and wondered how much he knew—or guessed. Maybe—maybe he'd seen Wesley today.

Not that it mattered, really. He'd find a way to take care of Wesley.

Out on the street he walked slowly and envied the people who brushed past him. Untroubled, they seemed, and unconcerned.

He decided to see Baldy's landlady.

In a way, I've been lucky, he thought. Sure, maybe it was lucky I got the call from the old lady. Maybe my luck is turning, after all. Maybe I can ride out the storm.

At least, with everything piling up, things were bound to get better soon.

But his very luck scared him. When things get so bad that you need luck, it's time to blow. Luck plays out, eventually.

What's happened to me? he thought. Once, not so long ago, I never worried. Never thought about luck, good luck or bad luck. Hell, all I need do is play the cards right, and everything will come out in the wash.

But he wondered if he'd played things wrong. He'd made more money with Baldy alive. And, maybe he'd have made more money with Wesley as his partner.

Ah, no. Baldy was going to quit, and Wesley couldn't be trusted....

People stared at him. They knew about last night. The news about the Barrick boys must have spread.

The clucks, he thought. The dumb clucks. Pulled around by their noses and robbed blind.

Ree started to turn the corner by the hotel, and then he saw Laura. Her car was parked at the curb, and she was sitting behind the wheel. There was a funny little smile on her face. Ree's steps faltered. He half stopped, half turned toward her.

Not now! he warned himself. Don't be seen with her in public, in case something happens to her.

He walked on, conscious of her eyes following him, wondering if the funny little smile was still there.

At the steps of the Hall he changed his mind, decided not to go in, and recrossed the street to his car. Laura's car was still at the curb when he drove by the hotel, but Laura wasn't in it.

The greedy bitch! She had smiled, but she wouldn't smile long. Not long, she wouldn't smile, for he who smiles last smiles best and she might be smiling now, but....

He crossed the railroad tracks and turned left on Oak. The street was paved for several blocks. He passed a lumber yard, a machine shop, a junk yard, and a feed store. The pavement ended and he was in shack town, surrounded by Negro shanties, Mexican hovels, poor white huts. Children played in the street and chickens scratched in the dust.

Shack town thinned at the edges. Only scattered huts flanked the street. He passed the last shack and had the street to himself, unmindful of the flanking mesquites, scattered sage, dusty sunflowers, and the railroad.

The house rested among elm trees, long ago transplanted and watered in this bare land. It was an old house, high-roofed and shabby white, with a porch extending along its entire front.

A dog ran around the corner of the house, stood near the car and barked.

"Here, pooch, good pooch, here pooch!" Ree called. The dog backed away, growled, and then made a stiff-legged advance.

"Josh!" It was the old woman, standing on the front porch. The dog backed away.

"He doesn't like me," Ree said.

"Don't know what's got into that dog. He's usually a friendly animal," the woman said. She was old, incredibly old, her hair white and her face lined with wrinkles and leathery. She wore a black dress, long and billowy. "You don't look like a policeman," she said.

"I don't wear a uniform."

"So I see."

"If you'll show me the room...."

"Of course. Come with me."

He followed along a high-ceilinged hallway, dark and quiet, cluttered with massive marble-topped tables, and funny high-backed chairs. Pictures of men and women, long ago dead and gone and half remembered, stared from the depths of mahogany frames, dim in the gloom.

The old woman stopped at a door. "In here," she said. "All his things are in that trunk."

"Thank you."

The trunk was in the middle of the room, resting deep in the rug, iron-ugly and looking out of place. No pictures of men and women, dead and long remembered, on these walls. There were prints in graceful frames. A dresser, chest of drawers, bed, desk, and easy chair. Antiques, but not heavy brought-from-the-east monstrosities. These were imported-to-the-South-before-the-War antiques, graceful and warmly glowing with rich color.

Baldy—in this room? he thought.

It took a few minutes to go through the trunk, but there was little to see. Shirts, a couple of suits, underwear, handkerchiefs, two pairs of shoes. No papers, no diary, no money.

"I'll put these things back like I found them," he said. "I'll make an inventory and give you a receipt."

"And I'll make some tea." She closed the door behind her.

He examined the trunk for a false bottom, knowing Baldy was too smart to trust such an obvious hiding place.

Where did the old boy hide his money?

Maybe the old woman knew. Or maybe she found it, though not likely. Baldy wasn't a trusting sort of person, and she wouldn't have guessed he had money in the first place. He sat on the trunk and surveyed the room. Pictures? Too simple. The first place examined for hidden objects. Same with the mattress and the rug. Light fixture? Taped to the bottom of the dresser or chest of drawers? In this room at all? Maybe in the house, but not in this room.

The old woman opened the door. "The tea is ready."

He followed her down the hall and into the living room, and knew he was looking at a fortune. The room was huge. It wasn't necessary to know furniture, for the feel was there, in the harmony of the curved line and the feel of the upholstery, the thickness of the rug. Part of the wall was paneled, part papered in a hunting print. Drapes at the windows blended with the panel work, in contrast to the paper. Sedate marble-topped tables flanked a marble fireplace. A hanging lamp sent a cone of light toward the ceiling, high and ornate.

There were two pictures on the wall, and he knew—without knowing—that they were fabulously valuable.

And Baldy lived here. Or did he?

"Mr. Lemuelson loved this room," the woman said.

What had she said—Baldy?

"You are surprised," she said. "I really didn't want to know what to do with his things, he was my brother."

"You just wanted to get me out here, Mrs. Lemuelson."

"You killed my brother."

"He was a burglar."

"So are you."

"No," he said, and knew it was useless to argue.

"Yes, he told me."

"Was there a diary?"

"No. There was no diary, Mr. Ree. I just wanted to give you a scare. I knew the Barrick boys were fighting you. I read their paper. So, I just said that about the diary to scare you."

"What do you want with me?"

She smiled. "Shall we have our tea?"

"I've never cared for tea."

"You'll have a cup with me."

"No."

Her smile was not the smile of a sweet old woman.

"What do you want?" he asked again, his voice trembling, tense.

She chuckled, threw back her head and chuckled. "Maybe I want revenge," she said.

"You're crazy."

"No, I'm not crazy. You're the crazy one, I'm afraid."

"I merely did my duty. You knew what Baldy was."

"Oh, yes, I knew my brother was a burglar. He never tried to hide his occupation from me." She laughed again, her old body shaking. "If you had been an honest police officer doing his duty, Mr. Ree, I couldn't find it in my heart to blame you." Her voice became shrill and a pale blush tinged her withered cheeks. "But you are worse than my brother! You hide behind the law—but you are a robber and a thief! And a murderer! You killed my brother for his share of the loot!"

"There was no loot! I tell you, there was no loot!"

"Oh, yes, there was!" Her voice was calm again. "He told me there would be forty thousand dollars in that safe, Mr. Ree! He was going to take his share and retire, here with me. We were going to live our lives out here, together!"

"You're crazy! I'm leaving here."

"No you're not leaving, my friend! Not until I tell you to leave. We'll have our tea now."

"You think I'm nuts? You think I'm going to drink poison?"

The old woman sat in a chair beside a table, quietly chuckling, her shoulders bobbing. She motioned toward a silver service. Her gnarled old hand looked like a claw. "We'll have our tea," she said.

"You'll have the tea," Ree said. "You'll drink tea, but I won't. You'll drink the tea you made for me." He walked toward her.

"I know how to use this, Mr. Ree," she said. There was a tiny gun in her hand.

"A pop gun," he said, wondering if all this could be true. He took another step.

"That's just a pop gun, old woman."

"It's a small gun," she admitted. "It might take more than one shot to stop you, but I'm prepared to shoot."

She would shoot. He knew she would shoot. She was crazy as a bed bug, and she would shoot. His scalp prickled, and chilly pin pricks shot up and down his back, between his shoulder blades, to his neck. And he thought, A little old woman. A cold, crazy, deadly little old woman. There was nothing he could do—for the moment.

"This is crazy," he said. "Silly."

"We'll have some tea," she said. "Maybe you're just imagining things. Maybe the tea isn't poisoned. Perhaps I just want to scare you."

"You've succeeded."

"Or, then again, perhaps there's poison in the tea."

"You're bluffing, lady. This is fantastic—silly! Not in cold blood you wouldn't poison me!"

"Maybe you're right."

"We'll have the tea," he said.

"We will." Her pale, thin lips spread in a smile. "Have a seat, Mr. Ree."

He was forced to sit across the table from her. She was smart. The little gun snuggled in her hand, and she used it to point at one of two cups, saying, "That is yours, Mr. Ree. Do you take lemon or cream?"

"Suit yourself."

"Then we'll have lemon. Sugar?"

"One lump."

"We'll see if you're a brave man, Mr. Ree. I have a theory about brave men, and I doubt that you are one. Only cowards shoot men in cold blood, and that's the way you killed my brother."

"No."

"Yes. And now we'll see if you're brave. You have to die, you know, for the crime you committed. If your crime became known, you'd have a trial. But the result would be the same. You'd die—in a different way, perhaps. In the electric chair or on the gallows. I believe in an eye for an eye, Mr. Ree. Don't you?"

"You're crazy, or I'm dreaming."

"I'm not crazy, and you certainly aren't dreaming, my friend. This is happening, fantastic as it seems to you."

"Here's where I get off."

"I wouldn't try to leave. I have the gun."

"A pop gun!"

"It will kill!"

He sat still, hand touching the hot cup.

"Do you have a sister, Mr. Ree?"

"No."

"That's a shame. That would have made your death equal—a brother for a brother." She tittered, gasping for breath. "But you must have had a mother."

He said foolishly, "Yes."

"Then it'll be a son for a brother."

"You'll be arrested."

"Does anyone know you're here?"

"There's the car...."

"I have a barn in the back of the house."

"Someone might have seen it."

"Oh, someone saw you come here, no doubt. And I shan't deny it, if they ask me. I'll say you came to investigate the prowlers I reported yesterday."

"You're crazy all right."

She giggled again, a ghastly and tittery giggle, her body shaking.

"I've listened to all the foolishness I can stand for in one day, lady."

"Sit still, son. I warn you!"

"I'd advise you to put that gun on the table, Mrs. Lemuelson. If you do, we'll forget this. If not—"

"I'll shoot!"

"I don't think so."

She cackled, "Oh, but I would! Be assured of that, Mr. Ree! I truly would, and if I miss—and you succeed in getting away, I would be forced to tell the police you were my brother's partner!"

"They wouldn't believe you. It would be your word against mine. Besides, you could be arrested as an accomplice if you made them believe you."

His hands were sweating.

"I do hope you show some courage," she said. "One way or the other, you must die. Believe me, Mr. Ree, it's better to go like this than die in the chair or on the gallows."

His laugh couldn't fool her.

He could see the humor in the situation. The whole thing was crazy funny, but he didn't feel like laughing.

"Tell me," he said. "What do you intend to do with my body?"

She seemed pleased he had asked. "You know, I have that all figured out! Did you see that old well on the railroad right-of-way?"

He stiffened.

"You must have noticed it." She leaned forward, eyebrows arched. "It's a covered well, you know. Believe me, Mr. Ree, it would be a perfect place to hide a body!"

Was she playing cat and mouse?

"Why, Mr. Ree," she tittered, "I wouldn't be a bit surprised if a body or two had been thrown in that well before now!"

She's crazy, screwy, he thought. The old bat would have used the same tone of voice if she'd been speaking about someone discovering her favorite recipe for jelly.

He threw the cup of tea in her face. It was easy. She didn't have time to raise her gun—didn't even have time to think of raising the gun. He slapped it out of her hand.

The dog, the crazy dog, came for him when he cleared the porch. He kicked out viciously and his toe caught the brute in the ribs. Sprinting, he reached the car and slammed the door closed behind him.

He drove fast, thinking, Maybe this was all a dream, and surely this was all a dream.

Aloud, he said, "I wonder what she would have done with the body."

Crossing the railroad track, edging into the business district, he began to laugh.

Chapter Twenty-four

"Some dame has been trying to get you on the phone," Swing said.

Ree sighed, mopped his face with the back of his hand. "She leave her number?"

"Said she'd call back."

Ree tried to lose himself in routine work, but shifted most of the work to Swing. His nerves were shot.

The day wore on.

The Telegraph hit the street. There was a short story about the Barrick boys, saying both were injured while resisting arrest—drunk and disorderly charges—on and on.

Ree smiled. So much for that.

Halliday had pull.

Swing answered the telephone. "Yeah, he's right here," he said.

It was the waitress.

"I've gotta see you," she said.

"Sure, babe. Tonight. We'll dance."

"No—I mean, all right, but I've got to see you now!"

"What's up?"

"Maybe I'd better not tell you over the phone."

"Okay, Barbara. I'll drop by."

It had to be trouble, again trouble, more trouble, piling up.

He admitted it now. He was scared. Part of his mind warned him that scared plans would be bad plans, but he had to make plans. Some kind of plans.

Things had been going hit or miss, and things weren't working out. Some little something had gone bad somewhere, and a chain reaction of bad happenings followed the first little something that had gone bad.

Now, until his plans were made, he had to take things as they came along.

There were several customers in the café. He sat in a corner booth and watched Barbara.

She was scared, all right. She wasn't faking. Her face was white, pinched.

She came swinging toward him, bent over his table and mopped it with a cloth. Her dress was stiffly starched, buttoned at the front, and bulged down and out. He could see her breasts, wide spread and outward and upward pointed, not small, not large.

"It's Slick," she murmured.

"Slick?"

"Slick Macklin, the cook. He must have seen you give me the money. Now he claims he saw the trouble. He says he's going to talk. He says he's going to the Barrick boys' lawyer and tell him what happened."

"Is he in the kitchen?"

"Yes."

"I'll go talk to him."

She went back to the counter, her buttocks wriggling, and he was amazed that desire could come at such a moment.

The curious eyes of the customers were on him as he walked toward the kitchen. Whispers, nudges, curious eyes probing. He pushed the swinging door.

The cook was tall and skinny, sunken faced and thin lipped, dull eyed and sullen, with stringy hair falling over his forehead. He was slicing pickles. His white cap was dirty, and his apron was filthy.

"You say you saw the fight in here," Ree said. "Did you?"

"Yes. I saw it."

"Why didn't you tell the county attorney?"

The cook pursed his lips and examined the knife blade. "That wouldn't have made me any money," he said.

"You want to make money?"

"Who doesn't?"

"How much do you want to make?"

The cook selected another pickle and began to slice it. "How much did Barbara make?" he asked.

"Two hundred."

"That's what I want to make."

"O.K., cookie. I'll give you the two hundred. Not that you've got me over a barrel, understand. It's just that I like your looks. If you tried to talk now you'd be in trouble up to your neck. You waited too long, and they'd want to know why. But I've got a job and I don't want trouble, so you get the two hundred. Understand?"

"Yeah."

"Here's the money."

"Thanks."

"If I hear any more out of you, cookie, I'm liable to pick you up on a charge of molesting children. In fact, we've had a couple of complaints about you already."

"There won't be a peep out of me."

"Just make sure of that."

Barbara was at the coffee urn. He smiled at her, and winked.

"What time do you get off?" he asked.

"Ten o'clock."

He whistled. "Do you work all the time?"

"I had four hours off this afternoon."

"I'll pick you up at ten."

"All right."

He drove to the edge of town and had a beer at a drive-in.

Thinking of the day, the past days, he shook his head. It had been one long cat and mouse game, and he had been the mouse. The cat, some invisible force that seemed determined to trap him, had toyed and pawed, toyed and pawed, but hadn't ended it.

It had been that way a long time. Closing in, closing in, time running out and closing in, closing in. Time, some huge pincer that would snap shut at some predetermined time, closing in.

He had another beer.

It would be a joke if he could figure out ahead of time just when the pincers would close and time would run out—and be gone just ahead of deadline.

That would be a joke. Smart, too. Manage to get the forty grand and blow just before the deadline.

He had another beer.

Time was a cat, a black cat with blazing green eyes, toying with him and pawing him, playing with him and getting a little closer and a little rougher all the time.

Wesley and Baldy and Laura, Ed Barrick and Cliff Barrick and Wesley's landlady. Baldy's sister and the waitress and the cook. Wesley's car and the sheriff.

Closing in.

He swigged one more beer, paid the check, and returned to the Hall. On the way, nearly there, he changed his mind and drove to his room.

Better to see if his money, hard-earned money, was safe. He might not get the forty grand, but he had money, some money, a lot of money.

There was a bottle of liquor in the bureau drawer with his shirts. He poured, drank, poured, drank. Again. And again.

Head spinning, but no matter. No mouse like a drunk mouse and to hell with the cat.

The money.

Poor old Baldy. Old Baldy took most of that money out of safes. Store safes. Or was it saves? Safe, save, plural of mouse is mice and there's only one cat and the plural of cats is kites, and to hell with the cat.

Half a glass. Neat.

Now the money.

See if the money's safe, save, and be quick about it. Safe. That's a hell of a word. All words are a hell of a word if you get right down to it.

Take Laura, for instance.

Hell in bed.

All there, no inhibitions, but maybe the little waitress would be better.

The money. In the lining of his top coat. He had split a hole in the pocket, stuffed in the money, sewed up the hole in the pocket and who in hell would think of looking there?

He went to the closet and found the coat. The money was still there, safe and sound, that word safe again, still there.

Why not blow? That's a lot of money. Blow to Mexico and buy a ranch. Before the cat pounces.

Like hell!

Get the forty grand from Laura and then blow! No girl's gonna take forty grand from Willa Ree and get away with it.

Take Laura along.

Take Laura and so what good is forty grand? With forty grand you won't need Laura, for forty grand will buy all the Lauras in Mexico.

Another drink.

Something trying to close in, something big. Something. Everything going wrong. One thing leading to another thing and everything piling up, trying to close in. Like chain reaction.

Go see Laura. Maybe he should. Getting dark.

His head was spinning, but he felt good. He circled, avoiding busy streets, and was careful.

Laura was home. He saw the light.

For the first time in a long time, suddenly, he felt gay. Happy and gay, light hearted and gay.

"Maybe I love the girl," he said and giggled.

That would be a good one.

But maybe it was true, for he realized he wanted Laura. Wanted to be with Laura, feel her close and hold her close—safe.

Safe?

He wanted her, desperately. He wanted to hold her in his arms, be held in her arms, and tell her all about it. Tell her all about everything.

Whistling, staggering a bit, he went inside.

She had been in the bathroom doing something to her hair. When she heard him open the front door she came out.

He whistled.

Grinned broadly and whistled.

She wore panties and bra and house slippers. And she was beautiful, tall and beautiful.

"Hello, honey," he said.

"Good-by, Ree," she said.

"To hell with good-by, honey. Tell you what, tell you what, let's never say good-by. What say? Tell you what, Laura, tell you what. Let's get a good night's sleep and in the morning you get the forty grand and I'll grab my top coat and we'll head for Mexico. What say?"

He held his arms wide and stepped toward her.

She fiddled with her hair, stepped back.

"You're drunk, Ree."

"Sure I'm drunk. What the hell, you've seen me drunk before. Bit of drunk, maybe, I am, but what the hell, Laura? I mean it. I'm serious. I've got a good-sized roll, myself, and with the forty grand you've got we could go to Mexico and buy a ranch. Live like kings! Like kings, Laura! No more of this crumby town!"

"But I don't have forty grand, Ree, and even if I had it I wouldn't go anywhere with you. Your money's got blood on it, Ree."

"Oh, no, Laura." He laughed and pointed a waggish finger. "You must be drunk yourself. There's no blood on my money! It's clean, green and crisp and clean!"

"You'd better go, Ree. I'm telling you, you'd better go. I know you're an ex-convict, and I know you're no good. You don't care about me and never have. You never will. I was just someone to sleep with. So get out."

He shook his head.

"Nope. Tonight we're going to sleep with your head on my shoulder and I'm going to make you love me."

"No Ree."

"And tomorrow, Laura, we're going to leave this crumby town. You're going to take the forty thousand and I'm going to take my little old topcoat and we're going to Mexico. We'll buy us a ranch and settle down. We'll live like kings, Laura!"

"What forty thousand, Ree?"

Laughing, he waggled his finger.

"You're not so dumb, Laura, but you don't have to play innocent with me! I'll admit you were pretty smart to figure it out, though."

"Figure what out?"

"About the chair."

"What chair?"

"The red chair."

"The red ch—"

"Wait a minute," he said. "Wait a minute. Maybe you didn't—"

"So you took forty thousand dollars from Wesley and hid it in the red chair."

"It's just a gag," he said.

"It's no gag," she said. "Where did Wesley get the money? From you? Where did you get the money, Ree?"

"Go to bed," he said. "Sleep with your head on my shoulder."

"Wrong again, Ree."

He looked at her and forgot the money.

Almost.

"The trouble with me," he said, "is that I never appreciate what I have. The first time, that is. You're more beautiful than any girl I've ever seen."

"Thank you just the same. But it's too late."

"Why?"

"I think I know what happened. You stole the money. And I'm beginning to wonder about that poor little burglar! I know there's something about the Barrick boy. And you slapped me around! I loved you, Ree! I really loved you, but I know you played around with the Halliday woman while you were sleeping with me, loving me, and you played around with that cheap little blonde down at the Hall! You make me feel dirty, Ree! Dirty all over, dirty and scabby and whorey!"

"Laura," he said. "Laura, I think I love you. I don't know for sure what love is, but I think this is it."

"It doesn't matter. Maybe I love you, too, but it doesn't matter! You're filth, Ree, rotten filthy! I'm no angel, but I'm too good for you!"

"We'll go away."

"I think you'd better go."

He tried to take her in his arms, but she pushed him away.

"To hell with you, then!" he said. "There are other fish in the sea!"

She laughed. "That's you, Ree. You'd turn on your mother, if she didn't do to please you."

"Good-by, Laura."

"So long."

He slammed the door.

In town, with traffic heavy, he nosed into the curb and walked a block to the café. His head was spinning and he cursed himself for drinking on an empty stomach. Two cups of coffee helped, and he ordered a steak.

So Laura's father had the money. He'd taken the chair and found the money.

Well, the preacher would be easier to handle than Laura would have been. At least he wouldn't have to marry the preacher.

That Laura.

Long legs, beautiful body, and what a dream she'd been tonight.

The steak tasted like ashes, but he ate it all.

Have to go see the preacher, but not tonight. Tomorrow night. Tonight, the waitress—Barbara.

He had more coffee and smoked. His mouth hurt, his face hurt, and a couple of teeth felt loose. *That damned Barrick!* The steak was heavy in his stomach, but his head had stopped spinning. He decided to have a bath and change of clothes.

One eye was black. His face looked haggard, worried, eyes stary in the mirror behind the counter. He paid his bill and left.

The loose teeth began to ache.

He had a drink as he dressed and one after he dressed. His head was spinning again, but the worried look was gone from his face when next he looked in the mirror. Time to pick up Barbara.

He sat in the car until he saw her switch off the lights in the café then got out to meet her at the door.

She wasn't any bigger than a minute.

"Tired?"

"A little."

He helped her into the car.

"Where do we go from here?" he asked.

"I'll have to change. I live on Oak Street."

"Rooming house?"

"Garage apartment."

"Oh."

"Did you—fix things?"

"The cook? Yeah, I talked to him. He was just talking. When I got tough he admitted seeing things just like you did."

"Good." She laughed a shaky little laugh. "You know," she said, "I've been worried all day."

"What about?"

"About what happened. And if I did the right thing."

"You did right, honey. Believe me, I'm pretty torn up about what happened. I'm not kidding... I wouldn't have hurt that kid for anything in the world!"

"You've been drinking," she said.

"Do you object?"

"It's a waste of time," she said.

"I guess you're right, Barbara. I don't drink usually, but I was upset because of last night."

She pointed out the turn and told him when to stop.

"It'll take a little while," she said. "I'll have to take a bath and fix my hair."

She expected him to wait in the car.

He went around and opened the door, took her by the arm and walked down the drive leading to the garage. He felt the hesitation in the stiffness of her arm.

"You didn't need to get out," she said. "It won't take but a minute. Could you just wait in the car?"

"And let you go in that dark house by yourself? What kind of gentleman do you think I am?"

"I do it every night."

"But not tonight."

He followed her up the outside steps and waited while she unlocked the door.

"I don't know what Mrs. Callon would think if she saw you going inside with me," she said. "She's my landlady. She teaches Sunday School and is the president of the PTA, and I just don't know what she'd think if she saw you going...."

"Don't worry. She'll never know."

She closed the door before switching on the light. It was a one room and kitchenette apartment, with a couch that made into a bed, an overstuffed chair, a worn rug, bookcase, coffee table and dresser.

"Sit down," she said.

"Thanks."

She rummaged in the dresser and he stifled a chuckle as she rolled panties and bra into a small ball and tucked them under her arm. She made a trip to the bathroom and returned without the underclothing.

"How old are you?"

"What?"

"I said, how old are you?"

She was at the closet, selecting a dress. She turned around and made a face.

"I'm twenty."

"Ever been kissed?"

"Once or twice."

She spread the dress on the couch and returned to the closet for a housecoat.

"It won't take long," she said, and went into the bathroom.

He heard the splash of water, fragments of her song.

She had wanted him to wait in the car.

Quiet in the bathroom.

He grinned.

She had left the housecoat with the dress on the couch.

"Would you hand me my housecoat, please?" she called.

"Sorry."

The bathroom door opened a crack, and her head appeared. She smiled and wrinkled her nose.

"Be a good boy."

"Sorry."

"Please. I'm cold."

"Sorry."

She stamped her foot. "I'm cold!"

"You'll have to get your own housecoat."

"I'll stay in here all night."

"It'll be awfully uncomfortable."

"Stop teasing," she begged. "Really, I mean it."

"I'm not teasing, little one."

"You're not—you wouldn't—"

"Don't play hard to get."

"Look," she said. "Please. I'm not that kind of girl. Forget the rest of the money, Mr. Ree, but please go."

"I can give you something better than money."

She threw the door open and made a dive for the housecoat, bare legs flashing and black hair flying.

Ree grabbed the wrap and held it behind him, but she picked up the dress and rushed back into the bathroom. He followed, grabbed at her, caught a shoulder, a smooth bare shoulder.

She wrenched away, and he saw the red mark of his fingers on her flesh.

Her eyes were wide and frightened when she turned to face him, and he stepped back to look at the small perfection of her body.

She stood, defiant and unashamed.

Upturned breasts, hidden by bra. Pink, bare flesh dimly visible through the sheer pink panties.

He put out his hand and took her by the hair.

"Please," she said, left arm instinctively covering her breasts. He pulled her hair.

She let her arm drop.

"Please," she said.

He caught her in his arms and bent to kiss her.

She lifted her head and stared into his eyes, and then she kicked him, hard.

He rolled on the floor, doubled hands to crotch, groaning and trying not to retch.

"Go!" she screamed. "Go away!"

He got to his knees, felt pain lessen, subside.

"Not now, baby! Not now!"

She tried to push him away from the bathroom door, but he shouldered forward, still on his knees, and held her tightly.

"Not now," he panted. "Not now."

"I'll scream!"

"What would your landlady say?"

He wrapped both hand around her knees and pulled her to the floor.

She fought savagely, crying silently, and clawed, writhing, at his face.

"I'll kill you," she said. "So help me, I'll kill you!"

She bit him.

"I'll tell them I lied about the fight!" she said. "I'll tell them you paid me to lie! I'll tell them! I'll tell them!"

"It's too late, baby."

She gave up. Exhausted, too tired to cry, she went limp in his arms.

"I'll kill you," she said. "So help me, I'll kill you!"

"It would be worth it," he answered. "So help me, it would be worth it."

Chapter Twenty-five

Swing pounded on the door, but Ree didn't answer. At last, irritable, he got the landlady to unlock the door.

Ree had gone to bed fully dressed.

"You must have had quite a night."

"I did," Ree said, fingering the stubble on his chin.

"Well, so did I. While you played, I collected."

"How'd you do?"

"Good. Damned good. The money's in the car."

"Bring it in and figure the divvy while I clean up."

He had finished shaving and was taking a shower when Swing finished the count.

"Hey, Ree!"

"Yeah?"

"It comes to fourteen hundred and four dollars!"

"Not so loud."

Swing came to the door. "Seventy of them paid off."

"Figure up the cuts. Messner gets ten per cent of the total, so if fourteen hundred is one fourth, the girls took in fifty-six hundred. Ten per cent of that is five hundred and sixty. Take five-sixty from fourteen."

Swing scribbled on the wall. "Leaves eight hundred and forty."

"O.K. Halliday gets half, so that leaves me four hundred and twenty. You get half of that."

Swing whistled. "Not bad for a week, but the whores do better."

"We'll do better when we start making the gamblers and bookies come through."

"That reminds me, Ree. You're supposed to see Parnell."

"Yeah."

"I told him you'd see him. He wouldn't talk to me. Said he'd have to be guaranteed protection by someone with authority before he pays a cent."

"I'll talk to him."

Swing divided the money into stacks while Ree dressed. Ree took some envelopes from a bureau drawer and marked them. He put Messner's cut in one envelope, sealed it, and slipped Halliday's cut into another.

"Let's go. Stop somewhere for coffee."

"I hope this keeps up forever," Swing said. "I'll buy a house and a new car."

"Buy a new car and start people talking. You'd better be careful how you throw money around."

Swing laughed. "We're counting our chickens before they're hatched."

"They'll hatch, sonny boy. They'll hatch. Just stick by me, that's all."

"I'll stick."

Ree had hotcakes and black coffee.

"I'll deliver these envelopes and meet you at the office," he told Swing. "You know, I hardly know the routine of that damned department. Don't know what I'd do without you and Pounds."

"Don't worry about the department. You get everything organized and we'll take care of the routine. Anyway, you're the chief. All you have to do is supervise."

"Well, you keep the wheels turning and you'll be in clover. We're just playing penny ante now. Wait'll we break that gambling setup."

He walked to the courthouse and entered the sheriff's office. Blondie, the deputy he'd socked for teasing the Negro woman, was seated on the desk. He scowled and grunted at Ree's greeting.

"Where's the sheriff?" Ree asked.

"In there." Blondie pointed at Messner's office.

Ree opened the door without knocking. Messner was reading a newspaper.

"Morning, sheriff."

"Howdy, Ree."

He tossed an envelope on the desk.

"There's your cut from the girls, figured at ten per cent. Do you want to check the figures?"

"I'll take your word. How much does it come to?"

"Five hundred and sixty."

Messner whistled. "That's better than I was doing."

"We've got more girls in town now. I did all the work and only made two hundred and ten."

"Maybe you're paying your friends too much."

"I want them to be happy."

"Well, I'm not going to cry about your troubles, Ree. After all, it was my deal to start with."

"I'm not bitching. I'd rather have crumbs than go hungry."

"You'll do better when we get everything organized."

"I intend to. What say we have a talk with this Parnell guy."

"Parnell?"

"You know the man, sheriff. Don't spoof me, and don't be coy. It doesn't become you. He's running all the games in town."

"He's a tough customer."

"So what? You're not afraid of him, so what?"

"He represents the syndicate."

"So what?"

"That's dynamite, that's so what!"

"Way out here in the sticks?"

The sheriff grinned. "Well—we'll talk to him. But I suggest we use a flat fee instead of a percentage. He's paying off all over the state as it is."

"How about a couple of thousand a week?"

"Too much. This is not a big town, son, and we can't get that kind of money."

"A thousand?"

"If he'll pay it. I'm not guaranteeing he'll pay it."

"He'll pay."

"What makes you think so?"

"We're the law. We can close him down."

"You're sure."

"Hell yes, I'm sure! Aren't you?"

"Well... maybe. Again, maybe not. It takes more than a chief of police and a sheriff to make a thing like that stick."

"We'll get cooperation."

"Maybe."

"I'll call him today and tell him we want to talk."

"O.K."

"I'll give you a ring."

"O.K."

Blondie stared as he passed through the outer office.

"Friend," Ree said, "you look like a poodle with the piles."

"Any time you want trouble," Blondie said, "you just say the word."

"Word."

"Be careful, Ree. You're liable to wind up in a ditch with your little toes turned up."

"I'll be careful, son. You wouldn't care to step outside, would you?"

"No, thanks just the same. The sheriff says it'll be my job if I get in any more brawls."

Ree spat on the floor and walked out.

Halliday was in his office, and Ree handed him the envelope.

"Very good," Halliday said after he had counted the money. "We should do very well when you get things organized. Okay, take it easy from now on out. You had a narrow escape. People are talking, and one more mistake will get the whole town on your tail."

"I'll tread lightly."

"Do that. Oh, one more thing. Cliff Barrick made bail and he's out. He may want trouble."

"I'll dodge him."

"Run from him if you have to. We can't prosecute him for jumping you and he knows it. We can't stand the publicity. Knowing that, he may jump you again. He may want trouble, just so he can tell his story in court. And he can still tell his story in print. We're not out of the woods yet. He may be able to sue, if he can get that waitress to tell things his way. So dodge him."

"I said I'd dodge him," Ree snapped.

"Good."

"I've seen Messner about the gambling racket. A guy named Parnell has things sewed up. We're going to soak him a thousand a week."

"How'll we split?"

"We didn't talk about that, but I suggest a three-way cut. We can split with the others out of our own cuts, any way we like."

"Fair enough, but Messner may hold out for more dough."

"I can handle Messner. I think."

"O.K. Work it out."

Messner trotted up the steps to Fry's office, nodded to his secretary and barged in without knocking.

Fry looked up and frowned.

"How's the honest county attorney today?" Messner greeted him.

"As honest as he was yesterday."

"But not as honest as he was before the election."

"What can you do?" Fry spread his hands. "It's the company I keep. My political bedfellows. Corrupt sheriffs and police and county judges."

"I've never asked," Messner said, "but I know you give the judge part of your take. Does he cut you in on any of the county take? Like road funds and the like?"

"Ask the judge."

Messner shrugged his shoulders. "I've got something for you."

"Tainted money?"

"Well, it's money." He tossed an envelope on the desk. Fry picked it up and slid it into an inside coat pocket.

"Willa Ree came through with that a little while ago. That's good old tart money."

"Well, that gives you some of your money back," Fry said. "Personally, my wife takes care of me. When I have to pay for it at the window I'll do without."

"That's funny, Fry. Coming from you, that's funny!"

Fry grinned tightly.

"Let's change the subject."

"O.K. Ree's planning to cut in on gambling."

"He won't get very far. I don't care for him cutting in on the whores. That's penny ante stuff. But he's going a little out of his depth when he hits gambling. That's been a good return."

"The big boy'll stop him cold. I strung him along, but the big man will push him down hard."

"What if he doesn't."

"What can Ree do?"

"He could make some raids."

"We can stop that. We might have to get Halliday to put the clamps on him, but we can stop it."

"And if Halliday can't handle him?"

"Fire him. Get rid of him. We can't have a man we can't control."

"He's an eager cookie."

"He's dangerous! Look at the trouble he's been in already! It's a damned wonder the whole town's not on our ear—and may be yet, if the Barrick kids tell their side of the story in the newspapers!"

"The Barrick boys shouldn't be given the opportunity to print their story," Fry said. "Halliday oughta be able to put the screws on that rag. The kids can't have much money. They tell me they're operating on a shoe string."

Messner removed his hat and massaged his scalp, the fingers working rapidly, making a dry scratching sound.

"There's something about Ree that bothers me," he said. "Damned if I don't think he's got a pretty bad record somewhere. And—Wesley disappeared too damned slick to suit me."

"It's fishy," Fry agreed.

"More than that. Wesley's car was found out at the edge of town. There was blood on the seat."

"You think Ree and Wesley had trouble? Think Ree may have bumped him?"

"Well, would Wesley go off and leave all his personal belongings in his room? And a bank account he's never touched? What do you think?"

"I think we ought to damned well find out! I think we ought to sweat Ree until we do find out! I think we ought to get rid of Ree before he drags us all down!"

"I think you're right."

Sam Byrd was sitting at his desk working a crossword puzzle when Halliday entered. He grunted, but didn't look up. Halliday took a roll of bills, circled by a thin rubber band, and stuck it in Byrd's shirt pocket.

"What's that?"

"Money, Sam. It'll buy a lot of liquor."

"That's all it's good for."

"This money came from Ree. He's working out pretty good, but he's too ambitious. He wants to move in on gambling."

"What's wrong with that?"

"Nothing, if he can swing it. He can pull more out than Messner's been getting, but I don't think Messner's going to sit around and let Ree move in."

"He didn't yelp about the whores, did he?"

"No, but Messner's smart. He threw that to Ree hoping it would satisfy him and keep him quiet."

"Well, if there's trouble, leave me out of it. All this was your idea, anyway. You've got to have the last ounce of blood. Can't be satisfied with big stuff, you've got to have screw money."

Halliday made a moist clucking sound with his tongue.

"You're being vulgar, Sam."

"Well, hell! Can't you see trouble brewing? You get Ree started on this, knowing he'd be bound to clash with Messner some time! What did you expect?"

"To tell the truth, Sam, I didn't know. For one thing, I wanted him to organize things another way. It didn't occur to me that he'd be spending his time on small stuff like prostitutes."

"You wanted him to rob and steal, crack safes and knock off honkytonks," Byrd said. "That's what you had in mind, wasn't it?"

Halliday didn't answer.

"You know something?" Byrd asked. "I think Ree did pull some jobs in this town."

"No!"

"Don't be sarcastic. I'd hate to think you had anything to do with it."

"We've been friends a long time, Sam."

"I wonder."

Halliday stalked out.

Ree sat in his office, doors closed, and felt the walls closing in. He thought, and the more he thought the more he thought, and the more he thought about. The more he thought, the more convinced he was it was time to clear out.

Something was behind him, close behind, breathing down his neck and ready to reach out and grab. It was time, good time, past time, to clear out.

He wanted to run, get up and run blindly and wildly, until the panic cleared out of his mind and body and he could think clearly.

Instead, he sat and thought.

Run without a plan and whatever it was, whoever it was, behind him would trip him up.

He knew that.

The town was a net, was a web, was a prison.

Time was running out.

He knew, perhaps by instinct, that the bubble was about to burst. Halliday, Messner, Fry... Byrd, and all the rest... would turn on him when the chips were down. That he knew. Only a bubble had prolonged the bursting of the bubble, and even Laura could prick that bubble.

And the Barrick boys—and Wesley, four little three little Indians, and he'd been lucky they hadn't pinned him down by now.

The girl, Barbara, might talk.

That was a stupid thing to have done!

He could have gone to Laura. She would have relented, if he'd worked on her enough. Anyway, it would have been better to pay for it than take it away from a girl like Barbara.

Laura still thought he'd killed Wesley, but something had kept her from talking. That something... could it be love?

Only Halliday had kept the Barrick boys from suing the city. And even Halliday couldn't keep them from printing their stories.

The hours ticked away, and as they ticked away, slowly ticked away, Ree made his plans.

First, the forty thousand. He would get the forty grand from Laura's father.

How?

By force, if necessary.

It would be worth it. He had to take the forty thousand to do what he wanted to do, add it to the money he had and do what he wanted to do.

Once he had the money, he'd see Laura and ask her to go away with him.

That was important.

She must go with him, far away with him. For one thing, she'd guessed where the forty grand came from.

And... besides... she was much of a woman.

But, if she wouldn't go?

She'd go.

She'd better go.

He thought of the little waitress, Barbara.

Last night she had insisted he pay her the three hundred he'd promised. Her voice had been dead, her eyes dull and lifeless, though she had responded with passion after he'd placed her on the bed.

He had laughed at her.

"You think I'm just talking," she said, "but I'll kill you."

"Don't kid me," he said. "You enjoyed it as much as I did."

"That doesn't make it right," she said.

"Aw, hell," he said. "Quit kidding. You were no virgin."

"That has nothing to do with it," she said. "It was still rape."

And then he said a foolish thing. Glibly and without thinking. The words just spilled out.

"Might makes right," he said.

She fingered the panties and bra he'd torn from her body. Sitting in the middle of the bed, legs drawn up under her, naked and unashamed, making no attempt to cover her nakedness. There were tears hiding behind her eyes, but they were held back.

"I'll kill you," she said.

"Kill me in bed, then. Kill me with your body. Kill me with passion and I'll die gladly."

"If I thought that would kill you—"

"You'd have fun murdering me."

Thinking of her now, remembering her small body, the tiny wide-apart up-thrust breasts, her hair loose around her shoulders, desire came again. He shut his eyes and saw her, and beside her—on the easel of his mind— he painted Laura.

Two perfect women.

If Laura refused to go with him, he'd take Barbara.

Time ticked away as he dreamed his plans. Five o'clock came and he saw himself winging across the sea. Five-thirty ticked away, and he was in Mexico City; then Brazil, Paris, places he'd never been, might never see.

Six o'clock came and he was in his office at the Hall again, surrounded by trouble, submerged in trouble, up to his neck in trouble.

A fine September mist was fogging the windows.

This crazy flat country. Still hot in September.

He went up-town and ate in a greasy spoon café, sitting near the window and watching the mist cover the street outside with a gleaming sheen of wet. Street lights were turned on early, and neon blossomed on store front vines of wire.

As he left the café, he saw Cliff Barrick, arm in a sling, standing on the other side of the street. Halliday had told him Barrick had made bail, but he had pushed it back into his mind and covered it, buried it, hidden it, scratched dirt over it. Forgotten it.

Cliff Barrick disappeared around a corner, and Ree went across the street to the car.

Forty miles to Rockford.

The asphalt was shining black under the film of rain. Lights of approaching cars were dim and round and ghostly. The motor purred comfortably, punctuated by the click-clack of windshield wipers. It was lonely, friendly lonely and cozy, in the rain and the night.

Few cars drove the streets of Rockford, and few dotted the curbs. He drove around the town, a window down and one elbow stuck out into the wind. The tires swished, swished, rhythmically.

There were lights in the church, and many cars were parked at the curb. He pulled in, switched off motor and lights.

Music—organ music and singing.

On and on, voices singing, voices sweetly singing off key and shrill and loud, but sweetly sweetly singing. On and on, voices sweetly singing, and organ soft and droning behind the voices, a curtain of throaty music for sweetly singing voices.

The song ended.

And then the organ again, and the voices.

He got out of the car, slamming the door with savage violence, sudden and surprising savage violence, and walked across the wet grass to stand near a window. Rain was soft on his face, intimate and soft and caressing, but wet, and warm as tears.

Faint and far away, so far, a voice prayed.

"...and see us through the days and nights to come, and help us live as Thou wouldst have us do, O Lord, in Thy Name and in Thy service. Amen."

The organ music, again, and the voices. And then the organ played on alone, the voices still, and the peal of the organ swelled and soared and died.

Voices, not singing now, not musical, but happy and gay, and feet tramping the floor, doors opened and slammed. And the rain was cold on his face now, and he shivered, wiped a damp sleeve across his face and hurried back to the car.

He sat slumped down in the seat and watched people file out of the church, walk to cars, drive away.

And, finally, the last car light dimmed out far up the street, and the church lights snuffed out.

All but one, the light in the study.

Preacher Green was seated at the desk. Before him, on the desk, was the package of money. He sat staring at it, his hands spread to each side of it, not touching it. When he heard the door open behind him he whisked the package into a desk drawer.

Ree hit him as he turned.

It was a glancing blow.

The preacher threw himself backward, far backward so that his chair overturned, and the barrel of the gun glanced off his forehead.

There was blood on the preacher's face, but he was getting up.

He made no sound.

The blood welled from a cut on the preacher's forehead, into his eyes, and he wiped it away with his sleeve. Slowly, with deliberate slowness, he picked up the chair and sat down.

Ree stood, the gun heavy, out of place heavy, in his hand.

It was too late now.

The preacher had seen him.

That first blow should have been enough, and wasn't.

He'd bungled.

"Sit down, son," the preacher said.

"No."

"You've come for the money?"

"Yes."

"It isn't yours," the preacher said.

Ree slid open the desk drawer with his left hand, grasped the package and stuffed it into his coat pocket.

The preacher wiped blood from his face with his sleeve, stared at the sleeve, and then took a handkerchief from his coat pocket and held it to the cut.

"The money wasn't yours, either," Ree said. "But you had it."

"I was going to call the police."

Ree laughed.

"You've had plenty of time to do that, preacher. Plenty of time!"

Preacher Green nodded, shrugged his shoulders. "I won't try to fool you," he said. "I've had plenty of time, as you said. I brought the chair from Laura's apartment. When I brought it into the study I carried it upside down and noticed the taped place on the lining."

"You meant to keep the money," Ree said. "You meant to keep it."

"No."

Ree laughed again.

"I was tempted," Preacher Green said. "I opened the package and counted the money. There's enough there to do a great deal of good—for the church and for a great many people. I thought of that and I was tempted. But I won't try to fool you, son. I thought of myself, too. I thought of myself and my wife and my daughter. I remembered all the years I've lived on half enough money, in run-down parsonages. And I've remembered the dresses my wife has worn—given her by some church member who wouldn't wear them again because she'd grown too fat or because they were too threadbare....

"But I was going to call the police, son. I wanted that money. I was tempted. I needed it. But I wasn't going to keep it."

"You've had plenty of time," Ree said.

The preacher smiled, "That's my sin, son. You're right. I had plenty of time. But I wasn't going to keep it."

"Well, you should have called the police a long time ago, preacher. It's too late now."

"It's never too late to right a wrong, son."

"Don't hand me that crap!"

"Leave the money," Preacher Green said. "Leave the money and go away."

Ree smiled, lips curling.

"Leave it for you?"

"Then let me call the police before you leave. You can listen. I'll tell them I found the money, and that's all I'll tell them."

"No soap."

"You can go away. I don't know you. You can listen to me talk to the police, and then you can go away."

"Preacher, you're wasting your time."

"I've wasted a lot of time in my life, son. But I've planted a lot of seed, too. Some of that seed has borne fruit. I don't know what you've done. I don't know. But you're a troubled man, a mixed-up man, and I'd like to help you. Believe me it's not too late!"

"Cut out that crap!" Ree said. "Don't give me that not too late business!"

"Then what are you going to do?"

What?

Ree stared at the preacher, the gun heavy in his hand.

What?

"You should have stayed out of this, preacher. You should have called the police when you found that money."

"Let me call now, son. Don't do... what you're thinking."

Ree felt the sweat pop, felt it trickle, on his face and under his arms.

"Don't do it," the preacher said.

The gun was heavy, so heavy in his hand, and the preacher's face floated, inflated and floated, and he tightened his grip on the gun.

Preacher Green lunged, straight across the desk, on his belly with arms extended and hands clawing and grasping for the gun.

Ree hit him.

A crunching sound, a sickly and moistly thumping sound, and the preacher sighed, slumped, slid downward face first to the floor, his back arched as he fell, to lie doubled up on the floor.

Hit him again?

No need.

Maybe he should hit him again. Just to make sure.

No need.

The preacher was, or had been, a big man, a handsome man, florid and broad featured, full of good humor, bubbling over with personality.

It was plain to see. Plain there on the face, the wide unwrinkled face with its thick nose and puffy cheeks, the widespread mouth, open and gaping now. He looked dead enough.

Now what? Leave the preacher there? No. He'd be found too quickly.

But where? Leave him where?

And then he knew. He knew just the place. The well. He lay the gun on the desk and stooped, grasped the preacher around the waist and lifted. And then he remembered the lights, dropped the preacher and went over to switch off the lights.

The preacher was a big man, a heavy man.

Ree half dragged him, half carried him, arms around his chest, hands clasped, walking backwards and half dragging and half carrying.

Rain and darkness felt like friendly arms, reaching out and enfolding him, holding him safe from fear and punishment.

It was dark, pitch dark, womb dark.

Once he stumbled and fell.

He reached the car, lowered the body to the ground, gently to the ground, and opened the door.

It was hard work, stuffing the preacher through the rear door, and he was breathing hard when he closed the door.

Breathing hard, and trembling.

And now for the gun.

But there were footsteps.

Clickity-clack, clickity-clack, clickity clickity clickity-clack. A woman's footsteps on the walk leading from the street to the study.

The preacher's wife?

Or some silly Sunday School teacher with an adolescent crush, returning after church to ask the preacher a question, as a school girl lingers after class to consult the teacher.

He heard a door open, and then the lights in the study flicked on.

It was Laura.

The gun was in there, and in there was blood, all over blood, and it was Laura silhouetted in the doorway.

Ree drove away, fast, and knew he wasn't driving fast enough.

The speedometer climbed to eighty, and he knew that wasn't fast enough.

Once he slowed down, determined to dump the preacher's body beside the road.

But no, he decided.

No use to give them a corpse so soon.

Let them look for it.

He caught a glimpse of the side road leading to the well, a fleeting glimpse as he passed it. He braked the car to a stop, backed up, and nosed down the road.

There was the well.

He stopped, flicked off the lights, and got out.

The preacher was too heavy to lift over the fence.

Ree climbed the fence, caught the preacher's arm and dragged him under.

He dragged the body.

But the wind will blow and the rain will fall and the sand will blow before the wind, and there'll be no track.

It couldn't be far to the well, not far, but it was miles and still there was no well. His feet slipped on the gravel of the embankment and the body twisted in his arms. The body sagged to the ground limply.

He pulled the wire down and slid the body over it.

Head and shoulders first.

The wire caught the preacher's clothing, but he pushed harder. Something tore. He swore.

The body was balanced on the wire. One more shove—he found himself holding his breath.

One shove, one hard shove, and the weight was gone, the preacher gone, and he held his breath, clenching fists, cringing.

A splash. That was all, just a splash, and he wondered if the body would float.

No flowers on that grave. Baldy had flowers, but no flowers for the preacher.

Chapter Tweny-six

Laura recognized the gun.

There was blood all over, and blood on the gun.

She'd seen that gun before.

She drove the forty miles to Breton in forty minutes. She circled the courthouse square, driving slowly, and parked near the driveway leading from the street to the courthouse basement.

Why tell?

Keep quiet and kill him.

Ree would leave town, she knew. He would go far away, and she hadn't much time.

The man wasn't human. He hadn't looked human the night he beat Wesley, and he must have looked the same when he killed her father tonight.

She left the car and walked across the wet grass, under the trees, in the quiet still of the night, conscious that her feet were cold and damp, but not caring.

...and I, Laura Green, do solemnly swear and depose and further saith that on a certain night the said Willa Ree did willfully and with malice aforethought and with some degree of pleasure beat unmercifully one Wesley and I further believe did later kill said Wesley further and moreover that on this night tonight with further malice aforethought and for all I know no little pleasure club my father a preacher of the Lord's gospel on the head until he was dead and further I do solemnly swear that on many previous occasions the said Willa Ree did with malice aforethought willfully and with no small degree of pleasure and satisfaction sleep with me and make love to me as well as he was able and I do further say and depose that a murderer makes love as well as or maybe a little better than do other men and further the witness sayeth not....

Her heels clicked on the worn stone steps. She paused at the door and brushed hair back from her face.

Why go in? Why not find him and kill him? They'll try to smear you, Laura, because they're all in it, all of them.

She pushed the door open with her shoulder, click-clacked down the dark hall, and entered the sheriff's office.

He was using the telephone, but hung up.

"What can I do for you, Miss Green?" the sheriff asked.

She tossed the gun on his desk.

"That belongs to Willa Ree."

The sheriff stared at her.

"Tonight Ree killed my father!"

"Tell me about it," the sheriff said.

"I went to my father's study. In Rockford. He's a minister. There was blood. Blood everywhere. And the gun was on the desk."

"And your father?"

"He wasn't there."

"Maybe he isn't dead."

"He's dead."

"But his... he wasn't there?"

"No, but there was blood all over."

"You know that gun belongs to Ree?"

"I've seen it before."

"Why would Ree hurt your father?"

The sheriff motioned her to a chair.

"It began on the night of the Johnson Tool Company robbery," she began. "Ree came to my apartment and I knew—instinctively—that something was wrong. But it was the next night that it happened...."

The sheriff asked no questions. As she talked, he smoked.

Laura told all she knew about Willa Ree.

The sheriff was polite, even considerate. When she finished talking, he walked with her to the car. She drove to the apartment, drank a glass of whisky straight, and then fell on the couch, face down, and cried.

Maybe I'm not going to make it, Ree told himself. Maybe it's not in the cards for me to make it. Maybe all the things you do, good and bad, add up and add up and then something or somebody or something subtracts the smallest from the biggest and throws the book at you if the biggest is the bad things you do.

There's been too much trouble, too damned much trouble. You can't run like hell out of hell, and this whole thing has been hell. A nightmare.

Should never kill, never kill, never kill. Steal and rob and cheat, but never kill.

Two things. Don't cross a state line and don't kill.

Forty grand in the coat pocket, and that should be enough. So take off now and don't stop and look back and don't come back, ever, never, and cross not one state line but any and all to far away and hell and gone.

Twenty grand in the lining of the coat in the closet. Forty and twenty makes sixty, the sum total of forty and twenty thousand dollars adds up to one ranch in South America or Mexico. Easy living. Women, plenty of women, and no hard work and no worry and no scheming and no looking back at all the things it took to get sixty thousand dollars.

A rabbit runs and the dogs chase.

Run and there'll always be somebody to chase, even if they don't know why you're running or why they're chasing.

So don't run.

Walk, don't run, to the nearest exit.

Take it easy, slow and easy, and hand in a resignation and take off.

Only the old lady, Baldy's sister, knows the truth about Baldy. And she's just guessing. Who would listen to her?

But Laura knows about the preacher. So there's no time to waste.

Don't walk, run. To the nearest exit.

Too bad to miss all that gravy. It was just beginning to get good. Gravy, hell.

Ree, you've had the meat. Leave the gravy for the hungry amateurs.

It stopped raining.

Everything was going to be all right.

He'd go away. Far away.

He wondered why Laura had gone to see her father. Could she have known he was going—followed him? She guessed that the money—or something—was in the chair, and... well, what the hell.

Messner called the deputy, Blondie.

"That old woman—the one we thought was screwy—where does she live?"

"Out on the railroad," Blondie said. "Oak Street, I think. Anyway, that well she was talking about is on the railroad track."

"I want you to get some men and go out there," Messner said. "Get down in that well and see if you can find Wesley's body."

The deputy cursed. "You don't believe that old hen's story? For cryin' out loud! I went out there and examined that well! There's net wire around it and there's not a tear in it anywhere! There was a loose place at the top, but I'll bet it hasn't been touched in years!"

"Get yourself out there," Messner said. "Go down and have a look."

"Sheriff, that woman's nuts! Everybody knows it! And she admitted she was just guessing!"

"The car was out there, and there was blood on the seat. I'll meet you out there."

"O.K.!"

Messner hung up, walked to the window and stared into darkness.

He'd known all about Laura Green. He'd made it his business to know, because she'd been Ree's girl and he felt it was important to know everything possible about Willa Ree.

But he hadn't believed Ree had killed Wesley. The woman, that wrinkled old woman, had marched in and told him Ree had dumped Wesley down that well. She'd heard shots the night before Wesley's car was found, and when she'd heard about the car, with blood on the seat, she'd known Ree had killed Wesley.

Well, she could be right. After tonight, if Ree'd really killed the preacher—it wouldn't do any harm to have a look in that well.

He could still hear her voice, her cracked old voice.

"That Willa Ree did it," she had said. "Wesley's in that well."

But he hadn't believed her.

He'd sent Blondie out there, and Blondie had said there couldn't have been more than a couple of feet of water in the well, and that he could have seen a body if there'd been one.

Now he wasn't so sure. Blondie was cocksure, but not too bright, and more than a little lazy.

Now, after what Laura Green had said, he'd have to take a look in that well. If Ree killed the preacher, he could have killed Wesley.

He left the courthouse and drove out of town.

Blondie had picked up the janitors, two Mexicans, and old Pete, the handy man at the courthouse. He'd cut the fence and had driven the county pickup close to the well, using its lights to work by.

It was still raining.

Old Pete was grumbling, standing around and grumbling, while the two Mexicans tore the net wire from the framework of the well covering. Blondie was fastening a block and tackle to a beam lying across the top of the well.

"Somebody's tampered with this wire since I was here last," Blondie said.

"You got a flashlight?" Messner asked.

"Yeah."

"You going down?"

"Yeah."

"Hurry it up."

"O.K., but you stand by and see they don't lower me too fast."

Messner sat on the beam and waved directions as the Mexicans and Pete handled the rope.

"This is one deep bastard!" Blondie called, his voice muffled. "It's darker'n the inside of hell!"

"Yell when your feet touch water," Messner said.

He peered into the well.

"I hope we got enough rope," Blondie called.

"What?"

"I said I hope we have enough rope!"

"Oh. We got plenty of rope."

"Tell them to take it easy. I see water now. About ten more feet."

"O.K."

"Stop her!" Blondie yelled.

There was a body, pin-pointed by the flash.

"It's not Wesley!" Blondie called. "This guy hasn't been here long!"

"Okay, we'll pull you up. I know who it is."

Messner helped lift Blondie.

"Get the coroner and some more help," he said. "Get the body out of there. I'm going to go get Ree."

"Maybe I'd better go with you," Blondie said. "There's nothing I'd like better than getting that bastard."

"You do like I said. I'll handle Ree."

"Who the hell is this guy?" Blondie called as he drove away.

It had stopped raining.

Messner drove straight to the courthouse.

He called Halliday.

"This is Messner," he said. "All hell's broken loose now, and we've got our asses in a sling."

"What now?" Halliday asked. "What's happened that hasn't already happened?"

"Ree's killed a man," Messner said. "Found him in a well out on the railroad tracks, and by morning everybody in town'll know Ree killed him."

Halliday cursed.

"Listen, Halliday, you call Byrd and the mayor and Swing. I'll get Fry. Come on down to the courthouse as quick as you can and we'll figure what to do."

"Right away."

"Yeah, right away. This time hell is going to bust wide open."

"Do you have any ideas?"

"Yeah, I have an idea, but it'll have to wait until you get down here. I can't tell you over the telephone."

"Go ahead and call Fry. I'll get the rest and come on down."

Messner called Fry.

Messner sat down and smoked.

So they were coming down, all of them, and he'd tell them what had to be done. The only thing that could be done... if they wanted to go on living in this town as respectable citizens.

They were not going to like it.

But they'd have no choice.

Swing would be the man to take Ree's place, because he had things pretty well lined up and he had been doing Ree's work, anyway. And Swing would be easy to handle, a helluva lot easier than Ree had been. Fact, Ree couldn't be handled. He'd been doing the handling. They had given him plenty of rope and he'd hanged himself. Only trouble was, he almost hanged the whole kit and kaboodle before he got snubbed himself.

Arthur Fry was the first to arrive. And he was scared, plenty scared.

"What's up?" he asked. "What's happened now?"

"Have a seat, Arthur. The others are coming."

"What's Ree done now?"

"Killed a man."

"How do you know?"

"We know, Fry. And by morning the whole damned town will know."

Fry sank into a chair.

"So, what'll we do? Throw the book at him?"

"We can't, friend. He's got us by the ying yang and we can't risk a trial."

"I don't see—"

"You will, Fry. You will. Just wait for the others and I'll explain it slow and simple like."

Swing was next, and Halliday arrived with Byrd and the mayor.

Messner led the way upstairs to the district courtroom, carefully locked the doors, and joined the others at the press table near the jury box.

"Spill it," Halliday said.

"The other day an old woman told us Ree had killed Wesley," Messner said. "We thought she was nuts. Remember that little bald burglar Ree killed at Johnson Tool? Well, he was this old woman's brother, so we thought she just had it in for Ree and was making up this story about Wesley being dead."

Halliday started to speak, and Messner silenced him with an upraised hand.

"The old lady said she heard shots out by that old well the night Wesley disappeared. Said she'd seen car lights down there, and heard the shots later. Says she knows for sure Ree was mixed up with her brother in the Johnson Tool burglary and some others. Said Ree killed her brother to keep from having to split the take. She said Wesley was down in that old covered well out on the railroad track."

"Well, was he?" Halliday asked, half rising from his chair.

"No. I sent Blondie out there for a look around. He said the net wire around the well hadn't been tampered with. He used a flash to look down the well and didn't see a thing."

"Get on with it!" Fry yelped.

Messner grinned, a tight cold grin.

"Tonight this Laura Green came in. She was Ree's girl friend. She says

Ree hid the Johnson Tool take in a chair at her apartment. The next day her dad came and got the chair. So, tonight, Ree went over to Rockford to get the money. The girl's dad is a preacher over there. Or was. Ree killed him. The girl had gone over and found Ree's gun and a lot of blood in her dad's study. But no body."

"Then what the hell do you mean that Ree killed him?" Fry asked. "How do you know—"

"We went back out to the well," Messner said. "I decided Wesley could be in that well after all. He wasn't, but the preacher was."

"Who knows about this?" Halliday asked.

"Blondie and Old Pete and the Mex janitors," Messner said. "And the girl knows for sure Ree killed her father. So the whole town will know about it by morning."

"We'd better do something," Halliday said. "We've wasted too much time now."

"Sooner the better," the mayor said. "Run him out of town."

Swing and Fry said nothing. Byrd squirmed in his seat.

Messner cleared his throat, fished for a cigarette and accepted a light from Swing. He could feel all their eyes on him, and he took it slow, made them wait, let them sweat.

"We can't let him leave town," he said easily.

"Why not?" Halliday asked.

Messner knew Halliday was just asking, just talking. You didn't have to draw any pictures for Halliday.

"He'd be caught," Messner said. "We'd have to put out a wanted call on the guy if he skipped, and he'd be caught. He wouldn't get a hundred miles."

"And if he's caught?" Fry asked. "What then?"

"He'd drag us down with him, and you know it," Messner said. "That baby's not going to take a rap by himself. He'd tell all he knows about us— and a lot he just guesses. He'd make up things, bad things, and the town would believe it because people like to believe things like that."

"We'll have to take that chance," Byrd said.

"What chance?" Messner asked. "You wouldn't have a chance! This town would launch an investigation that could put every one of us behind bars! Ree wouldn't just talk about vice pay-offs and things like that! He'd talk about contract pay-offs and special funds and liquor licenses and all kinds of deals, and there's not a one of us clean enough to get out of it clean! Not a one! Swing would have the best chance because he just collected the money from the whores on Ree's orders. The rest of us would be trying to explain how we bought ranches and rental property and big homes on the salaries we get!"

Halliday plucked a cigar from the mayor's coat pocket, got it going, and leaned back in his chair.

"Messner's right. Ree would try to implicate us in everything he's done, up to and including murder."

"He can't do that," Fry said. "My hands are clean."

"Are they?"

"As clean as yours!"

"Watch yourself, Fry," Halliday said. "Just remember Ree doesn't have to prove a thing! Not a damned thing! All he has to do is talk—and we're ruined!"

Fry stood and pointed a trembling finger at Halliday.

"We should have run him out long ago! He's caused nothing but trouble! Remember what I told you! I said—"

"Shut up," Messner said scornfully. "We don't give a damn what you said! It's what we do now that counts! This Ree murdered a man and threw him down in that well! For that he can burn, but before he does he'll drag every single one of us down! Every single one of us!"

Fry gasped like a fish out of water and sat down. Swing sat up straight in his chair and Sam Byrd beat a nervous tattoo on the table top with his fingers. Halliday arched his brows and cocked his head.

"Why haven't you—well—why haven't you arrested him?" Fry asked.

Sam Byrd looked up, his eyes slightly out of focus with drink.

"I'll tell you why he hasn't arrested Ree," he said. "It's because he's afraid to, that's why. He's going to kill the poor bastard."

Halliday leaned forward to stub out his cigar in the tray. Fry raised his hands and held them close to his face, seemingly fascinated with their trembling. Byrd laughed, explosively, and was as suddenly silent. The mayor looked at Halliday, a hurt look on his face.

"This is insane," the mayor said.

"I'm getting out of here," Fry said.

"You'll stay," Byrd said. "You're like me, Fry. You got in too deep and you'll stay."

"We'd better decide something," Messner said. "We'd better get down to brass tacks."

"It's your worry," Sam Byrd said. "You're the sheriff. Arrest him."

"Listen, you bastard!" Messner almost, not quite, shouted. "Arrest Ree and bring him to trial and he'll pull us all down! All the way down!"

"Ree can't prove anything," the mayor said. "Not a thing."

"Prove it!" Messner hissed. "He wouldn't have to prove it. All he'd have to do is tell it, you dumb bastard! There'd be investigations then and the city books can't stand investigation! Neither can county books!

"Oh, we're not the only crooks in town! The judge and county commissioners will suffer just as much as we will if an investigation is made. But they're not in on all the things we've been in with Ree, so they wouldn't appreciate this little meeting."

"This is no place for me," the mayor said. "I haven't had anything to do with this Ree. Whatever was done is not my responsibility, and I feel that the voters will understand if I...."

"Crap!" Halliday said. "This is not a question of taking your story to the voters! You'd be in front of a jury, brother, and don't you forget it! You're in just as deep as the rest of us!"

"I say it's time we cut out this stalling and decide what to do," Messner said.

"Let's don't jump too fast," Halliday cautioned. "Of course you're right, sheriff. The whores would back him on the pay-off business, even if that is a minor point. But if he proved that, they'd believe anything else he said. That would be enough to start a general investigation, and none of us could stand that."

"What'll we do?" Fry bleated. "What are we going to do?"

"That's what we're here for," Halliday said. "That's why the sheriff got us down here."

They all turned to Messner. He got up, stood rocking on his heels.

"I'll have to arrest Ree," he said. "There's no doubt but that he'll try to make a run for it. Since he's a killer—and probably would be sentenced to death in court for the murders he's committed—I couldn't just stand there and let him get away. I'd have to shoot him."

Byrd got up and started for the door.

"Where are you going?" Messner asked.

"I'm going home. I'll not have anything to do with any of this."

"You'll stay," Messner said, walking toward him. "You'll stay and make your vote right with the rest of these men. I'll do the work, and there won't be any blood on your hands, but you're going to vote."

"Why?" Fry wailed. "If you had your mind made up why did you drag us down here?"

"I'm going to make damned sure I'm not going to be left standing alone," Messner said. "This way nobody will be able to put the blame on my shoulders."

Halliday laughed. "What he means," he said, "is that he'll make us vote and then he's got us around his little finger. He could have killed Ree and not a soul could have said a word, because by tomorrow everybody will know Ree killed the preacher."

"I'll stay and I'll vote," Byrd said. "But my vote is no, and that's the way it'll stay."

"It doesn't have to be unanimous," Messner said.

"Yes it does," Halliday said.

"How will you vote, gentlemen?" Messner asked. "How about you, Halliday?"

"I say arrest Ree," Halliday said.

"Finish the thing," Messner told him. "Say the rest of it."

"That's all of it," Halliday said. "Arrest Ree."

"Arrest Ree and see to it that he stands trial?" Messner asked. "Is that what you mean?"

"I didn't say that," Halliday said. "You're only human, and Ree might not submit to arrest. For all I know he'll make a break for it. If he does—why, then—do your duty."

"In that case, what should I do, Halliday? What should I do if Ree makes a run for it?"

"Do your duty, sheriff."

"That's good enough for me. All right, Fry. What do you say?"

Fry had his hands clasped on the table in front of him, the fingers twisting and weaving and twining.

He didn't answer.

"What do you say, Fry?" the sheriff persisted.

"I say do your duty," Fry muttered.

The sheriff laughed.

"All right, mayor," he said. "Let's hear your little speech."

"You took certain oaths when you took office," the mayor said. "You know your duty."

Messner laughed, "You vote aye, then, mayor."

The mayor left the room.

"All right, Byrd," the sheriff said. "How do you vote?"

Byrd was still standing by the door.

"No," he said. "You can stay here all night, but I say no."

The sheriff looked at Halliday.

"Let it go at that," Halliday said.

"Then," said the sheriff, "I have work to do. Good night, gentlemen."

"What about me?" Swing asked.

"All right, what about you? Do you want to be chief of police?"

"Yes."

"Then that takes care of you. Good night."

Sam Byrd was sober, cold sober, for the first time in a long time sober.

He didn't like himself, couldn't stand himself, but for the first time in a long time he had a faint glimmer of pride in himself, for himself.

I bucked them, he told himself. I bucked them and didn't back down. Even Halliday rode along, even when he didn't want to go along, because he was afraid not to go along. What he has and what he is means more to him than his conscience.

He paused on the courthouse steps, wondering what he should do.

Halliday came out the door.

"Want me to give you a lift, Sam?" he asked.

"I'll walk."

"What do you think about all this?"

"What do you think?"

"I think I'm sorry it went this far. Ree's gone, of course. Long gone, and we won't ever hear anything about him."

"They'll catch him if he's gone."

"No they won't. The sheriff won't ever send out a wanted message."

"He'll have to. Ree will be indicted and they'll have to."

"He won't be indicted. The sheriff can cover things up. He can say there's not enough evidence."

"You're kidding yourself," Byrd said. "You're kidding yourself so that later you can tell yourself you only voted yes because you thought Ree would get away. You can kid yourself, but you can't kid me."

"I'm not kidding myself," Halliday said. "Ree's gone by now. He won't be around when the sheriff goes to get him. If I didn't know that for a fact I'd have strung along with you."

"You're just trying to ease your conscience in case he hasn't skipped," Sam Byrd said.

"No, I'm not. Messner wasted too much time, and by now Ree's long gone. I know he's gone, and that's the only reason I didn't take a firm stand against Messner."

"I hope you're right, but I don't think you are."

"Well, at any rate, I'm getting out of town. I'm going home and pack some things and get out of town."

"Where you going?"

"I don't know. But when the sun comes up I'll be a long way from here, in a hotel, and I'm not coming back for a week."

"I hope you sleep well."

"Oh, I'll sleep, but things are going to be different when I come back. I'm going to stay on the council, but things are going to be different. We're going to run things right. I've got all the money I need and I don't want any more. We'll run the whores out of town, stop gambling and keep the city's business on a sound basis."

"It's too late."

"It's never too late. I'll see you in about a week. Sure you don't want a ride home?"

"I'll walk. Thanks."

"Well, good night, Sam."

"Good night."

Sam Byrd walked up the street, slowly, wondering if Ree had skipped town and knowing he hadn't. He had no reason to believe he hadn't, but knowing it just the same.

Messner will kill him, he thought, and I'll spend the rest of my life in hell.

There's only one thing to do, he thought. Call Ree and warn him. That way I can always know that I was against what Messner said. Even if Ree doesn't believe me and stays and is killed, I'll know I did what's right.

He ordered a cup of coffee in a café and asked to use the telephone.

A woman answered. Ree's landlady.

"I'll knock on his door," she said, "but I know he isn't here. I'd have heard him come in."

She left the phone for a minute.

"He doesn't answer," she said. "I knocked and called and he doesn't answer."

"Thank you," Byrd said. "Thanks a lot."

Ben Halliday packed a bag. He didn't want to talk to Martha, though he felt she was awake. He left a note saying he was called out of town on business, then picked up his bag and left the house.

After he put the bag in the car he went back, found a check book and an envelope.

He wrote a check for five thousand dollars, payable to Martha's church, addressed the envelope and put it on Martha's dressing table. He added a postscript to the note.

"Please mail this for me," he wrote.

He drove two hundred miles and checked in at a hotel. Though he stayed in bed eight hours, he slept only in cat nap snatches.

The mayor turned on the desk lamp in his study, found paper and pen, sat down and wrote his resignation as mayor.

He gave failing health as his reason for resigning. When he had finished writing, he found envelope and stamp and left the house.

He walked three blocks before he found a mail box, but when he dropped the letter in the slot he felt better. When he returned home, he went into the bathroom and vomited.

And then he went to sleep.

Arthur Fry scraped a fender against the garage door, but it didn't matter.

"Where have you been?" his wife asked.

"Something came up at the courthouse," he said. "Go back to sleep."

Because she was awake—and because he wanted privacy—he went into the bathroom and closed the door. He stayed a long time, on his knees, trying to pray.

Sam Byrd stripped.

Nora was still up, reading.

As usual, she wore a sheer negligee. The black bra and panties were sheer, too, so that he could see the blacker black than the black panties beneath the black panties, and he marvelled that he hadn't noticed the blacker black before, though he had seen it night after night and sometimes day after day just as he was seeing it now.

She let the book fall to her lap. "Where have you been, Sam?" she asked.

He didn't answer, just stripped, and a puzzled frown crossed her face.

"You might pull the curtains," Nora said. "After all, we do have neighbors."

He stripped, and then took off his shoes, standing up.

"Stand up," he said.

"Why?"

He caught her by the hand and pulled her up, ripped the negligee from her body, then the other clothing, until they fell around her ankles. He put his arms around her legs, buried his face in the soft warm flesh of her thighs.

"You've been with Halliday," he said. "I should hate you but it's my fault. I'm sober, Nora, cold sober, for the first time in a long time, but that's the way it'll be from now on and from now on I'll give you all you need and all you want and if I catch you even thinking about another man I'll leave you."

"Yes, Sam," she said.

He stood up and turned her around. Three times he spanked her, as hard as he could, until his hand burned.

"Now let's go to bed," he said.

Martha Halliday heard her husband come in. She watched as he packed a bag, wondered what he was doing when he left the room, and closed her eyes when he looked her way.

When he left the first time she got up, turned on the light and read the note. She heard his footsteps on the walk, switched off the light and jumped back in bed. When he left again she got up and opened the envelope he had left.

Five thousand dollars, to her church.

Ben's conscience must be bothering him, she thought. A hell of a lot.

At first, when he was packing the bag, she had thought he must have found out about her and Ree—or someone else.

She thought of Ree, wishing he would come, knowing he wouldn't because how would he know Ben had left town at this hour and wondering if he would come if she called and knowing she wouldn't call.

Sam Byrd got up and went to the bathroom.

He dressed.

"Sam?" Nora called. "Where are you going?"

"I've got some business to see to."

"At this time of night?"

"Yes."

"What kind of business?"

"I'll be back in an hour or two," he said, turning off the lights.

Arthur Fry made a pot of coffee and smoked. His hands trembled, and there was a lost and gone feeling in the pit of his stomach and in his chest.

After a while he called the sheriff's office, but there was no answer. He let the phone ring and ring, but there was no answer.

He went back to bed and couldn't sleep.

Martha Halliday heard the car pull into the driveway and thought Ben had returned.

She heard footsteps on the walk and was sure of it.

The door opened, the front door, and the click of the living room light.

Maybe I should get up, she thought. After all, it might not be Ben.

"Who is it?" she called.

"Sam."

"Sam? Is something wrong? Are you drunk?"

"I'm cold sober and there's nothing wrong."

She got out of bed, found her robe and slippers.

Sam appeared in the doorway.

"I came to sleep with you," he said.

"Sam Byrd!"

"Maybe I'd better tell you why I'm going to sleep with you, Martha. Ben has been sleeping with Nora, for several weeks now, and I've come to get even."

She gasped, audibly, and then wanted to laugh. Not that it was funny, except Nora was so pretty and Ben had a paunch and she wondered how Nora could have stood Ben's paunch.

"Get your clothes off," Sam said.

She stood up, slipped out of the robe, and stood still and straight while Sam pulled the gown over her head.

"Now undress me," he said.

Her fingers trembled, fumbled, but he wouldn't help. She felt silly.

He even made her take off his shoes and socks, and she had to get down on her knees.

"Now get in Ben's bed," he said.

"That's taking things a bit too far," she giggled.

"Just the same," he said, "get in Ben's bed."

He wondered, later, why Ben wanted anybody's wife but his own.

The mayor's wife listened to him snore.

I wonder, she thought sleepily, where the old fool has been?

She went back to sleep, but came wide awake when the mayor screamed. She sat up in bed and called to him.

"What's the matter? Are you sick?"

"Just a nightmare," he said. "Go back to sleep, my dear."

"I told you to stop eating so much," she said.

Swing left the courthouse alone. His feet hardly seemed to touch the pavement. He felt he was twenty feet tall and that nothing could hurt him, touch him, bother him.

He was in.

He'd taken their crap, listened to their orders, had done as he was told.

Now he'd be in the driver's seat, and there'd be money, and he'd run this town and squeeze it like a lemon.

Ree was finished.

All this business about killing Ree was screwy, of course, because by now Ree would be far away and long time gone.

Swing drove home, fast, sliding around the curves and pushing on the gas to take the kinks out.

Ree would be gone by now.

Of that he was sure.

Chapter Twenty-seven

Messner was alone in the courtroom, sitting at the press table.

He heard Fry's footsteps fade away on the stairs, clatter down the ground floor hallway. The squeaky old door slammed shut, and the courthouse was empty. Except for Messner—and a couple of Negroes in the jail upstairs.

Deliberately, he spat.

A window was open and he closed it, then clicked off the lights and walked down the stairs in the darkness. In his office, with the door closed, he sat at his desk and thought of what he must do.

Must do?

He didn't have to do it. No. It was of his own choice.

Hell, yes, he told himself, his image behind his eyes facing him, talking, hell, yes, you made the choice.

Messner stood up, took in a notch in his belt, hunching at the middle in that peculiar way soldiers and officers, men who carry guns, have of hunching in at the middle to take up a notch in the belt. He patted the gun at the hip, tugged it down, pulling the belt down from the waist to the hips, slapping the gun butt until he was satisfied it hung just where he wanted it to hang.

He tipped his hat down over his right eye and left the office.

It was time for a showdown, past time, and he was looking forward to it and dreading it a little, anticipating it and afraid of it, but not scared.

As yet, he hadn't decided how he would handle it. He wasn't even sure he could make a plan, because Ree didn't seem to be the kind of man to allow a plan to be made. The guy went off at tangents, unexpectedly, so that you could never figure what he was going to do next. As far as that went, he wasn't sure Ree hadn't skipped town. He didn't think so, but it was possible. Maybe it would be just as well if he had....

He drove slowly, but it wasn't far and he was there before he expected to be there, parking the car and getting out in the darkness and circling away from a street light and crossing a street.

The rooming house was bulky in the darkness, squat and ugly in the darkness, but that was good, too.

He knew Ree's room, for he'd been there before. Once, just once, he'd been there before on the hunch that Ree had something lying around, papers or something, that would tell something or prove something.

The porch, old and creaky, was dim and shadowy, half dark and half light in the dim refracted rays of the distant street light.

The front door was open.

There was no light in the hallway.

He flicked a match with his thumb nail and moved swiftly down the hall to Ree's door.

Something was wrong.

He heard something, or didn't hear it, felt maybe, but whether he heard it or not he knew there'd been sound in that room moments before.

No sound.

He stood, tense and still, but there was no sound. His hand moved to the knob, turned it, and he threw the door open.

There had been sound.

Now he could hear the sound of breathing, heavy and labored breathing. He closed the door behind him.

"Ree?"

"Yeah. Swing?"

He stood with his back to the door and fumbled for the light switch, found it, and flooded the room with light.

Ree stood in the middle of the floor with blood streaming at his chest, dripping to the floor.

Wesley was on the floor. Not dead, just on the floor. Unconscious on the floor.

Ree had a knife in his left hand, but his right hand hung limply at his side.

"The crazy fool slipped in here to kill me," he said.

"Where's he been?" Messner asked. "We figured you'd killed him."

"No. I should have, but he got away. He was waiting here for me tonight, in the dark, and he knifed me."

"I half figured you'd be gone by now."

Ree smiled a wry smile. "I would have been, but I passed out. I managed to club the bastard and then I passed out."

"Let's go, Ree."

"I need a doctor."

"We'll see a doctor. Let's go."

"What are you doing here, Messner? What do you want?"

"You know well enough. I want you. As of now you're under arrest."

"What for?"

"Murder."

"Listen, call me a doctor and stop talking silly! I'm bleeding, man, bleeding!"

"You'll notice I'm wearing a gun, Ree. If I have to, I'll wrap the barrel around your head. Now, let's go!"

"Bleeding like this?"

"Stop bleeding if you want to. Just come with me."

"To hell with it! I'm calling a doctor and to hell with you! If you think I'm going...."

Messner had drawn his gun.

"Do you mean it?" Ree asked. "Do you really want me for murder? Are you nuts?"

"We found the preacher in the well, Ree."

"The hell you did! I don't know what you're talking about! So you get me a doctor and stop me from bleeding to death!"

"We looked in the well tonight, Ree, and found the preacher. We thought we'd find Wesley!"

"You're nuts! Get me a doctor!"

"Your girl friend says you killed him, Ree. And she found your gun in the church."

"Call me a doctor!"

Messner stepped in, fast, and Ree tried to step back, bringing the knife up, but not quickly enough, and Messner hit him on the forehead with the gun barrel.

Ree fell to his knees, shook his head, slinging blood, and then stood up.

"Okay," he said. "Okay, you bastard, there'll be another day."

"Drop the knife, Ree."

Ree flipped it, end over end, and it stuck in the floor, quivering.

"Let's go," Messner said.

Ree staggered and half fell on the bed. He breathed deeply, shook his head and wiped the blood from his eyes. The gun had left a gash, slightly longer than wide, edge bruised and bluely swollen, dripping blood thickly.

"I think you would kill me," he told Messner. "I think you could do it."

"I'm just putting you under arrest."

"Maybe. I doubt it. You wouldn't want me to stand trial."

"Hurry it up."

"We'll soon know, anyway," Ree said.

Messner shepherded him down the hallway, across the yard, across the street, into the car.

"Don't try anything," he warned Ree. "Don't try to jump me while I'm driving."

Ree didn't answer.

Messner drove away from town, left the asphalt roads and drove swiftly on graveled lanes, the gravel tinkling against the inside of the fenders.

"So you're going to kill me," Ree said.

"You're talking too much."

"Have you ever killed a man, Messner?"

"I have."

"In cold blood?"

"You talk too much."

"I think you have."

"Just don't start anything, Ree, because I can kill you before you got start-ed good."

"I know that. I'm not stupid. I've lost too much blood."

"It's pretty and quiet out here, isn't it?" Messner asked. "I always liked to drive out here and watch the flares in the distance. Sometimes jackrabbits jump up and run in front of the car."

Ree had felt someone there in the darkness. He'd opened the door to his room and stepped inside, and felt someone there in the darkness.

"Wesley?"

"Yeah. How'd you know? Guilty conscience?"

"Take it easy, Wesley."

"Oh, I'm taking it easy, Ree. You're going to die but you'll have your chance! I wouldn't kill you in cold blood, but nobody could blame me if I did!"

"You're talking like a kid."

"Well, think like that if you want to, pal, but I'm not playing. I've got a knife for you and a car outside and we're going out in the country and play for keeps."

He felt Wesley move in, and that's when he lunged, grabbing at where Wesley should be, at the sound of his voice, the arms spread wide.

The knife was like a red hot poker, starting beneath his left arm and rak-ing across his chest and digging deeply into the arm above the muscle.

He struck wildly and moved in. Wesley went down and Ree started kick-ing with both feet. As hard as he could.

Finally, at long last finally, Wesley was still.

Ree searched for the light, stepped on the knife, stooped to pick it up, felt himself falling and didn't know when he hit the floor.

Someone was at the door when he regained consciousness.

The door opened.

It must be Swing.

"Ree?"

He stood up, Wesley's knife in his hand.

"Yeah. Swing?"

The lights clicked on, and it was Messner, and he knew his number was up. He should have skipped. By now he should have been long gone.

Messner meant to kill him, that he knew. He tried to bluff, but it was no use. Messner herded him to the car. When they left the city limits there was no longer any doubt.

Messner stopped the car, finally. Ree was glad, because he was sick at the stomach. The blood had spurted and spurted, but now it oozed, and he was weak and dizzy and sick at the stomach.

"Is this the spot, Messner? Is this where you pull the job? Have you consulted Halliday about this?"

"Get out of the car and shut your mouth." The sheriff's tone was mild, only the words hard, but the sheriff wasn't mad and he could be mild.

Ree opened the door.

Luck was with him.

He stepped on a rock.

It was a round rock, round and smooth and fist sized, just right, and Messner, the fool, was getting out of the car on the far side and walking around.

He stooped down, fought off the dizziness, and picked up the rock.

With his left hand.

He switched it to his right hand, feeling the numb fingers close around it, and wondered if he could throw, if he could even lift that right hand, much less throw. Nothing else for it. He had to throw.

Messner was a blob, walking slowly, but the gun in his hand glinted.

Ree threw.

The gun went off and a firecracker exploded in Ree's chest. The world upended crazily and he was flat on his back, looking up at the stars, and he was numb all over. Things went black, snuffed out, for a while, and then he was looking at the same stars.

He wondered why Messner didn't finish him off.

He was cold. Rocks were digging into his back, hurting, and he shifted his position.

Maybe, he thought, I can get up and look around.

The car was still there, so Messner was still there.

On his knees, feeling something bubbling in his chest, he saw the car. Messner was gone.

Why?

He wouldn't leave the car.

A cough came, burbling deep inside his chest. He wanted to feel his chest, feel the wound, but he was afraid.

Doggedly, slowly, he moved along, knees scraping on the gravel beside the road, until he fell across Messner.

The rock had hit.

He scrounged around, looking for the gun, but couldn't find it.

Messner was breathing.

Well, he could kill the bastard with a rock. Or choke him. The choking would be better, but the rock would be messier, and he'd use the rock if he could find the rock.

No.

Leave the bastard alone.

Why?

Well, hell, why not?

Let him live and maybe that'll make up for some of the things that happened, that happened—just happened.

Get Laura and get out of town.

He fought his way to the car, on his knees, and pulled himself erect. It was easier then to get into the car, half crawling, pulling and clawing.

Under the wheel, ready to go, he passed out again. Not all the way out, but some of the way out, and he didn't come awake until he coughed and choked on something, blood maybe, and came awake struggling for air and thinking he wouldn't get air.

He started the car, then, backed it around, thinking once to run the wheels over Messner and deciding against it.

It was slow going, like being drunk.

He drove back to the room, fought his way out, stayed on his feet and made it to the room to get the money in the topcoat. Wesley wasn't there. Ree found the topcoat and made the long trip back to the car.

And now for Laura.

Laura could drive. Laura could drive, fast, and take him away, far away, to Mexico or somewhere.

But, first, she'd call a doctor and fix him up and he'd feel better and they'd go away, long away, and never come back.

Laura's light was burning.

At this time of night?

She'd be drinking, and full of love, and she'd be alarmed because he was so bloody but she'd call a doctor and then they'd go away.

It was hard, climbing the stairs, and once he almost fell. Once he had to stop and cough, choking, and then he went on, fighting his way, feeling the blood run again, swallowing blood.

Laura opened the door.

He pulled the package of money from the coat pocket and handed it to her.

Laura stared at him. Her eyes dead and frozen.

"We've got to get away, Laura," he said.

"You'll never get away, Ree. I'm going to call the sheriff."

"I need help, kid."

"You must be crazy," she said. "You killed dad and now you come here."

She put the money on the table beside the telephone, picked up the phone, then returned it to the cradle.

"You look like death," she said.

"Maybe you'd better get a doctor."

"Police or doctor," she said. "It doesn't matter. A doctor would turn you over to the police. But I think you're dying."

"Get me a doctor."

"Get your own doctor."

She wouldn't help. He knew she wouldn't help, wouldn't leave with him. He'd have to leave. By himself. She was sitting at the table, one hand on the package of money, the other on the telephone.

"Give me the money, kid."

"No."

He staggered toward her, hand clawed for the money, but she stood up and pushed him.

Ree fell.

Sprawling, he fell, flat on his back and hard on his back, the blood gushing into his throat until he thought he would choke. He rolled over, pushed himself up, and moved toward the door on hands and knees.

"You won't get the money," she said. "You'd better get out of here before I call the police. Go somewhere and die."

He tried to speak... and gurgled.

He coughed, the blood streaming from his mouth, and then he could breathe again.

"We could go away, Laura! We could go to Mexico or South America and buy us a good big ranch! I've got money, plenty of money, and we could be happy!"

"You're bleeding."

He crawled toward the door, pulled himself up, and turned around.

Laura didn't look up. She was sitting at the table, one hand on the telephone and one on the package of money.

"Give me the money, kid," he said.

"No."

"I'll be back for it."

"No."

"I'll get patched up and come back."

She had taken her hand off the telephone and was looking at the money. She didn't answer, didn't look up.

He had to have a doctor, and fast. Better if he could go to a hospital, but that wouldn't do. They'd hold him, drug him, wouldn't let him go. A private doctor would do. Even a quack would do.

He tasted blood now. The cough was more frequent, and blood came with it. The car was hard to handle and he was weak, dizzy and weak, and he wanted to sleep.

Sleep.

Once he closed his eyes, let go, it would be all over. This he knew, and fought it, but he felt it wasn't too late if he could get a doctor.

What was it? Plasma? Sure, plasma. That would do the trick.

But he couldn't go to the hospital.

Something told him to go to Swing, but something else told him to find Barbara.

And he decided to go to Barbara.

It took a long time, too long, and he lost his way twice. But, finally, there was the garage apartment, with the long stairs, and he was out of the car, floating across the yard and up the stairs without effort.

He knocked on the door.

No answer.

Again he knocked, harder now, and heard someone call sleepily.

"Open up!" he said. "It's important! Open up! It's life or death, Barbara, open up!"

And he coughed.

She opened the door and he moved inside.

"Turn on a light," he said.

She moved across the room and he heard the click, blinded in the light. She wore a housecoat and her hair was in curlers.

She stared.

And now, suddenly, he knew it was too late. He was going to die.

She stared.

"Call a doctor," he said. "Call an ambulance."

"Why?"

"I'm hurt! Can't you see I'm bleeding?"

"Yes."

"Call a doctor!" he shouted.

"No."

"I'll die, Barbara! I'll die if you don't get help! Do you hear? I'll die and it'll be your fault!"

"I don't care if you die."

"Sure you do. Sure you care if I die."

"No."

It was crazy, completely crazy.

"I'll die."

"You should die, Ree."

"You shouldn't let yourself be the judge of that."

"I haven't hurt you."

"You could help me."

"I don't even have a telephone."

"Use the neighbor's telephone."

"No."

And now the cough came, the one he'd been expecting, a deep and shuddering, racking cough. The blood came, and soft gray nothing darkness, with pin-point stars, winking and blinking, and he felt himself falling.

When he could breathe again, after a long while, the blackness went away.

Barbara was standing over him.

"You're dying," she said.

"Look in my coat," he said. "The lining of my coat."

"You should pray," she said. "Do you want to pray with me?"

"It's too late."

"No. It's not too late now, but it will be soon. Will you pray with me?"

"Look in the lining of my coat. It's yours."

"All right. But pray."

"You won't call a doctor?"

"No. But I'll pray with you."

He smiled, wanted to laugh, but knew the blood would come so only smiled.

"Promise me you'll pray," she said. "Even if you don't say it. Even if it's just in your mind."

"All right. I promise."

"I'll pray, too," she said, "but I won't call a doctor."

"At least," he said, "at least, put me on the bed."

THE END

Stark House Press

CLASSIC MYSTERY AND DARK FANTASY FICTION

1-933586-23-0 **Wade Miller** The Killer / Devil on Two Sticks $17.95

0-9749438-0-0 **E. Phillips Oppenheim** Secrets & Sovereigns:
Uncollected Stories $19.95

1-933586-27-3 **E. Phillips Oppenheim** The Amazing Judgment /
Mr. Laxworthy's Adventures $19.95

0-9749438-3-5 **Vin Packer** Something in the Shadows /
Intimate Victims $19.95

0-9749438-6-x **Vin Packer** Damnation of Adam Blessing /
Alone at Night $19.95

1-933586-05-2 **Vin Packer** Whisper His Sin / The Evil Friendship $19.95

1-933586-18-4 **Richard Powell** A Shot in the Dark / Shell Game $14.95

1-933586-19-2 **Bill Pronzini** Snowbound / Games $14.95

0-9667848-8-x **Peter Rabe** The Box / Journey Into Terror $19.95

0-9749438-4-3 **Peter Rabe** Murder Me for Nickels /
Benny Muscles In $19.95

1-933586-00-1 **Peter Rabe** Blood on the Desert /
A House in Naples $19.95

1-933586-11-7 **Peter Rabe** My Lovely Executioner /
Agreement to Kill $19.95

1-933586-22-2 **Peter Rabe** Anatomy of a Killer /
A Shroud for Jesso $14.95

0-9749438-9-4 **Robert J. Randisi** The Ham Reporter /
Disappearance of Penny $19.95

0-9749438-2-7 **Douglas Sanderson** Pure Sweet Hell /
Catch a Fallen Starlet $19.95

1-933586-06-0 **Douglas Sanderson** The Deadly Dames /
A Dum-Dum for the President $19.95

1-933586-29-X **Charlie Stella** Johnny Porno $15.95

1-933586-08-7 **Harry Whittington** A Night for Screaming /
Any Woman He Wanted $19.95

1-933586-25-7 **Harry Whittington** To Find Cora /
Like Mink Like Murder / Body and Passion $19.95

If you are interested in purchasing any of the above books, please send the cover price plus $3.00 U.S. for the 1st book and $1.00 U.S. for each additional book to:

STARK HOUSE PRESS
2200 O Street, Eureka, CA 95501
707-444-8768
www.starkhousepress.com

Order 3 or more books and take a 10% discount. We accept PayPal payments. Wholesale discounts available upon request. Contact griffinskye3@sbcglobal.net

COMING SOON FROM

Stark Houʌe Preʌʌ

Danger in Paradiʌe / Malay Woman

A. S. Fleischman

1-933586-28-1 **$19.95**

Two south sea, cinematic adventure thrillers, with a new introduction by the author.

"Filled with a colorful cast of characters and wonderful noir dialog." MICHAEL CART, *Booklist*

SUMMER 2010

The Silet Wall / The Return of Marvin Palaver

Peter Rabe

1-933586-32-x **$19.95**

Two previously unpublished novels by one of the top noir authors of the 50's and 60's—a serious study of Mafia revenge, and a crazy con from beyond the grave.

"With Rabe, you never know how the plot is going to unfold." MICHAEL SCOTT CAIN, *Rambles*

WINTER 2010

Gang Girl / Sex Bum

Don Elliott

1-933586-34-6 **$19.95**

Two compulsively readable erotic novels written by Robert Silverberg under his Don Elliott pseudonym for Nightstand Books, back in print after fifty years with a new introduction by the author.

SPRING 2011

Dead Dollʌ Don't Talk / Hunt the Killer / Too Hot to Handle

Day Keene

1-933586-33-8 **$21.95**

Three short erotic thrillers of mystery and suspense from the golden age of the paperback.

"He knew how to tell a story that gripped the reader immediately and held him to the end." BILL PRONZINI

New introduction by David Laurence Wilson.

SUMMER 2011

 STARK HOUSE PRESS
www.ʌtarkhouʌepreʌʌ.com